10/2001

LB

ESAU

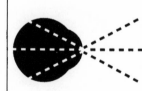

This Large Print Book carries the
Seal of Approval of N.A.V.H.

ESAU

James R. Shott

Thorndike Press • Waterville, Maine

Copyright © 1993 by Herald Press, Scottdale, Pa. 15683

People of the Promise # 4.

Published in 2001 by arrangement with Herald Press,
a division of Mennonite Publishing House, Inc.

Thorndike Press Large Print Christian Fiction Series.

The tree indicium is a trademark of Thorndike Press.

The text of this Large Print edition is unabridged.
Other aspects of the book may vary from the original edition.

Set in 16 pt. Plantin by Rick Gundberg.

Printed in the United States on permanent paper.

Library of Congress Cataloging-in-Publication Data

Shott, James R., 1925–
  Esau / James R. Shott.
    p. cm.
    ISBN 0-7862-3594-2 (lg. print : hc : alk. paper)
    1. Esau (Biblical figure) — Fiction. 2. Bible O.T. — History
of Biblical events — Fiction. 3. Large type books. I. Title.
PS3569.H598 E8 2001
  813´.54—dc21   2001041506

To Jodi and Jennifer,
grandchildren, who are
just now discovering the excitement
and wonder of maturity.

Part I

Isaac ben *Abraham*

1

The old woman pressed her ear to Rebekah's swollen abdomen. "T-twins!" she stammered. "Two nations . . . at w-w-war!"

"How can you be sure, Deborah?" Isaac squatted beside his pregnant wife and looked the ancient serving-woman in the eye.

But she only winked, bobbed her head, and sniffed.

Rebekah, who was lying on a mat on the floor of the tent, looked up into Isaac's eyes and smiled. "She may be right, Isaac. She's been right before. Don't you remember when Mari-baal gave birth to twins, Deborah had accurately predicted —" Rebekah tensed, her face contorted in pain. Her grip on Isaac's hand tightened.

Deborah pointed to the door of the tent. "Out!" She was the only servant Isaac had known who could order her master around and get away with it. He wasn't sure whether it was her strength of will or his weakness.

But he saw the justification in her command. "I'll be outside, Rebekah. May God be with you." He kissed his wife on the forehead, then rose and walked out.

Outside the night air was chilly. An evening breeze had sprung up and there was a hint of dampness in the air. The *yoreh* would come soon, the first rain. Isaac pulled his burnoose around him and walked to the fire one of the servants had kindled for him.

That same thoughtful servant must have anticipated his needs, for he was waiting for his master with a blanket. Isaac sat before the fire, his back to a rock, and wrapped the blanket around himself.

"Will it be long, Isaac?" The servant put more wood on the fire.

"Not long, Jubal. Her birthing pains have begun."

The servant nodded, murmured a ritual blessing for Rebekah, then walked toward the small brown tent near the well where he and his family lived.

Isaac watched the central black tent, now shrouded in darkness. Light from the oil lamps inside silhouetted grotesque shadows on the walls as the old midwife inside moved about the mysterious business of birthing a baby.

Isaac grunted. Deborah was as good a midwife as anybody. She had certainly had enough experience. Rebekah said she had been doing it for years back in Haran, before they were married twenty years ago. She was even present when Rebekah was born.

How old was Deborah now? Rebekah was thirty-five; the servant must be at least forty-five. Yet she looked as young as Rebekah. She must be ageless.

Isaac shook his white head, and his wiry white beard jutted out from his chin. Rebekah. His wife of twenty years. Twenty years waiting for this moment! The baby to be born tonight would be their first child.

Or would it be children? Could Deborah be right, that twins struggled in her womb, fighting like two warring nations, scrambling to get out? Isaac shrugged under the heavy blanket. Unlikely. Deborah was just an addled old lady.

The night air grew colder; Isaac shivered a little even under the comforting wool around his shoulders. He gazed up at the familiar stars. How often he had studied them during those long nights out in the field with his sheep! Their very familiarity steadied him now and brought him comfort. And the moon — full tonight — was just beginning to make its appearance above the hills. In a few minutes the whole clearing would be bathed in silver light.

Rebekah's pregnancy had been hard. He hoped the birth would be the easiest part of the experience. There was certainly enough activity inside her body. Could Deborah be right about twins?

His thoughts were interrupted by a baby's cry, coming from the tent. *Ah!* he thought. *I have a son! God be praised!*

Then the thought struck him: *What if it's a daughter? No, God promised a son. He will fulfill the Promise.*

There was much more to it than just the promise of a son. His father, Abraham, had been a deeply religious man who walked intimately with God. God had spoken to Abraham and had told him about the Promise. The descendants of Abraham would fill the earth and bring a blessing to all people. He, Isaac, was Abraham's only son by his first wife, and he had the birthright. Now he too had a son. The Promise would be fulfilled, the birthright continued.

Then another cry! He distantly heard two babies crying inside the tent. Was Deborah right then? He would know soon enough.

But he had to wait longer than he had anticipated. The moon was high in the sky and limning the camp in its soft light by the time Deborah beckoned to him from the doorway of the tent. He rose stiffly and hurried to her, the blanket forgotten on the ground by the dying fire.

"T-twins!" muttered Deborah. She winked, bobbed her head and sniffed, perhaps a little smugly.

He pushed past her into the tent. Another servant was hastily cleaning up, and he could smell the strange odor of the afterbirth. He knelt beside his wife and gently took her hand.

She opened her eyes and looked up at him. Although the classic lines of her face were still etched with pain, she smiled at him. He was once more struck by her beauty, even after the ordeal of childbirth.

"How is it with you, Rebekah?" he asked.

"It is well, my husband. Deborah was right. We have twins."

Even now, in this intimate moment, he was unable to speak to her in any way other than the formal phrases. A habit of a lifetime could never be broken.

Isaac felt the pressure of his wife's hand in his. "Look at them, Isaac. Tell me if they're all right."

Isaac nodded and left her side. Deborah was waiting for him by the brazier, which radiated enough feeble heat to take the chill off the inside of the tent. The babies were wrapped tightly in swaddling cloths and lying on a thick mat on the floor. One was crying; the other was silent.

"F-f-first born," Deborah muttered, as she unwrapped the squalling infant. Isaac reached for the oil lamp so he could thoroughly inspect this child who would fulfill the Promise.

The baby's squalls shrilled loudly in the tent, as though he were protesting the removal of his clothes for inspection. It seemed to Isaac that the child was not crying but angrily berating the old nurse for making him chilly. Perhaps this boy had a temper.

But something else struck him immediately about the baby. He was hairy! Fuzz enveloped the body. It covered his stomach, legs, arms. The head was blanketed with it. Not black, but a light color. Was it red? He would have to look again tomorrow in the daylight.

But the baby was big, strong, and apparently healthy. And blessed with a mean temper, to judge by the howling.

Isaac nodded to Deborah. She quickly wrapped the child in its protective covering of swaddling cloths. The squalling instantly subsided, and the baby closed his eyes. *Independent fellow,* thought Isaac. *He has gotten his way; now he has decided to go to sleep.*

Deborah unwrapped the other child, the one lying quietly. He too began to cry as the

14

clothes came off, but this time it was definitely a cry. He was complaining bitterly and feeling sorry for himself. Probably the weaker of the two, guessed Isaac. At least the stronger child had the birthright.

But this child looked perfect too: strong and healthy, although not as big — yet smooth, unlike his hairy brother. The skin, still purple and wrinkled from birth, gave promise of health and beauty. That would be his mother's child. The other was more of a man than this crybaby.

He chuckled as he nodded to Deborah to wrap the baby in the swaddling cloths. Only a few minutes old, and he was thinking of them as men, not babies. But that was as it should be. After all, they were a special family. God had chosen them to fulfill the Promise.

He got up and went to the other side of the tent where Rebekah was lying. Kneeling beside her, he took her hand.

"They are good-looking boys," he said gently. "The firstborn is big and strong and chastised Deborah loudly for taking his clothes off. He's going to be quite a man!"

"And the other?"

"He's a fine boy, too. Perhaps a little more delicate than his older brother, but he's in good health and well built. God be praised, Rebekah! We have two fine sons!"

His wife smiled. "Twins!" she said. "Isaac, are you sure which was the firstborn?"

"Of course I'm sure. Deborah pointed him out to me, and she ought to know. Besides, there's no mistaking which boy is stronger, more deserving to be heir of the Promise."

A slight frown momentarily marred the classic beauty of Rebekah's face. "Isaac," she whispered, "promise you'll treat them equally. After all, they were born together."

Isaac paused. His wife was tired and physically not equal to a prolonged discussion. "Of course, Rebekah. They're both our sons and equal in God's sight. Now take your rest. I'll see you in the morning."

He kissed her forehead and noticed that the frown had disappeared. *She's a beauty,* he thought, *even after giving birth to twins.* God had blessed him with a lovely wife and now two sons. God be praised!

Isaac stepped outside. The wind had died down, and the night was still cold. Moonlight bathed the area; he could see the many tents which comprised their little village. The fire had dwindled to smoldering embers.

He breathed deeply of the chilly night air. A son! After twenty years, God had given him a son! No, two sons. He must get used to thinking about having two children now. After so many years of being childless, that would take some getting used to!

Suddenly Deborah appeared by his side. The old servant winked, bobbed her head, and sniffed in her eccentric manner. She wanted to say something, Isaac realized, but she couldn't bring herself to utter it. Because of her stuttering, she said little, and when she did talk, it was in monosyllables.

But she obviously had something to convey, something which couldn't wait to be told to Rebekah tomorrow. Hesitantly she began. "S-s-second son. C-c-came out . . . gr-gr-grasping heel of f-first son."

Isaac smiled. He understood now why the old servant felt it important enough to overcome her shyness about stuttering to tell him immediately. She was a superstitious old lady, born and raised in the far country of Haran where they worshiped idols and accepted all sorts of superstitions. She would naturally see something sinister about this unusual incident at the birth.

"Thank you, Deborah." Isaac's voice was reassuring. "I'm sure it's all right. Please don't be troubled about it."

The old nurse winked, bobbed her head, and sniffed. She had done her duty, had told the master the problem. It was out of her hands now. Isaac nodded as she shuffled back into the tent.

Isaac walked to the dying fire and kicked one of the embers, sending sparks flying. He wondered what Deborah believed would happen because of the incident. Perhaps she thought the younger son would trip up the older boy some day. He chuckled. He'd tell Rebekah about this tomorrow. They'd both have a good laugh about it.

With that thought he turned and walked to his own tent to settle himself for the night. His next-to-the last thought before going to sleep that night was, *Praise God! I have a son who will fulfill the Promise! God is good!*

His last thought was, *If that younger child tries to trip up his big brother, as Deborah probably thinks will happen, he's liable to find a foot in his face! That older boy looks like he can take care of himself.*

It was a pleasant thought, one to go to sleep on.

2

On the eighth day after the birth of the twins, Isaac assembled his household for the circumcision. The day was cold and blustery, the sun was weak, and a threat of rain was in the air.

Before the circumcision would come the naming of the children. Isaac and Rebekah had discussed this during the past eight days and could not reach agreement.

Isaac insisted the boys be named for his ancestors: Abraham and Terah. Family names. Honored by previous generations in his family.

But Rebekah wanted to name the children herself, following the custom of her people in Haran. The older boy should be called Bethuel, for her father. The younger boy's name should be Laban, for her brother. These names might help them in later years, if they journeyed to Haran to find wives.

It was a contest of wills. In the past, Isaac had often bowed to his wife's wishes. She was stronger than he; he accepted that. In spite of the tradition of male mastery, he always seemed to give in to Rebekah.

But not this time. The two had clashed for perhaps the first time in their twenty years of marriage. Neither would yield.

Finally Rebekah offered a compromise. "Let's name them later," she suggested. "Perhaps when they reach puberty. Let's give them temporary names now, and permanent names later."

Isaac acquiesced, although he suspected that in the years ahead, she would contrive to have her way. She always did. But he had an additional suggestion, "Let me name the first-born with a temporary name. You name the younger one."

To this Rebekah agreed. But she wouldn't reveal the name she had chosen until the day of the circumcision. Perversely, Isaac did the same.

Isaac and Rebekah sat under the sycamore tree by the well of Beersheba, while the assembled household looked on. There had been great anticipation in the clan. They all knew about the disagreement between husband and wife. They were eager to know how the argument would be resolved.

Deborah stood nearby, holding the twins. Beneath his shaggy white brows, Isaac watched her. He could almost read her thoughts. She wouldn't approve of these proceedings. There ought to be at least some kind of idol on display. What kind of luck would these children have without a visible god to look after them? Later they were going to sacrifice animals on the altar, which was fine. But to whom? Isaac suppressed a chuckle. Deborah didn't have much confidence in his invisible God.

Isaac nodded to her; she handed the firstborn to him. In a loud voice, conscious of ceremony at this point, he asked her, "Is this the firstborn?"

Deborah winked and sniffed. In front of all these people, she wouldn't say anything. She nodded.

Despite the cold wind, Isaac unwrapped the carefully swathed baby. Then he held up the naked child for all to see. This was obviously a boy. The red fuzz on his head and body was emphasized in the sunlight.

"Behold my son, my firstborn!" Isaac sat and placed the child on his knees. "His name is Esau!"

There were smiles and nods from many. This was a good name, appropriate for this little red infant. Two words were melded together: *edom*, which meant "red," and *seir*, meaning "hair." Though a temporary name, it was likely to stick. What else would you call a child with red hair but "Red Hair"? Esau.

Isaac smiled, proud of the name he had chosen. He wrapped the swaddling cloths around the unprotesting baby. The chill in the air did not seem to bother him. He would be hardy.

Then Rebekah nodded to Deborah, who passed her the other child. Rebekah also took off the child's clothes and held him up for all to see. He too was obviously a boy, but smooth skinned and white. He had the beginning of black hair on his head.

Rebekah sat down and held the child on her knees. Here was the moment everyone awaited. Would her name for this boy be as good as Isaac's?

"His name is *Jacob!*"

There was a gasp from the audience. Isaac frowned. He, like many others, thought it a bad name.

The name meant "the grasper." By this time everyone had heard the story of how the second son followed the first out of the womb grasping the heel. The name was appropriate enough, but what kind of a name is that to grow up with? "The Grasper"! What was Rebekah thinking of, to name a child that?

Isaac shook his head and ran his fingers through his wiry white beard. A terrible name! He decided again that he liked the first-born better for several reasons, not least of which was the name.

Then the little boy began to cry.

What an inappropriate time to cry, thought Isaac. He was probably cold, for his mother was hurriedly wrapping the swaddling cloths around him and shushing him as best she could. But to cry at a time like this! A sign of weakness. The older boy had not whimpered because of the cold!

Isaac glanced at the stone table on which was carefully laid the little knife he would use for the circumcision. *All right,* he said to himself. *Now let's really give him something to cry about!*

At a nod from Isaac, the women retired to the tents, since the rite of circumcision was attended by men only. Isaac did not know why, but he suspected it was because of its bloody and painful nature. Women would see only the howling and suffering infants, the blood flowing from their mangled genitals, and miss the deeper religious meaning of the event. Whatever the reasons for it, the tradition had been established by his father, Abraham. Isaac would not dream of breaking a tradition.

Actually this was not the first time Isaac had performed the ceremony. All the servants and slaves in his company were circumcised when they joined his household, a custom established by Abraham. Their children were circumcised at birth. Isaac was becoming skilled at it, but this was the first time he had done it for members of his immediate family.

Esau would be first. Isaac performed the operation deftly and efficiently. The howl of pain and surprise which shattered the stillness and solemnity of the event was expected, but it was nevertheless shocking.

Isaac shook his head. This was the worst part of the ceremony. He could see why the women would be disturbed by this. Although his mind told him no real harm was done — in fact, the child would recover quickly and have a cleaner and healthier body because of it — he was nevertheless upset by the screams of the hurt infant. But it had to be done, so he closed his mind to the child's agony.

It had to be done again. The first child was bundled and sent for treatment of his wounds to the women waiting in the tents. The second infant was brought. The cutting stone and flint knife were hastily rinsed and dried, and Isaac repeated the process. More screams. But it was over in a few minutes, and the second child was banished to the waiting women.

Isaac wondered again if his imagination betrayed him, or were the screams of one child an angry scolding and the screams of the other a whining complaint? Maybe it was his own bias, but he was convinced one boy was strong and the other weak. Again he thanked God that the strong one was the birthright child. That was what really counted.

Next Isaac turned to the sacrifice he had prepared. A large stone altar had been erected on a high place overlooking the valley. A fire was already burning there when he arrived, panting, at the top of the hill. He had selected two bulls and twenty sheep for the sacrifice, one bull and ten sheep for each son. They were perfect animals, the best of his livestock. Nothing less was suitable to give to God.

He used the circumcision knife to dispatch the first animal. A deft slice on the jugular vein was all that was needed. Isaac stepped back as the animal threshed around in its death throes. Then it was spitted and placed on the burning altar. He did the same for all the animals.

When it was done, he offered a prayer — a ritual prayer he had learned from his father, Abraham. His father had extemporized his prayers, but Isaac was not fluent in praying. The words were the same he had heard Abraham say.

The stench of the burning hide and flesh

spread over the small valley, and a cloud of smoke lifted to the sky; the breeze wafted it off and dissipated it in the clear mountain air. A phrase spoken by his father came into Isaac's mind. "The sweet smell rises like incense to the nostrils of God." Of course, this was symbolic language, because God did not have a man's physical body. But . . . why say it that way? Those were Abraham's words.

He was not a theologian like his father; he was a traditionalist. Abraham walked with God and claimed God spoke to him and led him in these matters. But Isaac did them because they had to be done. He knew the God they worshiped was not a fickle god with a human brain who needed to be appeased and flattered — like the Canaanite gods, some of whom demanded a human offering.

This sacrifice was a substitute. God wanted no human sacrifice, only the homage of the sincere heart. And the animal on the altar was the symbol of that homage, a sign that the worshipers would be willing to give themselves to God if the deity so wished. But that was as far as Isaac's practical mind would go. He did what he did because his father had established the tradition.

As he stood there watching the animals burn and the smoke ascend, his mind returned to his son. The son of the Promise.

That was something he did understand. The line of the chosen people would continue. He couldn't deny the reality of God's existence, because the evidence of it was there: he had a son. That was real.

And so, from the tradition of his father, Abraham, and the reality of his son Esau, Isaac found more reason to believe in God than he did from the billows of smoke lifting from the sacrifice like sweet incense to the nostrils of God.

Part II

Rebekah asha *Isaac*

3

"No! He's mine! You had him last time!"

"Go eat sheeps' dung, Judith! You got what you want!"

Rebekah sighed. The two women were fighting again. Since Esau had installed the concubines in two tents in their little village at Beersheba, there had been no peace.

Judith's voice rose to a whine. "Moloch made me pregnant, but I still want Esau! Curse you, Basemath, I'll —"

"It wasn't Moloch who got you with child, you pig's bladder! It was Esau! I know we're taking turns, but I want to get pregnant too. Besides, you know what happens when you mix the seed in your body when you're already —"

"May ten pigs empty their bowels on you. . . ."

Rebekah wearily got to her feet, leaving the barley cakes she was kneading. She marched with long strides toward their tents. It was only fifty paces across the clearing, but slightly uphill over rocky ground, and she was panting when she got there.

They hadn't even seen her coming.

"May a camel bite off your left breast!"

"May a buzzard's droppings fall in your mouth!"

"May ants crawl in your womb when you and Esau —"

Rebekah pushed between the two women. *"Stop it!"* She glared first at Judith, then at Basemath. "I've told you before, as long as you live in Isaac's tents, you'll keep *quiet!* Do you understand?"

The two Hittite women scowled at her, panting heavily. Rebekah took a deep breath. *"Do you understand?"*

Again Judith's voice took on that grating whine. "But it's my turn. She had him last time."

Basemath tossed her head. "She's pregnant and I'm not! He should be in *my* bed!"

"Stop it!" Rebekah demanded through clenched teeth. "One more word and I'll have you beaten!"

Basemath was a few years older than Judith. She looked into Rebekah's eyes and said nothing.

Judith, however plunged boldly on. "It's not fair, Rebekah! She's —"

"Stop it!"

This time Rebekah's vehemence got through. The young Hittite woman cringed before her.

Rebekah took a deep breath and said evenly, "Furthermore, you will address me as 'Mother' or 'Woman.' Not 'Rebekah.' And . . . *you will do as I say!*"

"Y-yes, Mother."

Rebekah nodded. She would have preferred "Woman" because it was a term of respect for a nonfamily member. But as Esau's concubines, they had a right to call her "Mother."

There was silence for a full minute until Rebekah felt she had both women — and herself — under control. Then she spoke quietly.

"You will each go to your own tent and stay there until Esau comes home tonight. He will come to me first, and I will tell him which tent to sleep in tonight. You are not to come outside until tomorrow. Is that clear?"

"Yes, Mother." Basemath accepted the pronouncement stoically and turned toward her tent. Judith was about to say something, but caught her breath when she looked into Rebekah's eyes. Judith too went to her tent.

Rebekah sighed and turned wearily toward her own tent and her barley cakes. She squatted on the ground and resumed her kneading of the dough.

Deborah came out of the tent behind her. Evidently she had heard everything.

"C-c-cut switch. I c-c-call Jubal?"

Rebekah smiled. "No, Deborah." She sighed. "I think they'll be all right now."

"N-n-need beating. Esau t-t-too."

Rebekah repressed a giggle. Deborah was always saying something to cheer her up. The old servant seldom spoke, but when she did, she said something in her quaint style which not only amused Rebekah but showed an earthy wisdom.

Esau — a beating? Who would give it to a twenty-seven year old giant? Not Isaac, the only one here with authority. He was old, tottering, blind, confined to his tent. Not Jacob — he was no match for his brutish brother. None of the servants had the authority or the strength. Maybe Deborah! A giggle burst from her lips. Deborah just might do it!

The old servant shuffled around in front of Rebekah to see what she was laughing at. She sniffed, winked, and bobbed her head, then turned and hobbled toward Isaac's tent. It was time for the aged patriarch to sit outside in the sun while Deborah aired and swept the tent. Only Deborah could manage the testy old man.

Rebekah glanced around the clearing. Twenty tents were scattered in the rocky semicircle at the foot of several hills. The well was in the center, not far from Isaac's black goatskin tent. On the southern edge of the valley stood the only large tree — the stately sycamore under which ceremonial gatherings were held.

No one was in sight. Most of the men servants were with Jacob, tending the livestock. The large herd of sheep, goats, and asses were roaming far into the wilderness in search of pasture and water. This was the *sharav*, the hot dry season before the *yoreh*, the first rain. Only a few goats and asses were kept at Beersheba, and the four men and several women who tended them were in the next valley today.

The sun beat down as she placed the barley cakes on the stones by the fire. She pulled the cowl of her burnoose over her head and as far in front of her face as it would go. The small shadow it created for her face brought little relief. She wanted to go into the cool tent, but she had to stay here and watch the cakes so they wouldn't burn.

Rebekah lifted her eyes to the hills in the west. The sun still had a long way to go before darkness brought cooler temperatures. But when the cakes were done, she would go to the well for a cool drink of water.

She scooped up the barley cakes with her

thin wooden spatula and placed them on the stone plate. She would bring some still warm to Isaac, where he sat on the bench in the sun. By now he would be looking forward to a cool drink of water and a damp cloth to wash his face. That was one of his few pleasures in life.

She glanced toward the east, where the trail slipped between two hills. A cloud of dust. Someone was coming. If visitors, they would have to be entertained. That meant meat. Cooked meat. Barley cakes were not enough for guests.

She shaded her aging eyes and squinted. Several men. Six — no, ten. On foot. They wore the drab faded robes and head-pieces of any of the local Canaanites tribes.

Rebekah stood up, her mind whirling with plans for a cooked meal. Where was Jubal? Where were any of the servants? No one. She'd have to greet them herself.

She recognized them as they approached. Beeri and Elon, the two Hittite "kings." Proud, slothful men. They lived like barbarians, but called themselves royalty. And . . . they were the parents of Esau's concubines.

She went to them. Elon's bushy black beard covered his face so completely, his eyes looked like little dark berries in a bramble bush. Beeri's pointed black beard was trimmed so closely it failed to cover the perpetual scowl he wore.

Rebekah bowed her head. "Welcome, honored guests, to Isaac's tents —"

Elon snorted. "Get out of the way, woman!" His speech was heavily accented. Rebekah had heard once that in the Hittite language, the word for "woman" was the same as "slave."

Beeri's eyes stared down at her. "We come to see Isaac, not you. Where is he?"

Rebekah bit her lip. She was not accustomed to such rudeness. If only Jubal were here!

As though in answer to a prayer, Jubal opened the flap of his tent next to hers. She had forgotten; he was resting during the day, to take over the supervision of the flock at night. She breathed a sigh of relief.

Jubal was hurriedly adjusting the sash of his robe. He was barefoot and bareheaded, and his hair and beard were uncombed and unoiled. But he was a man, and the visitors would deal only with a man.

Beeri nodded his head briefly. "We would speak to your master, slave. Take us to him immediately."

"It shall be done, my lord." Jubal turned to speak to his wife, who had just come out of the tent. "Send Markesh to the flock. Have him bring a goat for dinner. Immediately!"

When the ten-year-old boy appeared, he spoke softly to him.

The two Hittites nodded. This was more like it. They enjoyed being treated like dignitaries.

Jubal was the most competent servant Isaac had ever had. He now turned to Rebekah.

"Go to Isaac, Woman. Prepare him for his visitors. I shall make preparations for a feast which will . . . honor our guests in the most appropriate way."

Rebekah looked into Jubal's eyes. He obviously had something in mind and tried to communicate it to her. But she couldn't guess what it was.

As she turned to walk to Isaac's tent, she noticed the boy Markesh running toward the next valley, where the livestock were grazing. She was halfway to where Isaac was sitting when she remembered she had forgotten the barley cakes and the water. Oh, well. She'd get the water when the visitors had been presented to Isaac. She would serve the cakes later.

"Isaac, my husband, we have visitors."

Isaac had been slumped on his bench, head down, cowl back, the sun beating down on his partially bald head. Hastily Rebekah pulled the hood over his thin white hair. He straightened.

"Who, Rebekah?"

"The Hittites, Beeri and Elon. Jubal went to prepare dinner for them. Here they are."

She helped the old man rise to his feet. No matter how old and infirm, it would have been a breach of manners to greet his visitors while still seated.

"Welcome to my tents, honored guests," croaked the patriarch with as much dignity as he could.

"Greetings, Isaac. May Moloch bless you and give you many sons."

Rebekah's mouth firmed in a thin line. To wish him many sons at his age was insulting. And to bless him with their god! They knew whom Isaac worshiped, but that didn't seem to matter to them.

Then Deborah came out of Isaac's tents with an armful of mats. She spread them for the visitors to sit. Only when the two "kings" and several of the other Hittites were seated would Isaac resume his seat on the bench.

The conversation began with a discussion of the weather, the drought, and the condition of the livestock. Rebekah went to the well for fresh water. She would offer the guests a drink, but she wouldn't wash their feet, no matter what they expected. She couldn't bring herself to do that!

As she walked back to Isaac's tent, the

bucket of water heavy in her left hand, she wondered why they had come. To discuss their daughters? They could hardly object to Esau's taking them as concubines. The girls were willing enough, and it meant that Isaac's household, not the Hittites, would be responsible for their lodging and food. What then?

Marriage? She suppressed a laugh. Preposterous! Isaac would never — or would he? Rebekah hurried a little, ignoring the slight twinge in her knees and left elbow. She wanted to hear this discussion!

4

"We've asked Moloch to bless you, Isaac," said Elon.

"We sent a sacrifice through fire for you," said Beeri.

Isaac nodded but said nothing. Rebekah poured water into two cups and handed them to the guests.

She shuddered as she heard Berri's words. Rumors of the Hittite worship of the god Moloch told of human sacrifices, in which a child was passed through fire. If he lived, which was seldom, it meant the god had rejected him. If he died, the sacrifice was acceptable. A male child for a blessing; a girl for a curse.

Isaac stared at the two men with sightless eyes. After a moment of silence, he spoke. "Your customs are not ours. We offer animal substitutes to God. But your thought was good."

The two "kings" wasted no more time on preliminaries. One of them, Elon, spoke hesitantly. "Your son Esau . . . ." He paused.

41

"My son Esau," said Isaac, "has accepted your daughters into his tents. Do you not approve?"

Beeri frowned. "As you said, our customs are different. We do not keep concubines."

There was a moment of silence. Then in a soft voice, Elon added, "We keep only wives."

Isaac nodded. Rebekah knew also what these two men were saying. A concubine, by Isaac's standards, had no official standing. Her children were servants, not heirs.

Beeri took a deep breath. "We have come," he said slowly, "to discuss the bride price."

So that was it! These greedy "kings" wanted to add a little of Isaac's wealth to their "kingdoms." Rebekah watched Isaac closely. She knew how he felt about Esau.

"No," Isaac's voice was firm. "My son Esau is my heir. His wife must come from our own people. Soon he will go to Haran, where our family originates. There he will choose a wife from the people of our own blood."

Elon rose to his feet, throwing his cup into the dust. "We're kings, Isaac! Royal blood flows in our veins. Esau will be marrying a princess. Is that not enough?"

Isaac struggled to rise. Rebekah ran to help him. When he was as straight as his old body could stand, he said firmly, "I don't recognize your kingship. Esau shall marry from his own kind!"

Now Beeri rose to his feet. "You pig, Isaac! No one can question my royalty. No one can refuse an offer of marriage to my daughter. For this you will die!"

Rebekah stepped in front of Isaac. "Leave him alone, please! You're guests. We want no violence in our tents."

Elon snarled, "Out of my way, woman. Or you die too!"

The Hittite men behind Elon and Beeri drew their knives. One had a heavy club. The eight warriors looked fierce.

Then Deborah was there, a large knife in her hand. She hobbled in front of Isaac and Rebekah, brandishing the knife.

"Go away!" she hissed. "I k-kill you!"

Beeri's mouth opened and his eyes were wide. "You?" Then he threw back his head and laughed. "You'll *what?*"

Elon wasn't laughing. "Kill her, Beeri," he sneered.

"No!"

The voice came from behind them. Rebekah looked up. There on a slight rise of ground about ten yards away was Jubal. With him were four men and a boy. All were armed with bows, arrows on the strings, drawn and ready.

The Hittites spun around. Nobody moved.

Rebekah held her breath. Five men and a boy, against ten Hittites. But Jubal's men were better armed. Esau had taught them to use the bow and arrow. They were not as skilled as Esau, but at this distance they were formidable.

Evidently the Hittites thought so too. Beeri shoved his knife back into the folds of his robes. "We wish no violence while guests in Isaac's tents," he muttered.

Elon too hid his weapon. "We'll go now, Isaac."

Isaac said nothing. It was customary to bless his guests as they left, but he remained silent. The Hittites marched along the edge of the clearing toward the tents of Esau's two concubines.

"Isaac," said Rebekah. "They're going to their daughters."

Isaac nodded. "So be it. If they take the girls away, they probably won't come back. I only hope we can stop Esau from following them."

Rebekah frowned. "He will, Isaac. You know his temper. How can we stop him?"

Isaac wearily sank down on the bench. "I don't know, Rebekah. Maybe this is the time to give Esau the blessing. Then we'll send him to Haran."

Rebekah bit her lip. She had been dreading this moment. Esau, the oldest son and heir, would be blessed and the Promise passed on. This mysterious Promise, which Abraham had received from God — or so the tradition said — predicted many descendants who would be blessed in the land and bring blessing to all peoples. Rebekah sighed. If only Jacob. . . .

Screams from the concubines' tents interrupted her thoughts. Evidently the girls did not want to go with their parents.

Jubal spoke to Isaac. "We can stop them. Shall we?"

"No." Isaac sounded weary. "Let them go. I won't miss them."

Nor will I, thought Rebekah. *Silence will return to Beersheba. Peace. No bickering over whose tent Esau will sleep in tonight. No jealousy over one girl's pregnancy —*

Rebekah caught her breath. One of the girls — Judith — would return to her father's tent carrying Esau's child. How would the Hittites feel about that? She let out her breath. There was nothing she could do. Did she even care?

More important, what would Esau do? Would that hothead take men, whom he himself had trained, and go after the Hittites? There would be bloodshed and death. If successful, Esau would bring the two girls back. She shuddered.

"Isaac, my husband."

"Yes, Rebekah?" He reached for her, and she took his hand. He could not see her, but she knew how much it meant to him to be able to touch her. He ran his fingers over her face and body. There was nothing sensuous about this. Long ago he had lost any physical desire for his wife. It was a loving caress, a need for assurance that she was there.

"Isaac, when Esau comes home tonight. . . ."

Isaac nodded. He too appreciated the problem. "What do you suggest?" he asked.

Rebekah ran her fingers through his beard, a gesture he enjoyed because it reminded him of her closeness to him.

"Why don't you send him to Haran immediately?" she said softly. "If he had a wife, he wouldn't need those Hittites."

Isaac nodded. "You're right. But first . . . the blessing."

"Isaac —" Rebekah caressed his hair. "Will you bless Jacob?"

Isaac's bushy brows came together. He wasn't nearly as interested in Jacob as in Esau. Rebekah remembered the years of struggle between the two boys. Just as Deborah had predicted at birth: two nations at war. For twenty-seven years, the tension had been there. Rebekah always sided with Jacob against the old patriarch and his declared heir.

"I can't bless Jacob." Isaac sighed. "He isn't in line for the Promise. Only Esau can inherit the birthright."

"But . . . Jacob deserves it far more than Esau. Look at the flocks! Under his management, they have grown and prospered. He stays home, while Esau roams —"

"No, Rebekah." Isaac's voice was as firm as when he spoke to Elon and Beeri. "We've been over this before. Esau, and only Esau, will receive my blessing."

Rebekah wet a cloth and wiped Isaac's face. He relaxed. No matter how deep the rift between them over their sons, she was his wife and met his needs.

Her thoughts turned to the two boys. They were men now, but they were still boys in her eyes. And one far more deserving of the birthright than the other. If only there were a way. . . .

As she poured oil into the palm of her hand and stroked Isaac's white beard, a plan began to form in her mind.

5

"Greetings, Father Isaac!"

Esau strode into the large tent, threw down his bow, and looked around. His red beard and hair were shaggy and dust-streaked. He smelled of sweat, unwashed flesh, and animal fur.

Rebekah caught her breath. Her fierce son frightened her. He was big, blustery, hot-tempered. Everything he said was loud.

Three people were waiting for him in the large black tent — Isaac, Rebekah, and Jubal. Usually when he came home only Isaac was there to greet him.

Esau stopped and stood flatfooted in the center of the tent. He looked first at Rebekah, then at Jubal. Turning to Isaac, he demanded, "What's everybody doing here?"

"Esau, my son." Isaac tried to keep his voice calm, but there was a tremor in it. "Please stay right there, until I tell you everything. You must listen to it all."

"Something's happened!" roared Isaac's

giant son. "Tell me!"

"Calm yourself, my son. Promise you'll not rush out and do something rash. Do you understand?"

"No!" shouted Esau. "Father Isaac, tell me what's going on!"

Isaac sighed. "Your concubines went away with their fathers."

"They *what?*" Esau's red beard jutted straight out from his chin. His red face turned a slightly darker red.

"Calm yourself, son —"

"Don't tell me to calm myself!" yelled Esau. "What happened? Did they leave willingly, or did those Hittite pigs force them?"

"Esau, listen to me —"

"I'll kill them!" Esau snatched up the bow he had dropped on the floor and ran from the tent. Rebekah heard him roaring orders to his servants outside.

Isaac shook his head. "Go with him, Jubal. Try to keep him from getting himself killed."

Jubal nodded. "I'll try," he muttered and hurried out.

Rebekah sat beside Isaac. "My husband," she murmured, "what shall we do?" Her fingers massaged his shoulders.

Isaac breathed heavily. "I don't know, Rebekah. There's no way to stop him. We can only trust that God will watch over him. After all, he *is* the heir of the Promise. . . ."

Rebekah glanced sharply at Isaac. Maybe Esau would be killed in this impulsive anger. He might dash off alone and attack the Hittites by himself. He'd probably kill most of them, but then. . . . She shuddered. The thought of her son being killed wasn't as disturbing as it should have been. It would mean her plan might not be necessary.

The small community at Beersheba settled down to wait. Jubal, Markesh, and the four remaining servants had gone with Esau, leaving about thirty women and Isaac in the village. Rebekah sent some of the women to the next valley, to be with the flock left behind. If only Jacob were here.

Three days later, Jacob came home. As always, he went straight to his mother's tent. "Mother, has Esau come back yet?"

"Jacob, do you know what has happened?"

Jacob leaned his staff against the tent. He refused to use the bow Esau had trained the servants to use. "Markesh came to us where we watched the herds in the valley near Beerlahai-roi. He told us everything. All but four of the servants went to join Esau and Jubal. I thought I'd better come straight here."

Rebekah looked closely at her favorite son. He was tall and thin, darkly handsome; a short beard outlined his face. His small black eyes showed intelligence and cunning. And he was practical, too. He knew Jubal could do what was necessary to support Esau. Jacob would be needed here.

She smiled, relieved that he had come. Let Esau run off and get killed. Jacob must stay alive to claim the Promise.

"Come wash yourself and eat some barley cakes, my son. Then go to your father; tell him what you've told me. He'll be glad to know our men have gone to be with Esau."

The next afternoon Esau returned. Rebekah saw him first, coming along the trail leading from the gap in the two hills on the east. The red-bearded youth was leading the concubine Basemath by the hand. No, by her wrist. He was dragging her. They went straight to Esau's tent.

Then Jubal and the twenty-three other servants came out of the hills, dust from the journey clinging to them. Their shoulders slumped. The men straggled across the clearing to their own tents. Jubal, still holding his bow, came toward Rebekah.

"Greetings, woman," he said formally. "I will report to Isaac."

Rebekah nodded. Jubal's words were an unspoken invitation to come to Isaac's tent to hear what he said. She called to Jacob, inside her tent. He hurried out and followed her to Isaac's tent.

As she pushed aside the tent flap and entered, she saw that Jubal had already started speaking. Jacob came in behind her, and they listened to the servant's report.

". . . he wouldn't say anything; just wanted to get to the Hittites and kill them. So I sent Markesh to Beer-lahai-roi for reinforcements. They joined us the next day, before we caught up with the Hittites."

"Tell me about the battle, Jubal. There was a battle?"

"Not yet, Isaac. Something else happened first."

Rebekah bit her lip. She knew Esau had not been killed or wounded, nor any of their men. What then?

"We found an altar to Moloch," said Jubal softly.

Isaac grunted. Jacob's breath hissed through his teeth. Rebekah clenched and unclenched her fists.

An altar to Moloch! That would mean a place where a fire had been. A wide place on a hilltop, where a body could be dragged through the burning altar. She shuddered.

"We found Judith lying nearby. She had been burned so badly we couldn't recognize her. But she was still alive."

Poor Judith. Rebekah had never liked the whining girl from the moment Esau brought her to his tent, but no one deserved this! She must have suffered horribly.

And then another thought struck her. A girl . . . sacrificed to Moloch. That meant a curse! On Isaac? Or Esau? But the girl still lived. To the Hittites, that meant the sacrifice had been rejected by Moloch.

Isaac's thoughts must have followed the same line as Rebekah's. "And Judith?" he asked. "Did she live long?"

"No, Isaac." Jubal hesitated.

"Tell me, Jubal."

Jubal took a deep breath. "She . . . she was suffering terribly. Her screams. . . ." His voice trailed away.

"Go on, Jubal."

"I could hear her begging Esau to kill her."

Rebekah went to Isaac. This would be the grisly part of the story. She sensed he wanted her beside him as the last part of the story unfolded. She was right; as soon as she pressed close to him, he reached out and grasped her hand.

"Then —" Hesitantly, Jubal continued. "Esau asked a question we couldn't hear. We did hear her answer. She said she stayed alive so the curse wouldn't work. She begged Esau to kill her. She wanted to die of a cause other than the fire. Then her father's sacrifice would be rejected by Moloch, and Esau would live."

Jacob spoke from the back of the tent. "And did Esau. . . ."

There was an uneasy silence in the tent. Jubal's shoulders slumped. He opened his mouth to speak, then closed it. He looked at his feet. Slowly, he nodded.

Isaac was breathing heavily. His muscles tensed under his robe. Rebekah's thoughts went from the horror of the scene Jubal had described to concern for her husband. How much of this could the old man take?

It was Jacob who broke the stillness. "Jubal, what then? What did Esau do after he — after he finished with Judith?"

Jubal raised his head, took a deep breath, and continued. "He roared, like a wounded lion. He took up his bow and ran in the direction the Hittites had taken. I left one of the men to bury Judith, and we tried to follow."

Jubal paused again, but at a word from Jacob, continued. "We had to run to keep up with him. By the time we reached the Hittite camp, it was night. Esau was wild. He dashed in among them, killing them as they lay sleeping in their blankets. There were more than fifty of them, and they might have killed Esau if we hadn't been there. As it was, we spread out and fired our arrows at the men as they awoke."

Rebekah felt Isaac's body shivering.

"Esau found both Elon and Beeri in the camp. He — he killed them both with his bare hands."

"With his bare hands?" asked Jacob, his mouth gaping.

"Yes. He picked up Elon, raised him over his head, and slammed him to the ground. Then he hit Beeri a hard blow in the stomach. When he bent over, Esau struck him with both fists in the back of the neck. I could hear the crunch."

He could do it easily, thought Rebekah. Esau had the strength of the three men, and in his rage, ten.

"There were women in the camp. Esau shot them too. He killed them all."

Rebekah gasped. What kind of a monster was this, who had come from her own womb?

"All — except Basemath. He flung her, screaming, over his shoulder and ran off into the night. We haven't seen him since, although the men glimpsed him up ahead on the way home."

Isaac was trembling uncontrollably now. Rebekah forgot about Jubal's tale of horror and turned to her husband. He was gasping for breath.

"Jacob," she cried, "go to Deborah. Ask her to come quickly."

Jacob left immediately, but Jubal went to Isaac. Together he and Rebekah laid the old man on his bed. Isaac was sweating now, as well as panting and shivering.

Deborah hobbled into the tent and hurried to Isaac's bed. "B-bring water!" she said to Jubal, who left to do her bidding. In a moment Deborah was bathing Isaac's face. Then she held the cup of wine for him to sip.

"Deborah!" gasped Rebekah. "Is he —"

The old servant took the cup and looked into Rebekah's eyes. She sniffed, bobbed her head, and winked. But she said nothing. She didn't need to. Rebekah could read the answer in her eyes.

"Rebekah." Isaac's voice was weak. "Call . . . Esau, I . . . must bless him . . . now . . . before it's too late."

6

Isaac's dying!

Rebekah's mind whirled. She wanted to give in to grief, despair, and tears. But she couldn't. Not now. There was too much to do, and it had to be done now!

"I'll get our son," she whispered into her husband's ear. "Right away."

Isaac nodded, and she eased him back on his bed. Then she hurried from the tent.

Jacob was standing there, just outside the tent.

"How is he, Mother? Will he be all right?"

Rebekah looked into Jacob's face. The sun-burnt skin almost matched the short black beard and dark brown eyes.

"Jacob, come to my tent. We have work to do."

"But, Mother —"

"I'll explain in a moment. Come along."

Jacob followed her into the tent.

"Be seated," she said, pointing to a mat.

Jacob raised his eyebrows but said nothing. He sat.

Rebekah eased down on the mat in front of him.

"Now Jacob." She looked into his eyes. "How do you feel about the birthright?"

"What?"

"The birthright? How do you feel about it?"

They had talked about this before. Rebekah knew how he felt about the birthright.

He was silent a long time. When he spoke, it was a question. "Mother, what are you up to?"

Rebekah bit her lip. She wasn't sure how to say it.

"Jacob, your father is dying. He wants to bless Esau."

Jacob's eyes widened. "What?"

"Isaac wants to give Esau the words of the Promise, and he wants to do it now."

Jacob stared at his mother. "What are you saying?"

"I'm saying you should receive that blessing. You deserve it more than Esau. We've discussed this before. Now, do you want it?"

Jacob's eyes narrowed. He pursed his lips. Rebekah breathed a sigh of relief. Of course he wanted it.

When Jacob spoke, his voice was low. "What should I do, Mother?"

Rebekah leaned forward and spoke softly.

"Go to Isaac. Now. He will bless you, thinking you're Esau."

Jacob gasped. "Mother, that's impossible! Father wouldn't give me the blessing! And he knows the difference between me and Esau. Why do you think —"

"You can imitate Esau's voice and manner. I've heard you do it many times."

"But Mother, he'll know me by smell. You know what Esau smells like —"

"That's easily taken care of, son. We'll rub you with the blood of a dead goat. In a minute you'll smell as bad as your brother."

Jacob pursed his lips. "Yes, it might work. But what if he touches me? He usually does, you know, since he can't see me."

"A goat skin on your arms and face and legs should make you feel like Esau."

Jacob snorted. "Come on, Mother. That won't fool anybody. Not even a blind man."

"Isaac is sick. He's dying. In fact, he's only half conscious. If ever it will work, now is the time."

Jacob frowned. He pulled on his short beard.

"But Mother, if it doesn't work, will he curse me?"

Rebekah was prepared. "If he curses you, what have you lost? Unless you have the birthright, you're cursed anyway."

Jacob nodded. His eyes glazed over, and he looked over his mother's head. He was holding his breath. Finally he nodded again. "All right, Mother," he whispered.

Rebekah let out her breath. She had been holding it almost as long as it took Jacob to make up his mind. Quickly she got to her feet.

"Go to the pasture and kill a goat. We'll cook its meat for Isaac. We'll tell him it's fresh venison from the field —"

"Even Isaac can tell the difference between venison and goat meat, Mother. How can you —"

"He won't even taste it. He's sick. All he can do is smell it."

"But it doesn't even smell like —"

"Jacob, do you want the blessing, or don't you? Now go do as I say."

"All right, Mother." He left the tent.

Rebekah went outside to stir up the coals of the fire. There was much to do. The meat must be cooked just the way she usually cooked venison Esau brought in from his hunting trips. Then she must rub the blood of the goat into Jacob's flesh and hair. The goat skin too must be cut and wrapped around Jacob's hair, his arms, even his face.

Now where were those old clothes which Esau had discarded? She had bundled them into a sack and thrown them in a corner of the tent several days ago, when the idea first came to her. She hadn't expected her plan to come to fruition this quickly.

An hour later, Jacob entered Isaac's tent. "Greetings, Father Isaac!"

Rebekah, who stood inside the flap of Isaac's tent, nodded in satisfaction. Yes, he sounded just like Esau. That big, blustery voice. . . .

"Come closer, my son." Isaac's voice was weak. He lay unmoving on the bed.

"I've brought you some venison, freshly killed, cooked just the way you like it. Eat hearty, Father!"

The old man didn't move. Finally he raised one hand feebly and beckoned. "Closer, Esau. I want to touch you."

Rebekah's hand went to her throat.

Jacob hesitated, then knelt beside his father. "I am here, Father."

Rebekah bit her lip. Jacob wasn't loud enough! Everything Esau said was a roar.

Isaac's hand reached out. Jacob took it and placed it on his arm, on the goatskin. Again the old hand reached up. The fingers went over the chest, across the old skin robe which Jacob now wore, seeking the face. The fingers played on the sham beard. Then weakly, the hand fell to his side.

"The voice —" Isaac croaked. "It's the voice of my son Jacob. But you are Esau. Or are you?"

Say nothing, Jacob, silently pleaded Rebekah. *Don't give yourself away again.* But Jacob couldn't hear her unspoken cry.

"Father, I am Esau!" Jacob's voice rose to a roar, sounding just like his brother's. "That pig's bladder brother of mine never killed a deer in his life! He's probably sucking a sheep's teat right now, along with all the other little lambs!"

"My son Esau!" Isaac's voice sounded a little stronger. "Kiss me!"

Jacob bent over his father for the ritual kiss. Isaac's hand grasped his son's robe. In the stillness of the tent, Rebekah could hear Isaac's deep breath. Then his voice sounded clear and sure.

"Ah, the smell of my son is as the smell of the wilderness which the Lord has blessed! May God give you of the dew of heaven, and of the fatness of the earth, and plenty of grain and wine. Many people will serve you, and nations will be blessed by you. You will be the ruler over your brother, and always your brother's sons will bow down to you. Cursed be every one who curses you, and blessed be every one who blesses you!"

The hand fell weakly to the bed. The old

patriarch closed his eyes. Rebekah ran to his side.

"Is he dead, Mother?" whispered Jacob.

Rebekah felt for the artery in the throat. It was still throbbing.

"No, my son. He's just asleep. Go quickly now, before he wakes."

When Jacob was gone, she bathed Isaac's forehead with a damp cloth. Her husband was still breathing, but just barely.

Then Deborah came in and knelt on the other side of his bed. She had prepared a mixture of herbs and broth.

"M-m-medicine," she whispered, taking the cloth from Rebekah's hand. She dipped it into the broth and squeezed a few drops into Isaac's mouth.

"How much longer will he live, Deborah?" asked Rebekah.

The old servant winked and bobbed her head. "L-long time. T-t-too long! He f-f-find out you t-tricked him!"

Rebekah frowned. She might have known nothing could be kept from her shrewd serving-maid. But there was little to be done about that now.

Yet the question hung in the air in the stillness of the tent. It was something which hadn't occurred to her before. What would Isaac do? Or worse, what would Esau do?

Esau . . . the man who killed Elon and Beeri in a fiery rage! Who slaughtered all the Hittites, even the women! What would he do to Jacob when he found out?

Rebekah sighed as she got up to leave Isaac's tent. She would have to think of something. Some way to keep Esau from killing his brother. Something . . . anything . . . to save her son's life.

The next day as she left Isaac's tent, she noticed Basemath sitting outside the doorway of Esau's tent.

"Greetings, Mother."

Rebekah noticed that Basemath's greeting was respectful and without the usual sneer. She nodded. The girl's experience of the past few days would subdue anybody.

"Basemath, my daughter." Rebekah's greeting was also respectful, using the word "daughter" even though Basemath was only a concubine. She squatted on the mat outside the Hittite girl's tent, where Basemath was already seated, repairing one of Esau's torn garments.

"How is it with you, my child?" The question was formal but sincere.

Basemath hesitated. "It . . . is well with me, Mother. I —"

She couldn't go on. Rebekah noticed the tremble in her lower lip.

Rebekah tried to make her voice as gentle as possible. "This time tell me the truth, daughter. How is it with you?"

Basemath dropped the garment she was mending. Her hands went to her face; sobs burst from her.

Rebekah eased herself over to be near the young Hittite. As she put an arm around the shaking shoulder, she wondered how old this girl was. Fifteen? No more than that.

Basemath buried her face in Rebekah's bosom and wept. All the emotion and distress of the past few days seemed to flow out of her. Rebekah held her tightly, rocking gently.

In a few moments the tears subsided; Basemath took a deep breath. "Oh, Mother." She looked up, her eyes swollen and red. "It was awful."

"I know, child. I know."

Rebekah marveled that such a close bond was knit so quickly between them. For the past year, since Esau had taken the Hittite concubines to his tent, there had been a great deal of friction between them and Rebekah. Now, it was different. Basemath had no one to turn to. She was orphaned. And Rebekah was sympathetic.

"He killed them all — my father, my mother, my brothers — everyone! Then he . . . he carried me away. Oh, Mother . . . what he did to me after that —"

"Hush, child. You don't need to talk about it. It's over now. You're safe here."

The tears came again. Basemath's head went down into Rebekah's lap. She shook with the violence of her sobs. In a few minutes it passed, and the girl lay quietly.

Rebekah could fill in the gaps which Basemath left unsaid. Esau was always a lusty man with a large sexual appetite, but some perverseness of nature would make his erotic demands even more urgent after the violence. He must have cruelly used the surviving Hittite concubine last night.

Rebekah stroked Basemath's head. "Where's Esau now?"

"I . . . I don't know. He left before dawn this morning. He took his bow."

Rebekah nodded. She knew her wild son. He would go south, into the wilderness he loved so well. North was where he went for the best hunting, but south was where he could be alone. The barren country suited his wild nature. He was probably more at home there than in Isaac's tents.

Basemath straightened and resumed mending Esau's garment. There was silence. Rebekah listened to the hot wind blow in from the south. The *yoreh* would surely come soon. That first rain was one of the most welcome changes in the season. Right now, dust hovered around the clearing like a cloud.

But more dust could be seen in the south. Someone was coming. Who would that be? As she got to her feet, Rebekah remembered that the women who were keeping the sheep at Beer-lahai-roi should be coming back now. The men who had gone with Jubal to help Esau would have relieved them. Rebekah could make them out as they emerged from the hills. She would have to greet them and assign them their tasks. Some would need to go to the next valley to watch the flock.

"Greetings, Rebekah," said Sarai, one of the older women. "We have come from Beer-lahai-roi."

Rebekah nodded absently. She was still thinking about the household tasks. "And is everything all right there?"

"All is well. We passed Esau on the way. I think he was going to the *tsai*."

The *tsai!* The word meant "wasteland." It was often used to describe the desolate country south of Beer-lahai-roi. Very little water and vegetation; plenty of rocks, sand and thornbrush; heat, lizards, and scorpions. Esau's country.

"Did he say anything?" asked Rebekah.

Sarai shook her head. "He didn't even look at us. There was a wild stare in his eyes."

Sarai reported this without emotion. She was used to Esau's moods. When he was this way, the people of Isaac's tents avoided him.

"Sarai. . . ." Rebekah's voice trailed off. She stared at the mountain beyond the clearing, not seeing it. Now was the time! Jacob was still in his tent; he would join the others at Beer-lahai-roi in a few days when his father's condition stabilized. She would go to him, and —

"Rebekah, what is it?" Sarai stood before her, looking into her face. "Is something wrong?"

Rebekah realized with a start that she had been gazing off into the mountains.

"Nothing, Sarai." She took the woman's arm. "Just thinking about all that needs to be done. First, there's the flock. We need to send at least four women there. . . ."

Several hours later, Rebekah entered her tent looking for Jacob.

"Where are you, my son?"

"Mother!" The muffled voice came from the dark corner of the tent. "Is he anywhere around?"

"No, Jacob. He went south, to the *tsai*. The women coming from Beer-lahai-roi passed him only a few hours ago."

"Does he know?"

Rebekah could dimly see her son crouching

in the back of the tent. "No. Not yet. Come outside, Jacob. I have a plan."

The young man followed her outside. They squatted on the mat in front of the tent. Jacob took a long drink from the jug of water.

"Mother, are you sure he doesn't know yet?"

Rebekah smiled. "Rest easy, son. He was in Basemath's tent all night. He left early this morning without talking to anybody. I don't think he even knows how ill Isaac is."

At the mention of Isaac's name, Jacob frowned. "Just how ill is Isaac, Mother?"

"Deborah says he's stronger than he looks. He may live for years yet. Then again, he might die before Esau returns."

"When will that be?"

Rebekah shrugged. "You know your brother. In his present mood, it might be a week."

Jacob nodded; the lines around his mouth relaxed a little. He looked closely at his mother.

"When he does come back and finds out what we did to him, what will he do? Will he — will he come after me?"

"Probably. But I think I know what you can do then."

Jacob was still staring at his mother. "Yes. You said you had a plan."

Under her son's stare, Rebekah lowered her eyes. If only she didn't have to do all the planning. Jacob was intelligent, as evidenced by the way he managed the herds. But when he was frightened. . . .

She took a deep breath and met his eyes. "I want you to go south, to the trail beyond Beer-lahai-roi which leads to the *tsai*. Wait there for your brother to return."

Jacob's eyes widened. "But won't he. . . ."

"Remember, he doesn't know what you did to him. I don't know what he will think when he finds you there. But I do know he'll be hungry. There's no game in the *tsai* this time of year, and not much vegetation. He'll be very hungry."

She paused. Jacob was still staring at her, saying nothing. So she continued.

"You can have a pot of stew waiting for him. He'll be so hungry for it, he would give you anything you ask for it." She paused again. "Even his birthright."

Jacob's eyes narrowed. He pursed his lips. Then he shook his head.

"It won't work. Mother. Am I simply to tell him he can have some stew if he hands over his birthright? You know how strong Esau is. What if he just decides to help himself?"

"He'll be weak from hunger and ravenous for something to eat. If you're emphatic enough, he may not think about taking it by force."

"I don't know, Mother —"

"Jacob, listen!" Rebekah stared at her son. She spoke as firmly as she could. "It will work. Esau will swear an oath, giving you his birthright. You'll see."

Jacob shook his head, frowning.

Rebekah continued. "Consider the alternative. Esau will come into Beersheba, learn that Isaac blessed you by mistake, and kill you. But if he has already relinquished his birthright, he may resign himself to it and not harm you."

Jacob's forehead wrinkled. "But . . . how will we know?"

This was a question Rebekah was ready for. "We'll listen outside Isaac's tent when Esau goes in to him. We'll hear his reaction when he and Isaac discover what we did. Then we'll know whether Esau accepts it, or whether you should leave immediately."

Jacob's fingers played nervously on his short beard. "I don't have much faith in this plan. First, Esau must give me his birthright just because he's hungry. Then he must decide it's all right for Isaac to have given me the elder son's blessing instead of him. That's a lot to ask of Esau."

Rebekah sighed. "You're right, my son. It

probably won't succeed. But do you have another plan?"

The young man's eyes dropped. "No, Mother," he said softly.

"Whether it succeeds or fails," said Rebekah, "I believe it's time you went to Haran. You'll be out of Esau's sight for a few months. And besides, since you're now the heir to the Promise, you'll need a wife from among our own people."

Jacob lifted his eyes. "Yes, Mother." He smiled. "You're right. I should go to Haran. But why wait until after Esau learns we've tricked him? Why not go now?"

This was something Rebekah hadn't thought of. "No, Jacob. Wait until after you try to buy Esau's birthright from him for a pot of stew. If that part of the plan succeeds, he may not try to follow you."

Jacob's smile made him look like a carefree boy. "All right, Mother. We'll try it. Now, what shall we put into that stew?"

7

Six days later, Esau returned to Beersheba.

He went straight to Basemath's tent. Evidently she told him of his father's illness, as he went immediately to Isaac. Rebekah watched as her wild-looking son boldly entered his father's dwelling place. Then she scurried to the back of the goatskin structure to listen to what was happening inside.

"How is it with you, Father Isaac?"

Esau's voice was softer than usual, even when muffled by the thick goatskins. *He really loves his father,* thought Rebekah. She hadn't been sure this animal from her womb was capable of love.

Isaac's voice was harder to hear. "My son! My son Esau! You have come from the fields. Have you brought me some meat?"

Rebekah smiled. Isaac, though blind, would have no trouble recognizing his son. The smell of the *tsai* clung to him.

"Father, there's no game. Wait till the *yoreh;* then I'll bring you a fat deer, and you can give me your blessing."

Rebekah caught her breath when she heard these words. Had the plan failed? Did Esau still expect to receive the blessing?

"But my son, I have already given you my blessing."

"No, Father, you have not!"

"But I have. Just one week ago, you came to my tent. Don't you remember? I thought I was dying, and at that time —"

"No!"

"What is it, Esau?"

Rebekah shut her eyes. She could picture the scene: Esau on his feet, hands balled into fists, pacing up and down, hair and beard shaggy and streaked with dust, and his eyes — his eyes wide open and staring!

His next words roared out. "That brother! May ten pigs empty their bowels on him! He has tricked me. Again!"

"What is it, son? What happened?"

For a moment Rebekah heard nothing except Esau's labored breathing. What he spoke, his voice was subdued.

"Isaac, my father. You must bless me. Bless me now! My brother — may his carcass be eaten by jackels — has deceived both you and me! *He* was here last week to receive your blessing; he waited for me as I was coming in from the *tsai*. He had a pot of stew cooking. I was hungry, and he gave me some. But he made me swear a sacred oath to relinquish my birthright! May he eat goat's dung forever!"

So Jacob had done it! The plan was successful! Or was it? That depended on Esau — would he accept what was done and resign himself to the loss of the birthright?

Isaac's voice was so weak she could scarcely hear him. "Can it be so? Has my son Jacob done that?"

"Father, listen to me! You must revoke his blessing. It's mine! You must give it to me!"

"No, my son."

"*What?*"

"The blessing, once given, cannot be revoked. And your sacred oath is binding. Jacob is now heir of the Promise."

"*No! It cannot be!* Father, bless me, *now!*"

Rebekah could feel the muscles in her throat contracting. Isaac would not — could not — revoke the blessing. But what would he do? There was silence in the tent for almost a minute. When at last Isaac spoke, his voice was frail and soft.

"Behold, away from the fatness of the earth shall your dwelling be, and away from the dew of heaven on high. By your sword and bow you shall live, and you shall serve your brother —"

"*No!*"

"But when you break loose from him, you shall break his yoke from your neck!"

Rebekah gasped. The last part of Isaac's blessing could mean anything — anything Esau wanted it to!

From inside the tent came a mighty roar. *"I'll kill him! I swear before the living God, before I die, I will do to him what Cain did to Abel!"*

Tiny needles seemed to be prickling Rebekah's skin; her vision blurred. Sweat started on her body. Her head ached. A strange weakness overpowered her.

She couldn't give in to this weakness — not yet! She must do something — anything — to protect Jacob from this madman. She had to think . . . think calmly, clearly, without emotion. She took a deep breath. Jacob must be warned. But he had already fled. Immediately after he encountered his brother and exchanged the birthright for the stew, he was to leave and go to Haran. But Esau would follow, quickly, traveling day and night. Jacob could never get away! Esau must be stopped! Now! But how?

There came a strangled cry from inside the tent.

"Father!" Esau's voice reflected concern now, rather than rage. "What is it? What's wrong?"

Isaac! The strain of this conversation, the

realization that his beloved son had been tricked and the birthright given to Jacob, and now the final oath by Esau to kill his brother must have been too heavy a burden. Rebekah's concern for her husband overcame the paralysis of fear that had gripped her a moment before. She ran to the entrance to the tent.

"Isaac!" she shrieked. "Are you all right?"

She knelt beside him. She noted the staring eyes, the cold clammy skin, the rattle of breath in his throat.

"Esau! Tell Deborah to bring the medicine! Hurry!"

With a grunt Esau left the tent. Rebekah turned her attention to her dying husband. That he *was* dying, she was certain. The rattle in his throat was stopped now. He lay staring from unseeing eyes.

"Isaac, my husband, my beloved!" Rebekah lifted his head from the bed and hugged it to her chest. "Isaac . . . oh, Isaac!"

Then Deborah knelt on the other side of the bed, and her fingers went to Isaac's throat. Rebekah would not let go of his head, but she lifted her eyes to look at Deborah.

The old servant sniffed, winked, and nodded. "He's d-d-dead," she muttered.

"Oh, Isaac! My husband! My beloved!"

Rebekah's voice rose in a wail. She gently laid the head on the bed, then ripped her dress. Her hands went to her hair, so neatly combed and in place, and tore it from its bindings so it fell across her face. "Oh, my husband! My beloved Isaac! Oh . . . oh . . . oh!"

Behind her, Esau roared. *"My father! Oh, Isaac, my beloved father!"* He too tore his clothes. Outside Rebekah could hear other voices raised in a loud lament.

Although Rebekah's mourning was sincere, a small part of her mind was rejoicing. Isaac's death could not have come at a more appropriate time. Esau would stay for a few days to bury his father. They would have to go to the caves of Machpelah for the burial. It would take several days or a week. Jacob would have a head start, perhaps even be in Haran by then. Her brother Laban would protect him.

Esau might even cool his temper in a week's time and accept the situation. He would be the sole heir now of the flocks and herds, and he would need to stay and manage the flocks and household. Yes, and she could even tell him he must remain until after her death. And she would live a long, long time!

These thoughts swirled in Rebekah's mind as her voice lifted in wails of mourning for her husband. "Isaac, my husband! My beloved!"

she shrieked. But inside, deep in her soul, she was saying, *Thank you, Isaac, for dying now. By doing so, you may have saved Jacob's life!*

8

"Oh Isaac! My beloved! My husband!"

Rebekah's throat was raw and her voice harsh as she lifted her lament just outside the cave at Machpelah. For the past week, she and the others had wailed and shrieked and moaned as they mourned the dead patriarch.

About a hundred women stood on a ridge near the entrance to the cave at Machpelah, which was shaded by two mammoth oak trees. Rebekah could see the black gaping hole in the side of the hill, just beyond the oaks.

She had never been inside. Only men entered this hallowed grotto. Yesterday the servants had gone in and prepared the burial chamber. They described with awe the large rooms, especially the one with the sarcophagus containing Father Abrabam's body.

A similar crypt had been prepared for Isaac. She would never see his final resting place. Some day she too would lie in a chamber in that tomb. The irony almost brought a smile to her lips. The only way she would get in there was by dying.

"Isaac, my beloved!"

She was croaking the words now, but she mustn't stop. It would show disrespect for her husband if she stopped mourning just because of a sore throat. Soon the men would emerge from the tomb, and the blessed silence would begin. She could rest her voice then.

She had been mildly surprised by the intensity of Esau's mourning. Under that gruff exterior, he truly loved his father. From the moment of his birth, there had been a bond between them. They respected each other. Isaac loved Esau for his strength and manliness; Esau loved his father for his constancy and wisdom. Esau had temporarily forgotten his sacred vow to kill his brother as he mourned the passing of his father.

The wailing sounds around her husband stopped suddenly as the men silently emerged from the cave, grim-faced and squinting in the sunlight. Jubal's tall form appeared, his robe torn according to custom, and dust strewn on his head and beard.

There was Markesh his son, beardless, but even in his youth he had taken his mourning seriously. His small robe was rent in several places, and his hair was dusty and uncombed.

The dirty face was tear-stained, evidence of the love he — and all the company at Beersheba — bore the old patriarch.

No word was said as the men packed their equipment on the asses and began the twenty-five mile trek to Beersheba. Rebekah recalled the funeral procession two days before to this place. There had been wailing and lamentation and waving of arms. They had been joined by the Canaanite nobles just outside the city of Hebron, their voices raised in weeping and shouting to honor the dead.

In contrast, this return journey was silent, emphasizing the small sounds of the caravan: the clop-clop-clop of the asses hooves, the snorts of the beasts, and the low moaning of the wind in the treetops. Rebekah listened for the birds' songs. There were none. Even nature mourned with silence the passing of the patriarch.

But there was another reason for nature's quiet. Rebekah lifted her head and sniffed the air. The wind — the dry, hot wind — was shifting. No longer from the east, it now came in from the north. It wasn't as dry now; she could definitely smell the moisture in it. The yoreh! At last the first rain would fall, bringing relief to the ravages of the dry season.

The others in the caravan walked more briskly, sensing it too. Not that there was a rush to get home and get under cover; these people were accustomed to weather in its extremes. But there was a feeling . . . a renewal of vigor, a freshening of spirit, a sensing of new life with the coming of the *yoreh.*

Rebekah squared her shoulders and breathed deeply. Her legs didn't hurt as much now, although the change in the weather usually made her knees ache. She felt good, as though she had just wakened from a refreshing sleep. This was an enthusiastic time, when people made plans, talked about new ideas, looked forward to gardening, selecting pasture, washing clothes, and cleaning tents.

She wondered where Jacob was. If he traveled fast, he would be in Haran any day now. The thought of his brother pursuing him would keep him moving. By now, he should be safe.

Rebekah was at the head of the women's procession, and she could plainly see Esau's broad form a few yards ahead. He gripped his staff tightly, the ever-present bow left behind for the funeral procession. His head was high and his shoulders squared.

As he turned his head, Rebekah caught a glimpse of his face. She caught her breath. What she saw on his face was as clear as the signs of the *yoreh.* His teeth were clenched, his mouth drawn back in a scowl, his forehead creased in a frown. And his eyes — she read in them pure hate. This was no silent mourning for a dead father; this was hate. Hate for his brother. Determination to kill.

Esau's vow echoed in Rebekah's mind. "I'll kill him! I swear by the living God, I'll do to him what Cain did to Abel!" It was a sacred vow, irrevocable, uttered before God and his now-dead father. She shuddered. Now that he had buried his father, he was free to fulfill his vow!

Night had fallen by the time they arrived at Beersheba. She hurried to catch up with her son. Custom demanded a respectful silence must continue until they arrived home, but then they were free to speak. And speak she must, before it was too late.

"Esau."

He spun around to face her. They were standing by the well, and the servants were hurrying by on their way to their tents. Esau's face still reflected the hatred she had seen earlier, not even softened by darkness.

He stared at her, saying nothing. The silence of the day had settled into his being, and he was unwilling to break it. The look in his eyes spoke clearly, however.

Rebekah drew her breath. "Esau, my son." What should she say? She decided on a direct approach. This was Esau, who didn't like to waste words. "You must not do this! Your father would not want you to kill his son."

Esau stared at her, eyes narrowed, but said nothing.

"Please, Esau. The vow you made can be revoked. You can offer a sacrifice. You can —"

She faltered. What she was saying was false and hollow. The vow was irrevocable. She knew it. So did Esau.

When Esau finally spoke, his voice was guttural and harsh. "I leave in the morning. I'll follow him to Haran . . . *and I'll do to him what Cain did to Abel!*"

Rebekah gasped. Impulsively she reached out and grasped Esau's sleeve. He shoved her aside roughly.

"Remember the curse!" she hissed. "Moloch's curse on you. If you try to fulfill this foolish vow, Moloch will reach out and kill you."

"Moloch — bah!" Esau spat on the ground. "That god can't do anything. He couldn't even take Judith —" There was a catch in Esau's voice at the mention of her name.

Rebekah knew it was true. Even if Esau believed in Moloch — and Isaac insisted there was no god other than the God of Abraham — the Hittites' sacrifice had failed and the curse was nullified. Desperately she sought another way to deter him.

Maybe if she called on her childhood gods. "May . . . Isht and Baal kill you if you try to harm your brother! They have power in their own land, and I will make a sacrifice to them to protect Jacob!"

Esau snorted. "More false gods! They have no power even in Haran. Abraham's God will utterly destroy them!"

She knew he was right. When she married Isaac many years ago, she had forsaken the gods of her family and accepted Isaac's God. During these years, she had become so accustomed to worshiping the living God of Abraham that she found calling on Isht and Baal hollow and meaningless.

Her voice was close to breaking. "Remember Isaac's blessing: 'You shall serve your brother.' You can't harm Jacob; he's under God's protection!"

Esau snorted. "I plan to break his yoke from my neck!"

Rebekah bit her lip. She recognized the words Isaac had spoken when he blessed Esau. She didn't know then what they meant; she didn't know now. But that was unimportant; what mattered was that Esau could interpret them any way he wanted!

Esau turned and strode off into the darkness toward his tent. Rebekah stared after him, clenching and unclenching her fists. She thought of Jacob, whom she hoped was in Haran now. Was there any way to save him?

At that moment the first drops of the *yoreh* splattered onto the clearing. They splashed on her bare head and face. Warm wet drops, kicking up the dust on the ground. The *sharav* was over; no more hot dry days. This was the *stav*, when frequent rains would turn the land green again. It was a time of new beginnings, of thanksgiving, of rejoicing.

A tear from Rebekah's eye mingled with the warm drops of rain. Rejoicing! How could she rejoice, when Jacob's life was in danger?

9

The gray light was softening the edges of the clearing as Rebekah emerged from her tent. The day had not begun; the stillness of night pervaded the tent community of Beersheba.

Rebekah walked swiftly toward Basemath's tent, hoping fervently that Esau had not gone yet. During the long hours of the night, she had rehearsed in her mind what to say to him.

Remember, she told herself, *don't plead. Speak firmly. Don't give yourself away. He must not know you are suffering.*

Outside Basemath's tent, she stopped. Should she go in? Or wait out here? She glanced around the clearing; no one was in sight. Everything was still. Clouds formed in the west; another rain would drench them today. The grass at her feet was still wet, although the shower last night had not fully soaked the dust.

Someone was moving around inside the tent. Then the flap opened and Esau stood there, his huge bulk filling the doorway. A pack was on his back and his bow in his hand. The quiver of arrows at his side was full.

"Esau, my son." She kept her voice low but knew it carried in the early dawn. Anybody awake would hear her. She didn't care. It must be said.

"Good-bye, Rebekah."

The curt dismissal, using her name rather than the more intimate "Mother," warned her the confrontation would be difficult.

"If you stay here," she said, forcing the tremor out of her voice, "you can marry Basemath and be patriarch of this clan."

This was the first part of her strategy. An offer of power. She didn't have much faith in it — not with Esau. But she had other arguments to back it up.

Esau grunted. "I have already decided to accept Basemath as a wife, not a concubine. Good-bye, Rebekah."

What did that mean? But she had no time to think about that now. Time for the next step. "Esau, I need you. With Isaac gone, and Jacob gone, I have no one to turn to. You are the only son I have left. Please stay!"

Esau said nothing. She had little faith in this argument either. She had never been close to her wild son in the past; he had always been "Isaac's boy." But there was the barest chance that Esau would turn to her as his only surviving family member.

The silence stretched out. A few sounds intruded. A mourning dove greeting the dawn. Esau stared at Rebekah.

"Jacob will be in Laban's tents now," she said.

There was no need to cover up where Jacob had gone. Esau had already guessed. Actually Jacob had nowhere else to go.

"Your brother will be under your uncle's protection. If you harm him, you insult Laban. Let there be peace between me and my brother, Esau. Please don't fight your uncle!"

Esau glared at her with unblinking eyes. She bit her lip. If he would only say *something*.

Time now for the last argument, the final array of ideas she had marshalled against her son's stubborn will. This was her last — and most desperate — chance.

"Isaac's blessing to Jacob," she said slowly, speaking softly, "said this: 'Be lord over your brother, and may your mother's son bow down to you'."

She watched his face to see what the impact of her words were on him. That face — that whiskered, sun-wrinkled face, the red hair clearly visible even in the dim light — was impassive. She wondered if he had even heard her.

"The last thing Isaac said to your brother was 'Cursed be everyone who curses you, and blessed be everyone who blesses you.' Think about it Esau. These are the words of the blessing, spoken on Isaac's deathbed. They are as strong as the words of God. Do you want to be under God's curse?"

She let the statement hang in the stillness. Still there was no sign of emotion on Esau's face. He stared at her as though she were a tree or stick of wood.

The silence stretched out into the increasing light. At last Esau spoke. "Good-bye, Rebekah."

He turned and strode toward the opening in the east between the two mountains.

Rebekah's feet seemed to be made of stone. Tears formed in her eyes. This must not be! She had to stop him!

She ran after him. Her voice — usually so carefully kept under control — now shrilled like a crow's. "Esau, don't do this! Isaac would be ashamed of you! If you kill your brother, I will denounce you! You will be an outcast from your own family! You —"

She stopped, gasping for breath. Esau continued with long strides toward the east.

Rebekah raised her voice. "To Isaac's curse upon you, I will add mine! If you do this, may God turn you into a wild beast! May you

91

dwell in the field, eating roots and wild honey! May you never know peace, for God's curse will be upon you! *O God of Abraham, destroy his soul!*"

Her voice wakened the morning. Birds shrilled. Nearby an ass snorted. Other sounds, undefinable, forced themselves into the dawn. But Esau never turned. He strode on toward the hills in the east. In a moment he was gone.

Rebekah stood there at the edge of the clearing. Her jaw muscles were tight. The sounds she heard were her own sobs.

The whole community at Beersheba had surely heard her. She didn't want to face anybody now. Where could she go? In the small clearing there was no place to hide. If she went back to her own tent, Deborah would be there. She didn't want to face Deborah, not now. But she had to go somewhere.

Basemath's tent. She would go there. Maybe Basemath would respect her need for privacy, for silence, for a few minutes to absorb the shock and grief of this moment.

Basemath was standing in front of the tent, her eyes red even in the soft light.

"Come in, Mother." She put her arm around Rebekah's shoulders and led the older woman inside. Only a week ago it had been Rebekah's arm around Basemath's shoulder.

Now the fifteen-year-old girl offered comfort to her mother-in-law.

She took a deep breath, trying to control herself. No use. Her emotions overwhelmed her, and she turned to Basemath's shoulder and sobbed. Together the two women sank to the floor, arm in arm, Rebekah convulsed in tears and sobs.

The fury of the storm raged within her, ravaging her ancient body, bursting out of her mind through her eyes in an overflow of tears. For several minutes she wept, forgetting everything, everything except the need to spend herself in grief. Then it passed, suddenly, unexpectedly. She took a few gulps of air and raised her head.

"I'm . . . all right now, daughter," she murmured.

Basemath nodded. "Mother," she said softly, "I heard it all. I too tried to talk him out of this folly. But he's like a madman. I think Moloch has cursed him after all."

Rebekah said nothing. Basemath must learn — as she had years ago — that all gods were false except the God of Abraham. This was not the time to teach her, however.

Rebekah sighed. She had no one now. Isaac gone. Jacob gone. Esau gone. Rebekah had never felt close to Sarai and the other servants, not even Deborah who had been with her all her life. She was more alone now than she had ever been.

She looked at her daughter-in-law. Just a child. A lonely, orphaned child. She needed a mother. And Rebekah needed a daughter.

Suddenly she recalled Esau's last words. "I have already decided to accept Basemath as a wife, not a concubine." Had he done this to hurt her? Or to insure for Basemath a place in Rebekah's household? No matter. Basemath was family now.

With a start Rebekah realized the depth of her love for this youth. A Hittite stranger. No, not a stranger. And no longer a Hittite. Yes, she was family now.

"Mother." Basemath's soft voice cut into her thoughts. "I have something to tell you."

"What is it, my child?"

"Last week, I —" Basemath dropped her eyes.

Rebekah reached for the child's hand. "Yes, my dear?"

"I missed my unclean time. I can't be sure yet, but. . . ."

Rebekah caught her breath. This could only mean —

The two women looked into each other's eyes. Even in the darkness of the tent, Rebekah could see the spark of joy glistening in the eyes of Esau's concubine. No, not concubine. Wife! Then the child in her womb now was Rebekah's grandchild!

Suddenly her arms were around Basemath, and they hugged each other. Gone was the storm which had so recently raged inside her. Gone was the cloud which had darkened her mind but a few moments before. Gone was the fear inside her stomach about her beloved son Jacob. They were still there, lurking in the recesses of her being to be brought out and dealt with later. But for now, they were gone.

Her child — her new daughter — had given her something to live for. Something with which to fill the lonely hours of her old age and bring purpose to her ebbing life. She could teach this child the truth about Jacob and Esau. Now she had a mission, a reason for living.

And companionship! She looked at her daughter-in-law and smiled. Outside, a woodpecker knocked loudly on the old sycamore tree. A wren sang a cheerful song to all the world.

And Rebekah continued to smile as she rose to go about the tasks of the new day.

Part III

Mahalath bath Ishmael

10

Mahalath's delicate fingers plucked the strings of the lyre. She looked around. About twenty men sat in the large tent. Lamplight flickered on their faces as they watched her. She took a deep breath, smiled, and softly began to sing.

> The hunter strode into the rising sun,
> His bow ready, an arrow nocked.
> His eyes alert, his footsteps soft,
> Searching . . . ever searching . . . for game.

The tall red-bearded giant, the guest of honor, was watching. Mahalath felt his hard gaze on her as she sang. Her song was just for him.

> The day was cool, the fields were damp.
> Dark clouds surged across the ashen sky.

The grass was wet, the trees were
    dripping,
But still the hunter pressed on, pressed
    on.

She had learned the song as a child. She
sang in her own language, because it was also
the language of the red-bearded guest. When
he arrived this morning, his attempts to communicate were frustrating. No one could converse with him. Mahalath was the only one,
because the language was her own.

She had asked her master, Sakkara the
Egyptian, if she could sing the old hunting
song from the folklore of her people. Sakkara,
old and shrewd, had said yes. He had stroked
his smooth chin several times when Mahalath
had made her request. He too knew that the
stranger was a skilled hunter, and a hunting
song in his honor would be most appropriate.
The sly slave trader had something in mind
for his guest. It took no prophetic vision to
guess what it was.

The hunter sniffed the morning air.
He knew the signs; soon it would
    rain.
The game would cower in the forest,
When clouds opened and the rain
    began.

The red-bearded guest stared at her, eyes unblinking. The venison on the plate before him was untouched. Others in the room had hungrily devoured their meat, the first they had enjoyed in ten days. No wonder the big hunter was honored tonight; when he arrived in camp this morning with a large gazelle over his shoulders, he was eagerly welcomed by the slave caravan.

> There! On the ground! A spoor!
> The hunter ran swiftly now.
> He was ready. His strong bow
> Held the hickory shaft with practiced
>   ease.

Mahalath knew a lot about hunting. Her father, Ishmael, was a renowned hunter in his day, and her brother, Nebaioth, carried on the tradition. She herself had never been on a hunt, but all children — boys and girls — who grew up in the red lands of the Arabah were steeped in the lore of the hunt.

Surely their giant guest would be impressed with her song! He was the only one here who would be; no one else could understand the words.

> There! There, grazing on the
>   dampened meadow,

Unsuspecting . . . downwind . . .
   secure . . .
The graceful gazelle bowed its head to
   the grass,
While the hunter stalked, with quiet
   steps.

Now Mahalath's fingers plucked the lyre softly but urgently, building up the suspense. The ten-stringed lyre from Egypt was quite different from the seven-stringed *mahalath* — her namesake — which she had grown up with. Her father had named her for the harp; perhaps that was why she learned to play the instrument at a very early age.

Now! The hunter's strong arm tensed,
He planted his feet firmly,
The arrow drew back to his cheek!
The gazelle still grazed unaware.

Now came the climax of the song, and her fingers flew over the strings. The music surged into the room, its tenseness and urgency capturing the entire audience, even those who could not understand the words.

The arrow flew from the bow!
Across the meadow it sped!
It whirred through the air swiftly,

Straight and true, at the gazelle.

The big hunter clenched his fist. His jaw was tight. Mahalath knew he was reliving the hunt.

> Just behind the beast's left shoulder
> The shaft penetrated the skin,
> And the flesh, and the heart.
> The arrow passed through, to the
>   other side.

> The gazelle leaped into the air;
> It turned to run!
> But alas, it had no strength,
> And it fell to the ground, dead.

Now the music softened, and the fingers on the strings of the lyre were gentle.

> The hunter approached respectfully.
> He spoke words of grief to his fallen
>   game.
> He mourned the death of the noble
>   beast,
> While he thrilled to the victory of his
>   hunt.

One more verse. Softly, almost inaudibly, she sang. The short strings of the lyre lifted the music to a high pitch.

> Now the hunt is done; the hunter can
>   go home.
> He dresses the beast carefully,
>   skillfully,
> Then shoulders it and walks away,
> Leaving behind the blood and the
>   memory.
>
> The light is failing; the rain is gently
>   falling.
> The song in the hunter's heart is sad.
> He has killed his game, but has
>   brought death,
> For he is the hunter, who lives by his
>   bow.

The last chord lingered in the silence of the room. Mahalath wondered how the strange guest would receive the song. If she had guessed rightly, the fierce-looking hunter had a sensitive soul. Often her father and brother expressed the sentiments in her song. The true hunter, she knew, respected the game he stalked and grieved at its death. Not all hunters felt that way, only the best, the most sensitive.

Was he a sensitive one? She looked into the big man's eyes. They were impassive — no, they were soft! She saw beyond the gruff exterior into his inner being. The sentiments of her song had found a true response in him.

Although only fifteen, Mahalath had learned long ago to look beyond the outward appearance of a person. Everyone said she was like her grandmother, Hagar, in that respect. She knew and understood people. They said she had a gift. She could look deeply into a person and *feel* what that person was like. And she was seldom wrong.

She met the bluff guest's eyes. Behind them was something impressive, profound. This was a thoughtful, lonely man, whose sensitive nature was probably misunderstood and unappreciated. He was the kind of man who could hunt with skill and strength, yet grieve at the death of his noble game. He was a man who would be gruff and abrupt with everyone, but whose real nature was warm and sincere.

Their eyes held for a long moment. She looked deeply into a sensitive soul and knew instinctively that this unknown stranger had come into her life forever.

"Well done, Mahalath." Sakkara's deep voice broke the tense hush in the room following her song.

Mahalath smiled at him. "Thank you, my lord."

The old slave trader's fingers slowly stroked his wrinkled face. "He understood your words?"

"Yes, my lord. That is his language also."

"I see." The Egyptian's eyes narrowed. "Who else speaks this tongue?"

"No one, my lord."

"Is he from your village?"

"No. I have never seen him before."

Sakkara's face seemed to relax. Mahalath knew why. She was a slave, captured six months ago by some bandits and sold to him shortly afterward. Someone from her own village — who knew her — would present a problem.

"Ask him," said Sakkara with a slow smile, "who he is and where he's from. But first, tell him he's welcome here."

Mahalath turned to the big guest. "My master greets you, sir. He extends his warm welcome to our camp. He would like to know your name and village."

The red-bearded hunter grunted. He had glanced briefly at Sakkara a moment before, but mostly his eyes were on Mahalath. Finally he spoke. "How is it that you know my language?"

Mahalath smiled at him. "It's also my own. But we can't talk of this now. My master is waiting for an answer."

"I'm more interested in you than that pig Egyptian." The big man sighed. "But you may tell him my name is Esau *ben* Isaac, from Beersheba."

She turned to her master. "His name is Esau, his father is Isaac, and his village is Beersheba."

Sakkara nodded. He probably knew the place, being a well-traveled man. She too had heard of Isaac and Beersheba; she thought perhaps her own family was distantly related.

"Tell him he is welcome to stay with us for as long as he likes. In fact, I would employ him as a hunter. Offer him Egyptian gold rings, or Babylonian *darics,* or Midianite *kesephs,* or Tyrian *shekels.* Whatever coin he asks."

Mahalath translated. Esau's impassive face absorbed her words. When she finished, he snorted. "He can keep his gold and silver. I want none of it. But there is something I will consider."

"Yes, my lord Esau?"

Esau ran his fingers through his shaggy red beard. "I need a slave," he said.

Mahalath frowned, but she dutifully translated.

The Egyptian was delighted. He had slaves to sell. "Tell him," said Sakkara, "that I will give him a slave in exchange for a month of hunting for us."

After the translation, Esau shook his head. "No. I can't stay that long. I have important business in Haran. Tell him I can give him no more than five days."

Sakkara heard the request, frowning. He was enjoying the bartering. This was his business; he should be able to outbargain a stupid hunter.

He's in for a surprise, thought Mahalath. *This hunter isn't as stupid as Sakkara might think.*

Through her translations, Mahalath was in the middle of the haggling. Sakkara claimed five days wouldn't buy a mangy dog. Esau said no slave was worth a month. Then Sakkara offered an old sick slave, saying this was the value of five days hunting — but only if he brought in a large game animal each day.

Esau snorted. "Ask him if he knows how much skill is involved in killing one large game animal a day."

Sakkara's reply to this was a counter-question. "Do you know how much a decent slave is worth these days?"

Esau's uneaten piece of meat was on the plate in front of him. Now he picked it up. All eyes were on him; the people of the slave caravan were starving for good red meat.

Slowly Esau took a bite. As he chewed,

some grease dribbled on his beard. There was a pause while he finished chewing. He didn't speak until after he had swallowed. "How much is a large game animal worth to you?" he asked.

As Mahalath translated, she admired his shrewdness. The professional hunter versus the profession trader — and the hunter was showing more skill at trading than the trader.

"Bas curse him!" muttered Sakkara. "Tell him ten days. That's it. One large game animal on each day. And he's getting a slave cheaply," he added.

Esau nodded. "Agreed. I'll begin tomorrow. I want twenty of his men to carry the meat back to camp."

As Mahalath translated the final terms, she wondered if Esau could accomplish this impossible task. Her father and brother had often come home empty-handed after several days of fruitless hunting. On their best days, they could kill perhaps three game animals a week. Of course, the early days of *stav*, before the rains became heavy, were the best time for hunting. But it was still an impossible task.

The big hunter threw down the piece of meat, only half eaten. As he rose to his feet in a lithe motion, he said, "Tell the pig's bladder I leave at dawn. His men better be ready." Then with long strides, he left the tent.

11

How pleasant to mold barley cakes again! This was the first time since her captivity almost a year ago that she had made the cakes, which was a daily chore in her youth. How she hated it then! Now it was a privilege.

She had gone to her master, Sakkara, earlier this morning and asked to be assigned this task. She was tired of being pampered. Just because she could sing. . . .

Sakkara had grumbled but eventually conceded. "Just be careful," he had said. Careful! How could she ruin her precious hands making barley cakes?

What she really wanted to do was go hunting with the men. She had never been on a hunt. That was men's work; making barley cakes was women's work. She remembered her brother Nebaioth's laughter when she asked to accompany him. She had never asked again.

She tried to imagine the hunt. Stalking the game. Testing the wind. Drawing the bow. And Esau. . . .

There! In her breast, that strange tingling! No, not her breast, her stomach. What was it? She felt it yesterday when she looked at Esau. Familiar. She had known that tingling sensation before.

She had been five years old. The movement inside her body frightened her. Was she sick? She asked her mother, but was brusquely turned away. So she went to her grandmother. Hagar was well known in her village as a wise woman. She listened patiently to her grandchild, nodding thoughtfully. Mahalath could not describe the feeling inside her and stumbled over the words.

Hagar smiled. "I understand, child. You have a . . . gift."

Somewhat comforted, Mahalath turned away. That night a devastating hailstorm struck the village. Houses were washed away. Sheep were killed. Crops were destroyed. And little Joel's body was found in a ditch next morning.

When Mahalath was nine, she again felt those mysterious sensations inside her. The tingling. The confusion. This time she went directly to her grandmother. Hagar shook her head, frowning. And that night, Mahalath's mother choked on a bone and died, gasping and writhing in agony.

Then last year, when she was fourteen,

Mahalath felt it again. Grandmother Hagar was ill and must not be disturbed. Mahalath had gone into her house anyway and sat by her pallet.

Mahalath's eyes clouded as she recalled the scene. In the dark musty room, Hagar lay unmoving, wrinkled, gray, and somehow peaceful. Mahalath hesitated to waken her.

The old lady's eyes opened. "Yes, child?" she whispered.

Mahalath gently took her grandmother's gnarled hand. "Grandmother," she whispered, "I have that feeling again."

Hagar's eyes closed. Had she gone to sleep? For a long moment, she was silent. Then, not opening her eyes, she spoke.

"Mahalath."

The child leaned closer to catch the whispered words.

"Cherish your gift. It comes from God."

Mahalath's hand tightened on the bony fingers. "But Grandmother, what is it? I don't understand."

A smile fluttered on the wrinkled face. The words were soft, spoken clearly. "I can't explain. You'll know, when the time comes. Just be aware. And child, listen to me!"

Her eyes opened, and the smile disappeared. Now there was an urgency in her voice. "Use it . . . only for good!"

The eyes closed; she would say no more. Mahalath waited, but no further word was spoken.

In the next twenty-four hours, two things happened. Hagar died during the night. And Mahalath was captured the next day by Horite raiders.

Mahalath shuddered, the barley cakes forgotten. She had promised herself never to think about the time of her captivity by the Horites. When they finally sold her to Sakkara the slave trader, she had felt immense relief.

Mahalath dropped a barley cake on the hot flat stone by the fire. She wondered about her gift. And Grandmother Hagar's dying comment: "Use it only for good."

Esau! Was he in danger? Was this what the gift meant? Or was it merely a warning that her life was about to change drastically? She shook her head. She was not good at mysteries and puzzles. She could only wait and see.

That evening four of Sakkara's men returned to camp, carrying two gazelles slung from poles. The entire camp gathered at Sakkara's tent to hear the news. Marduck, a swarthy Babylonian, told the story in halting Egyptian.

"Red hunter, he good. He make us wait while he go ahead. We wait, maybe four, five hours. Then we come when red hunter called.

113

There in field, two gazelles. Already gutted. Head tied under front feet. Ready to carry."

Mahalath looked closely at the nearest gazelle. It was skillfully dressed, entrails removed, even the poison glands on the legs cut out. The arrow wound behind the shoulder was clean and unsplintered. Not even her brother could have done a more masterful job.

But two of them! And in the space of four hours! Impossible. The skittish animals, even if traveling in herds, would be extremely difficult to approach for the killing of one, let alone two.

Sakkara's voice boomed out over the titter of excitement. "Build a smoke tent! I want both gazelles skinned, smoked, and wrapped before sunrise!"

The excited chatter turned into a groan as the women realized the amount of work ahead of them. But already they were planning how to quick-roast some small but succulent pieces of meat for their evening meal. There wasn't much meat left over for the women after last night's dinner, and they were starved for juicy red meat. Mahalath felt her mouth watering as she thought of the savory smell of fresh venison. She had had enough of barley cakes.

The next day, Mahalath watched for the

men to come with more game, but none did. She was the only woman awake when the sun set; the others tired, went to bed early. Last night Sakkara would not allow Mahalath to help smoke the venison.

Mahalath had pouted as she went to bed last night in the middle of the bustling camp. She wanted to stay up and help the women. But she was too precious a slave to do the menial work. She was being saved for better things!

Tonight all the women went to bed early. An hour later they were wakened by a shout. Mahalath knew immediately what it was. At last the men had returned with more meat. When she arrived at the open space before Sakkara's tent, she noticed that most of the other women were there too, despite their weariness.

Bakharra the Egyptian had brought in the gazelle which Esau had killed today. It dangled from a pole carried by Bakharra and the big Nubian with no tongue. In the moonlight Bakharra's gaunt face looked skeletal, especially when he grinned. He had no front teeth.

"That red hunter ith tracking a herd," he said, basking in the attention from the entire camp. He had momentarily forgotten the speech defect caused by the gap in his teeth. "Latht night we made camp on a hill. In the morning, he told uth to wait here until we thaw thmoke in the north. We thaw it about noon. When we got there, the deer wath all gutted and ready for uth to take back."

Again Mahalath admired Esau's skillful dressing of the gazelle. The arrow wound was in the heart, the only place which would kill the big animal immediately. A neck or back shot meant a long chase until the beast bled to death. A deer which ran before dying had a gamy taste.

The smoke tent was still assembled, the coals smoldering. The tired women began the tedious job of skinning and smoking the meat. This time, however, they did not show the excitement of yesterday; fresh red meat was not a novelty for them now.

Once again Sakkara would not allow Mahalath to work. "You're a singer, not a cook," he said. Although disappointed, Mahalath understood. With her talent — and virginity — she would be worth a big price on the slave market.

Just as this thought was darting through her mind, she felt the tingling again, deep inside. She frowned. What did it mean? Something about the slave market? Could her gift be warning her of difficulties ahead? Or was it that she would never live to see the slave market?

She pushed aside that thought. She knew what she had to do to keep those thoughts away. From her tent she brought her lyre and seated herself on a stump near the smoke tent. She would keep the women entertained while they went about their work.

> Look at me, all of you,
> Look at me today!
> My new gown, golden crown;
> It's my wedding day!

She had learned the quaint Egyptian folk song from an Egyptian slave, whose mother had sung it on her wedding day. Now its lilting melody and cheerful phrases brought smiles from the weary women.

The other slaves never resented Mahalath's pampered status. They had accepted this. She was the privileged slave of great market value. Mahalath went out of her way to be friendly and helpful to everyone in the slave caravan, but she sensed that they would respect and love her anyway. Perhaps she brought music and cheer to the women who faced a dismal life of slavery and childbearing and toil.

> My lover is a golden man,
> His arms are strong and true!

Our wedding night, he holds me tight,
And oh! What he can do!

The smiles turned to snickers as the song became ribald. It was a song for women only, for their giggles and knowing winks. When she finished, the ladies called for another.

Suddenly her fingers froze on the strings of the lyre. She had heard a laugh behind her — a man's laugh. She felt her face redden as she realized that the song sung only for women had been heard by a man. Who? Not Sakkara, surely; he never laughed like that. Should she turn and look? Or just play another song?

Then she knew who it was, without turning. Bakharra! The sly Egyptian guard was probably skulking around the nearest tent, listening, laughing, spying on the women at their work. She always felt uneasy in Bakharra's presence. What should she do? Ignore him. Keep singing.

The reeds grow wild in the Nile today,
The water is blue and green.
When families go out on their boats
    today,
Leviathan may be seen!

A harmless folk song, to discourage Bakharra. And there — that strange feeling inside her. Did it have something to do with Bakharra? No. She was sure it was Esau, and Esau alone, who stirred the waters in her breast.

The next day nobody came back to camp with freshly killed game. Mahalath watched the trail all day. But she wasn't surprised. Even Esau's skill as a hunter was bound to have limits.

Nevertheless, she would be glad to see Esau again. That mysterious feeling in her stomach would not go away. Hagar had called it a "gift." Gift indeed! Mahalath wondered if it might be a curse. *Please, Esau, come back!*

No one came the next day either. But the following day, about noon, everyone returned to camp. Mahalath was stitching a goatskin patch for her tent when she heard the shout. She ran to the clearing in front of Sakarra's tent.

Her eyes widened and her jaw dropped at what she saw. All the men in the hunting party stood there, and gazelles were everywhere. Large-antlered bucks, fat does, yearlings — enough meat for a month! She counted them: eight. But there were already three butchered and smoked and packed. That was a total of eleven — one more than the ten agreed on.

Where was Esau? Ah, there, striding into

camp with a fawn on his shoulders. Mahalath sensed his sadness. The hunter had made his kill, had accomplished a feat few hunters could manage. He probably even began a legend — yet the hunter was sad. He had killed. He had wiped out a whole herd. And, of course, the fawn. Otherwise it would meet a tragic death alone in the wilderness.

There were shouts, laughter, and a general hum of excited conversation in the camp. Finally Sakkara held up his hand. Gradually the buzzing subsided.

"Amenhamen," he said to the tall soft-spoken Egyptian, the foreman of the slave guards, "tell us what happened."

The lean, graceful man, clean-shaven and cultured, paused before beginning his narrative. He knew how to hold an audience, but that was unnecessary in the breathless hush as they awaited his words.

"The red hunter tracked a small herd of gazelles in the wadi north of the Jabbok River. We did not understand his words, but his sign language was clear. We made camp on a hilltop overlooking a valley where the herd grazed."

Mahalath looked around. The women were at the edge of the crowd, eagerly listening to his story. Even the men who had been there were absorbed. Sakkara stood frowning and stroking his beardless chin.

"He told us to wait until we saw a curl of smoke in the north. Then we were to come and bring the game home." Again Amenhamen paused. He was a spellbinding orator.

"We waited. Three days. In the rain. It was miserable, but at least there was small game in the area. And some fish in the Jabbok River. We waited. Waited. Until this morning."

This time Amenhamen's pause was unbearable. In the silence, Mahalath could hear a bird singing in a nearby tree.

Even Sakkara vented his impatience. "Yes, yes. Go on!"

Amenhamen took a deep breath and continued. "We finally saw the smoke in the north this morning. We hurried to the place at the north end of the wadi where he had made his kill. We found these!"

He indicated with a sweep of his hand the eight gazelles, all neatly dressed, their heads tied between their forelegs, their feet bound and held up by the carrying poles.

"Evidently the red hunter had cornered them in a canyon. Then he killed them all. I wish I could have been there to see it. His skill with the bow is beyond belief!"

Sakkara's deep voice asked the obvious question. "And the red hunter? Esau? Where was he?"

Amenhamen rubbed his chin with the back of his hand. "Nowhere in sight, my lord. So we cut poles and hoisted the gazelles for the long trip to camp. He joined us about an hour ago. My guess is that the fawn escaped the slaughter, so he tracked it and killed it."

Yes, thought Mahalath. *That's exactly what he did. With great sadness.* She looked around, searching for Esau. There, by the smoke tent, beginning the job of skinning the fawn. But that was women's work! She smiled. This man went his own way, paying no attention to customs and conventions.

He lifted his eyes from his work and looked at the gathering of slaves and guards in the clearing. His eyes found Mahalath, and he nodded. No smile, just a nod. But understanding passed between them, and Mahalath again felt that sensation inside her.

Sakkara's sharp voice broke the hush in the clearing. "Get to work! The meat is spoiling while we stand here talking. I want all the meat smoked, the hides processed, the camp tidied up by tomorrow morning. We leave tomorrow for Hazor! Mahalath! Bring Esau to my tent immediately!"

Mahalath rose to obey her master. The payoff. She was again aware of the tingling inside her. It was stronger now.

"My lord Esau." She stood before him and

bowed her head in salutation, a custom among her people when a woman greeted a man. "Sakkara wishes to see you in his tent. Will you come?"

At first she thought he would refuse. The bushy red eyebrows came together, and the slits of his eyes narrowed. But he wiped his bloody knife on a tuft of grass, rose, and followed her without a word.

"My lord Esau," whispered Mahalath as they entered the tent, "be warned. He's a shrewd trader and a greedy man!"

A daring thing to say, but Mahalath feared no beating if Sakkara had heard. She had been the pampered slave too long. Besides, Sakkara had never beaten a slave in the six months she had been with him. Not that he was a kind and loving man. He was just shrewd, since damaged, unhappy merchandise brought low prices at the slave market.

"What did you say to him?" demanded Sakkara sharply.

Mahalath hesitated. What should she say to her master? Telling lies had always been difficult for her.

"I told him, sir, to be warned. You're a shrewd trader."

Sakkara frowned; his thin lips compressed. He knew about Mahalath's inability to lie. She bit her lip, wondering what the next few minutes would bring. Strangely, there was no tingling in her breast now.

Mahalath looked at the two antagonists facing each other, preparing for the battle of words they both knew was coming. Sakkara was a shrewd trader; this was his profession. But Esau was his match. He had proven this on his first night in camp. It would be a sharp piece of haggling.

Esau. How grand he looked, standing tall and proud, his hair and beard shaggy and matted, his eyes flashing. And the bow — the ever-present bow — gripped firmly in his hand. The tingling in her breast surged uncontrollably.

Sakkara smiled. "Mahalath." His voice was smooth. "I want an exact, word-for-word translation. Do you understand?"

"I understand, my lord." Mahalath understood only too well. The bargaining would be sharp, the bargainers evenly matched. He wanted no advantage to go to Esau.

Sakkara's first words were a shock. "Ask him why he has failed."

"But, my lord —"

"*Ask him!* Just interpret; say nothing more!"

She turned to Esau. "My lord Sakkara wants to know why you have failed."

"Failed, Sakkara?"

"Yes, failed. We made a bargain. You haven't kept it."

Esau glared under bushy red eyebrows at the slave trader. "Define the terms of our agreement," he said.

Sakkara smiled, but his eyes were narrowed. "You were to provide at least one game animal each day for ten days. This is only the sixth day. For that, I'll give you Mashtesha. She still has a few good years left when she recovers."

Esau grunted. "Sakkara, you pig. The bargain was ten large game animals within ten days. I have brought in eleven, plus a fawn. You have far more meat than you can eat for the next month. I demand full payment!"

"Then I withdraw Mashtesha, and offer in her place —"

"No."

Esau's flat refusal required no translation. The two men glared at each other. In the hushed tension, Mahalath gasped. She knew then what the bargaining was leading to. She knew also the meaning of the strange sensations in her breast.

Sakkara frowned. Perhaps he too now saw what Esau wanted. It was obvious; she should have known from the beginning. Maybe Sakkara had glimpsed the truth before this. But all three of the people in the large tent now knew who was the final bargaining chip in the game of haggling.

"You may not have her!" said Sakkara softly. Mahalath translated word for word, her voice trembling.

"I will," said Esau, his voice hard.

A cold silence followed. It seemed to Mahalath that two unbending wills were locked in combat. The moment stretched out. Finally Sakkara spoke.

"Amenhamen!"

The flap of the tent opened, and the tall Egyptian strode into the tent. He was followed by seven others. They carried a variety of weapons — spears, knives, clubs, slings — but no bows. Only Esau carried a bow.

Evidently Sakkara had prepared for this moment. His men had been waiting outside the tent for his command. Now Mahalath felt the tension inside her mount to a roar. This was the strongest she had ever felt her gift.

The men spread out along the edge of the broad tent, ready to obey their master's command. Esau ignored them, continuing to glare at Sakkara.

Sakkara spoke, his voice almost cheerful. "Now, Esau, let us conclude our bargain. You failed to complete your ten days, and you have shown an uncooperative spirit in our discussion. I will now proclaim the final terms.

You will have nothing.

"I am sorely tempted to punish you further. But because I'm a generous man, grateful for the few items of game which you have brought to our camp I will let you go. If you leave now, quietly, you will be unharmed. Do you accept the terms of our agreement, my friend?"

What happened next was almost too fast to follow. Esau stood in the center of the large tent, bow in hand. Suddenly he reached up, swiftly drew an arrow from the quiver on his back, deftly put it on his bow, and drew it back to his cheek. It was pointed directly at Sakkara.

"Now, Mahalath," he said softly, "tell him if it comes to battle, he will be first to die."

Mahalath translated, but the words were superfluous. Sakkara's face blanched. He glanced at Amenhamen, who was looking to him for orders.

"Don't move," said Sakkara. "He's a madman."

Esau took a step backward, toward the door of the tent. "Mahalath," he said softly, "tell the men to step away from the front of the tent."

Mahalath translated. At first there was no movement. But at a nod from Sakkara, they sidled along the tent wall, leaving a gap at the front of the tent. Esau took another step back-ward.

"Mahalath, come with me." His eyes never left Sakkara.

She went to his side. Sakkara spoke sharply to her. "Mahalath, stay where you are. He won't harm you."

Mahalath paused. Now was the moment of decision. The feeling inside her breast calmed. Her gift had spoken. "No, my lord," she said in Egyptian. "I go with him. He has paid for me with a fair price. My destiny lies in his camp, not yours."

Sakkara's eyes narrowed. Mahalath knew he would not give up his most valuable slave easily.

"Then go," he said. "But know this: this is not the end of the matter. I will see you again."

"Yes, my lord," she said as she stepped be-yond Esau and went out the door of the tent.

Esau stood at the door flap, his arrow still pointed at Sakkara. "Tell them," he said to Mahalath, "that I will kill the first man who steps out of the tent."

Quickly she translated, lifting her voice so that all could hear. Then he turned and ran, and she followed.

At the edge of the clearing, Esau stopped and turned. He waited. Then came the order he was waiting for, and the first man dashed from the tent. Mahalath heard the whir of the arrow as it sped through the air, burying itself in the chest of the man who first came out of the tent.

It was Bakharra. His mouth formed an O, showing the gap in his teeth. He looked stupidly at the arrow in him, tried vainly to pluck it out, then fell to the ground.

Mahalath caught her breath. This was the man she feared most in the camp of Sakarra. His evil leers and sniggers were silenced forever. She was not sure whether she felt relief or horror at his death.

No one else appeared in the doorway of the tent.

"Let's go," said Esau calmly and began walking. He set a brisk pace, but there was no panic, no uncertainty in his actions. Mahalath followed, her heart beating wildly. There was no tingling in her breast now.

As they walked down the road, a troubled frown creased Mahalath's brow. Esau had killed. Ruthlessly. Without hesitation. What sort of man was this? He was a hunter who killed game with sadness. Yet he killed humans without remorse. He was sensitive and thoughtful — but savage. Brutal. This was the man to whom she had irrevocably linked her life!

12

Esau led the way up the Jabbok River, climbing eastward into the barren hills. The terrain grew more difficult. No caravans had pounded this trail into a thoroughfare. Most of the time, in the narrow confines of the Jabbok riverbed, they went single file, picking their way among boulders and waterfalls, while limestone cliffs loomed above.

Mahalath, unaccustomed to such difficult travel, was exhausted. Esau would want to put as much distance between him and any possible pursuers as he could, so she did not complain.

In the late afternoon, Esau turned off on one of many feeder streams which seemed to pop out of the mountains. It was hard climbing; there was no trail. At last they came to a narrow defile through which only one person at a time could go. Esau waded through, stopped, and looked around.

"We'll stay here for the night," he said briskly.

Mahalath stepped into the rushing stream and moved upward. She was in a narrow cave-like gully, sheltered from the rain with just enough ground to stand on. Not a large place for a camp, but a safe one. She began to gather sticks for a fire.

"No," he said. "No fire tonight." He offered no explanation.

Was he expecting pursuit? Would Sakkara send a squad of men after them? Probably. Mahalath smiled grimly. Not an enviable job, knowing Esau's skills in the wilderness.

Mahalath sank down at the foot of a terebinth tree which grew out of the almost vertical mountainside, its gnarled roots providing a chair-back for her. She had no blanket, and the night would be cold. Her linen dress was designed for looks, not warmth. Without a word, Esau unslung the small pack he carried, pulled out the woolen blanket, and threw it to her. Gratefully, she wrapped herself in it.

She hadn't realized until that moment how hungry she was. But Esau seemed to read her mind. He pulled from his pack a strip of dried venison and handed it to her. It was tough, but the flavor was good. She chewed on it, savoring the smoked juices hidden in it. Nourishing.

Esau was still standing, chewing his piece of

131

meat. He picked up his bow where he had leaned it against a rock. "I'll be back soon. Sleep, if you like."

Then he was gone. He slipped out through the defile downstream, probably checking his backtrail for signs of pursuit.

As she settled back among the terebinth roots, she had a disturbing thought. She was Esau's slave now. He was a man with strong sexual appetite. Would this be the night she would lose her virginity? Would Esau take her, then roll over and sleep? This was his right.

She smiled in the gathering darkness. She had no fear of Esau. If he came to her, she would give herself to him. All her life she had been taught that this was a woman's primary function — satisfying the male sexual appetite and bearing his children, both connected with the same act. And Esau, despite his gruff savage exterior, would not be repulsive to her.

But instinctively she knew he would not come to her tonight. If she had read his character correctly, he would wait until the right time. His giving of himself to her would be an act of love, not a frenzied lustful tumble. Esau, she was sure, was that kind of a man.

Although she went to sleep before he returned, her sleep was untroubled. There were no dreams, no tingling in her breast, no fears.

She was safe, because she was with Esau.

She belonged to him. Not just because she was his slave, bought and paid for at a fair price. There was something else, some mysterious awareness deep within her, which told her that she had found her destiny.

Next morning, she awoke refreshed and eager to continue the journey. She wondered where they were going. It didn't matter; she would always go with him. Esau spoke very little, but Mahalath felt he would tell her eventually.

Esau stood waiting for her as she bathed her face in the small stream. She smiled at him, hoping he would talk to her. But he looked sullen and said nothing. How late did he stay up last night? Where had he gone?

They set out at a more leisurely pace than yesterday. Back down the small stream to the Jabbok, then east up the riverbed on the difficult mountain trail. Although refreshed from her night's rest, she soon began to tire. They traveled uphill, often slogging along in the river, climbing over rocks and up the sides of the cliff to avoid waterfalls. Not much wonder she was exhausted.

Yesterday she had plodded along behind Esau mile after weary mile. Her drugged mind sought meaningless things to do. She studied the back of his robe, his sandals, the quiver of arrows. She had counted the arrows a dozen times. Nine. Today there were five.

Five!

She knew then where he had been last night. And she knew also that there would be no more pursuit today.

It rained on them most of the day, but Esau did not seek shelter. In the middle of the afternoon he stopped.

"We'll camp here." Esau's first words all day.

He had chosen a pretty place, set among some pine trees overlooking a ford in the Jabbok River. An overhanging ledge offered shelter from the rain. This time he did not stop her as she gathered twigs and sticks for a fire. Esau handed her his flintstones without word, then climbed the hill behind their campsite for hunting.

While he was gone, she struggled to make the fire. How easy it had been at home, or even in the slave camp, where a firepot was constantly smoldering. The problem was, everything was wet. During *shav*, nobody built a fire; great care was taken that the existing fire should never go out. She didn't even have a knife to cut small dry chips.

She found some dry wood, broke it into small pieces, crumbling the bark, and set to work with the flintstones. It took a long time, but eventually her patience was rewarded. When Esau returned, the smoky fire was blazing.

He said nothing in appreciation. Maybe he was too preoccupied with the difficulty of finding game at this time of year. He had shot one pheasant, a small one, and there was no way to boil water to completely pluck it. So they roasted it, feathers and all.

All day Esau had scarcely spoken. She wondered about his taciturnity. Was he always this way, a product of a lonely life in the wilderness? Or was something troubling him? That must be it. Perhaps he would tell her sometime. But she must respect his need for silence and privacy.

Many questions troubled her, questions only Esau could answer. In time, they might be answered. She must be patient. After all, she was still a slave.

She sighed. Slavery. Six months ago, she had accepted servitude as her destiny. Her future had been in God's hands, but she had determined to improve her lot. She remained optimistic, using her musical talent to charm whoever would listen. Any future owner would treat her well, as long as she was dutiful and cheerful and treated her master with respect and good will.

She was delighted to be Esau's slave.

Mahalath knew her future would have many problems and difficulties, but with Esau it would be bearable. In fact, even enjoyable.

Just before settling in for the night, Esau finally broke his silence. The fire had died down to coals, and Esau sat before them, staring into the soft red glow. Mahalath picked up the blanket he had given her. She was about to wrap herself in it for the night when he spoke.

"Have you always been a slave?"

The question surprised her; he said so little. Was he interested in her background, or was she just piece of property? The question implied that he sincerely cared about her.

"My lord Esau, I have been a slave for less than a year. Before that, I lived in my family's village of Punon."

"Punon? Where's that?"

"In the Arabah, south of the Salt Sea."

"And your family? Do they still live there?"

"Yes, my lord. My father still lives, or did when I last saw him. He is the patriarch of our clan."

"His name?"

"Ishmael."

Esau looked at her with new interest. "Ishmael? Is he the son of Hagar, Abraham's concubine?"

"Yes, my lord. Do you know my family?"

Esau snorted. "No. But you and I are related. We share the same grandfather — Abraham. I am the son of Isaac."

"Grandmother Hagar spoke of Abraham often. She liked him."

Esau nodded. "So did everybody. He was a man of great faith. But there was no family love between Isaac and Ishmael."

Mahalath had never heard the whole story. Hagar talked of Abraham, always with love and respect. Neither she nor her father Ishmael ever mentioned Isaac. Mahalath often wondered what this mysterious family feud was all about.

"My lord Esau." She hesitated. Would he resent a request from a slave? "Would you tell me the story?"

He nodded. Mahalath wrapped the blanket around her and sat on a stone close to him. Would her bold action disturb him? Apparently not; he began telling the story.

"Sarah was Abraham's lawful wife. When she bore him no son, she gave him her handmaid, Hagar, to give him an heir."

Mahalath understood. She had heard that it was common practice among many tribes to sire a child through a servant. If a boy, he would officially become the child of the clan's matriarch. Her people had never done that.

"After Ishmael was born, Sarah herself conceived."

Esau's voice dropped a little. Ordinarily loud, he was finding it difficult to keep his voice low.

"When Isaac was born, Sarah was afraid Abraham would not acknowledge him as the heir, since Ishmael was older. There were angry words between Sarah and Hagar."

Mahalath looked into Esau's face. The soft glow of the coals danced on his red beard and hair.

"My lord Esau," she said softly, "would Abraham cast out his concubine and son because of petty jealousy? Why could he not merely acknowledge Isaac as heir? Didn't he control his women?"

In many families, had this situation arisen, a sound beating of both wife and concubine would have solved the problem.

Esau smiled grimly. "He *did* publicly acknowledge Isaac as the heir. But he saw that the two boys could not grow up together in the same household. The story my father Isaac used to tell was that Ishmael laughed at Isaac."

Mahalath smiled as she recognized the play on words. In their language, "Isaac" meant "he laughs." What Esau had said was, "Ishmael *isaaced* Isaac."

"Did Abraham just send her away? With no provision for her?"

Esau nodded. "He gave her food and water, and she went to live with Ishmael. I don't know if they ever met again."

"I know where they went," said Mahalath. "Grandmother Hagar and father both talked about it. They lived in the wilderness of Shur. They survived on father's hunting skills. After a few years, Father married an Egyptian girl, and they went to live in Punon, where I was born."

Esau whistled through his teeth. "The wilderness of Shur! I know that country. Not a good place for a woman alone even with a man to take care of her." He looked at Mahalath, his eyes narrowing. "Your father must be quite a hunter."

Mahalath felt her face growing warm under his gaze. She turned and looked at the dying fire.

"He was, my lord, a legend in the Arabah. Now he sits by the gates and talks to any who would listen. Many do."

There was silence for a moment. Mahalath continued to stare into the hot coals, feeling Esau's eyes on her.

When Esau spoke, his voice was as soft as she had ever heard it. "Mahalath, would you like to go home?"

Mahalath couldn't breathe. Something was choking her inside — deep inside, in her breast, her stomach. Something like that tingling sensation — but different. Her hands trembled under the heavy blanket. It was a long time before she had enough control of herself to speak.

"My lord . . . I. . . ." What should she say? That she had resigned herself to slavery as God's will and expected never again to see her home or family? Then images flooded her mind. Her ancient father, bald now and growing fat, his beard white and stringy, sitting at the gates telling his stories. Nebaioth her brother, strong and silent, gone most of the time on hunting expeditions. Her many brothers and their wives, her nephews and nieces, neighbors and friends. She had never expected to see them again.

Esau was waiting for an answer. Mahalath took a deep breath and turned to face him. She wondered if the tears in her eyes glistened in the firelight. "Y-yes, my lord."

Esau's stare held her eyes for a moment. She sensed in him a tenderness, an understanding. So much gentleness in so savage a man!

When he spoke, his voice was soft again. "We will go, Mahalath. We will go. As soon as I finish my business in Haran."

Mahalath closed her eyes, breathing heavily. Tears ran down her cheeks. She should say something, tell him of her gratitude. But she couldn't. Her voice was frozen. She would go home. Home. To see her family. And because of Esau. Thanks be to God!

13

Although it rained during the night, Mahalath and Esau were snug and warm under the ledge with the small fire. When Mahalath awoke in the morning, Esau was gone. Had he gone hunting? They had little food. She wished she had barley flour to make bread, but even the steady diet of dried meat was good enough to keep away the hunger pangs.

When Esau returned, his arms were filled — not with a game animal, but with wood. Most of it was wet, and he stacked it by the fire to dry. Then he picked up his bow, which he had left behind when he went for firewood.

"Keep the fire going," he said. "I'll be back by noon."

He slung the quiver on his back. Four arrows. Her father and brother had never started out on a hunt with only four arrows. Nor had they ever promised to be back by noon.

There wasn't much to do while she waited.

Clouds swirled in the sky, promising rain soon. Perhaps along the riverbank she could find crayfish or frogs, or even wild onions or other edible plants. She wandered in a grove of balsams for a while, carefully avoiding the thorny branches of the small trees. All she could find was a small clump of *dohan,* a wild grass which could be ground into meal for a cake much inferior to barley or wheat cakes. She sighed. It would have to do.

Back at the ledge she now called "home," she used two stones to pound the grass into a coarse meal. She mixed water with it, patted it into cakes, and placed it on hot stones by the fire. The *dohan* made only three cakes.

About noon, Esau came home empty-handed from his hunt. Saying nothing, he sat by the fire and ate two cakes without comment. He left the third for her, although she expected him to eat that too, since she was only a slave.

After eating, Esau rose. "Keep the fire ready," he said. "I'll bring in something before sundown."

Mahalath watched him climb the hill, this time to the north, into very rugged country. She hoped he would be successful, not just because they needed the meat, but to save him embarrassment. She remembered the time her brother Nebaioth had made a similar boast. He had not come back for three days; his stubborn pride would not permit him to return home empty-handed.

Mahalath was tired. She was not accustomed to long hours of hiking, especially in hill country. In the slave caravan she had ridden an ass. She stretched out on Esau's blanket and closed her eyes. The gentle rain made a soothing sound on the rocks outside the shelter of her ledge.

Intending to sleep only for a few minutes, she was surprised to open her eyes and find afternoon shadows creeping into the ledge. The fire was almost out. Quickly she added wood, frowning while it blazed. When Esau came home, the fire should be coals, ready for roasting.

But where was Esau? Would he, like Nebaioth, stay out until he had fulfilled his boast? He had said "by sundown." He should be home now.

And there he was. He made his way carefully down the side of the hill north of the Jabbok, an ibex on his shoulder. An ibex! The mountain goat was extremely hard to kill, since its agile wanderings among the mountain crags made it the most elusive of all game animals. Esau's arrows were gone.

He splashed across the shallow stream and dropped the goat by the fire. It was neatly dressed as usual. Mahalath would have to skin it. She was not skilled at skinning and butchering a carcass, although she had done it a few times with her mother. She would need Esau's knife.

"My lord Esau," she said, "may I have —"

For the first time she noticed Esau. His clothes were torn and dirty. His hair and beard were more matted than usual. And his leg — a large red scratch ran diagonally from his knee to his thigh. It had bled profusely, running down his leg into his sandals. Although the blood had clotted and was not flowing now, the wound looked purple and inflamed.

With a cry, she ran to him. "My lord Esau, sit down! Let me bind your wound!"

"It's nothing, Mahalath. Take care of the ibex first."

"No, my lord. That can wait. This is more important."

She would never have contradicted Sakkara like that. But with Esau she was firm, commanding him to sit on a rock with his leg stretched out in front of him. She went to the river and tore a piece of her linen robe. Would it be enough? Modesty would allow her to spare no more. Her legs were now showing to her knees. Her father would be horrified.

She shrugged as she washed the linen strip

in the stream. She must not worry about modesty. She hurried back to Esau, knelt beside him, and washed the dried blood from his leg. One small part of the wound was deep. As she pushed the torn pieces of flesh together, it began to bleed again.

Mahalath frowned, wondering what she could do. Then she remembered the grove of balsam trees nearby. "I'll be right back." She picked up Esau's knife and ran to the grove.

It was getting dark. The bark was tough. She had trouble cutting the piece large enough. When she returned to the ledge, she placed it on a stone by the fire. Esau saw what she was doing, and silently handed her a small clay bowl from his pouch.

She nodded and placed the bowl under the bark. Soon it began to drip into the cup. She scooped some of it out with her finger — it was hot! — and spread it into the wound at its deepest place. A few more dabs of the resin and she was ready to bind it. The piece of linen made a makeshift bandage which she wound as tight as possible. Then she sat back and sighed; it was all she knew to do.

Mahalath was just about to ask what happened when she caught herself. No. Keep quiet. She had no right to ask, and she sensed he would be offended if he had to give a long explanation, possibly involving some awkwardness or ineptitude on his part. He would tell her if he wanted; otherwise, she would just have to swallow her curiosity.

She took the bowl to the stream and washed it thoroughly, using sand to scour the stain left by the balm. The bowl was made from clay and while not large was adequate for making a stew. She filled it with water and placed it beside the fire to heat. Then she picked up the knife and began her work.

In the dying light, butchering the goat was difficult enough. Then she realized Esau was watching. She became aware of her bare legs, and heat flushed her face and neck. Her hands felt clumsy at the unaccustomed task. Twice she tore the skin as she was peeling it from the flesh.

"Give it to me, girl," said Esau gruffly.

She bit her lip as she handed him the knife and dragged the carcass to him. He sliced a hunk of meat from the thigh and handed it to her, then skillfully skinned and cut. Women's work! He looked as though he had done it all his life. Not many women could do it that well.

Mahalath spitted the piece of meat and placed it on two stones so it hung over the dying fire. The flames sputtered as fat dripped into them; smoke drifted from under the ledge. The water was boiled, and she cut the meat into it. When it was done, she took two sticks to lift the hot bowl from the fire and placed it before him.

He had finished preparing the ibex. The meat had been cut into long thin strips, which Mahalath draped on the spit and strung above the fire. Smoke filled the small cave as the fat dripped into the fire and the meat was smoked and preserved for the future.

"Mahalath." He spoke her name softly. She turned to look at him. "Come and eat your supper."

He had left almost half the stew for her. With a murmured "Thank you, my lord," she picked up the bowl. She had tried to ignore the pangs in her stomach since the meat first began to cook, but now her hunger could not be denied. The meat was juicy, savory, and the remaining broth delicious. She lifted the still-hot cup and drained it.

Mahalath looked up to see Esau watching her. Their eyes met. In his she saw a wild animal look. It startled her. Lust. Need for a woman. And she was his slave.

She took a deep breath. What else did she expect? He would be gentle; she knew it. And she was determined to please him, even though this was her first time and she knew nothing about pleasing a man.

"My lord Esau," she said shyly, "how may I serve you?"

A frown drew his shaggy red eyebrows together, and he looked away. "Bring me water," he said gruffly.

Mahalath picked up the bowl, hurried to the stream where she rinsed it clean, then filled it with water. When she returned, she knelt beside him while he drank.

When he had drained the cup, he handed it to her. "Now," he said, "bring me my mantle. I want to sleep."

Pulling the heavy coat from the pouch, she wondered if he would take her tonight. She had no choice. She was determined to be cheerful and make it a pleasing experience. Pleasing, at least, for her master.

But he merely wrapped himself in his mantle and turned on his side to sleep.

Quietly Mahalath tidied up the cave where scraps of meat and skin remained. When the strips of meat had been smoked sufficiently, she hung them away from the fire to dry, then added more wood to the coals and went to bed.

But not to sleep. Her confused mind, as well as her restless body, turned and squirmed for hours. Why had Esau not taken her, to satisfy his sexual needs? It was his right, his privilege. She was his slave, and she had accepted concubinage as her lot in life. There was no mistaking the look in his eyes — he had wanted to. But he didn't. Why?

There was no answer. But another question nagged her. How did Esau feel now? He seemed to be sleeping soundly, his exhausted body renewing its strength to fight the battle of healing. But did his unfulfilled lust leave him with no feelings at all? Or was *his* mind in turmoil too?

When she finally felt her body relax enough to accept sleep, she was still perplexed. But finally she put it aside. Maybe someday she would know something about this strange man she thought she knew so well. Maybe.

Mahalath awoke next morning with a feeling of dread. She glanced at Esau, who still slept. Strange. Why wasn't he up gathering firewood? The fire smoldered, but there was no more wood. She went out into a drizzly dawn to find something dry enough to burn. She took Esau's knife.

Everything was wet. The sodden undergrowth and grass reeds wet her bare legs and soaked the bottom of her dress. About half a mile from the ledge, she found a rotted log which she turned over. Although brittle, the wood inside was still dry. She cut out the crumbling pulp and carried it home.

Esau was awake and staring at her with watery eyes. She touched his forehead, which was hot. She filled his clay cup with water; Esau drank it thirstily. Next she unwrapped the bandage. The wound's purple color didn't look too frightening. At least it wasn't bleeding. She washed the linen bandage in the stream and rebound the leg.

No word had been spoken. Esau was by nature taciturn, but this morning he was also sick. Mahalath assumed there would be no traveling today, and perhaps not tomorrow. They had enough meat for several weeks; firewood would be the problem. If she brought the blanket to the fallen log, she could carry more of the rotten wood in it.

She would gather *dohan* and make some more cakes. This would take time, but they had plenty of it. With Esau uncommunicative, she would need a way to fill the empty hours.

The day passed quickly in spite of Esau's silence. He slept most of the day. In the evening, he seemed better. When she cleaned and rebound his wound, she noted the beginning of a scab around the edges. A sign of healing.

While Esau chewed the smoked meat that night, he spoke his first words. "Mahalath . . . did I say anything while I slept?"

She knew what was troubling him. Esau

151

wasn't sure whether his sleep was filled with babbling, with telling his secrets, or just more silence.

"You said nothing, my lord." Then, impulsively, she added, "Why? Do you have a secret you won't share with me?" She marveled at her boldness, wondering how Esau would react.

But he only grunted. After a moment he said, "You ask too many questions for a slave."

Mahalath laughed. She sensed that her master was in a bantering mood, a good sign.

"My lord and master, would you like to beat your slave? In your condition, I think I could beat you if I chose."

Again he grunted, but his eyes held humor, not resentment. "Well," he said his voice reflecting his usual strength, "we'll leave tomorrow."

"Yes, my lord. We go to Haran?" He nodded. She was encouraged to continue. "What is your business in Haran?"

This time her boldness was rewarded by a scowl — and silence. Had she gone too far? She looked into his eyes and what she saw sent a chill up her spine. Hate. Bitterness. He was wounded on the inside, but this wound wasn't healing. It was festering.

Gently she took his hand. "My lord Esau," she whispered, "please don't do this."

He caught his breath and glowered at her. Then roughly he pulled his hand away. When he spoke, his voice was rough and loud. "Be silent, slave. This doesn't concern you."

She cringed. But her concern for Esau overcame her timidity, and she blurted, "But it does, my lord."

Esau's voice was considerably softer. "How so?"

She met his eyes, her gaze steady. "Because our destinies are intertwined. What concerns you now concerns me — for the rest of our lives."

Esau frowned. "How do you know that?"

She turned away. "Because, my lord, I have a gift."

"A gift? What do you mean? What kind of gift?"

She stared into the fire. What should she say? Would he understand? But how could he, when she didn't understand herself? She could only be honest.

"I don't know. I don't understand my gift. I know . . . things. Things I can't explain. But I do know them."

Her back was to him now, but she was aware of his hard gaze on the back of her head.

"And do you know what my business is in Haran?"

"No, my lord." She turned around to face him. "But I do know that you must not do it. It is evil. If you do this thing, you will be . . . cursed."

As she looked into his eyes, she knew she had spoken the truth. Surprise. Shock. Resentment. Then — fear?

The silence stretched out. She cleaned up the remains of supper and crawled out of the cave. The cup needed to be washed. She would take it to the river.

"Mahalath!"

She stopped and looked back at him. "Yes, my lord?"

"And what should I do?" She couldn't miss the sarcasm in his voice. "What does your *gift* tell you to command me?"

His words shocked her. Not just the words; the tone of voice. Such bitterness! She took a deep breath and answered him as though it were a responsible question. "My lord, take me home. Then you can save yourself — and me."

With that she turned and busied herself washing the cup. She took a long time doing it. When she returned to the ledge, he said nothing. He wouldn't even look at her.

For the rest of the evening, he said nothing.

At last he rolled himself in his mantle and slept. Mahalath wrapped herself in the blanket and tried to sleep, wishing she had brought in some balsam branches to make a softer bed.

Strange dreams troubled her during the night. Several times she wakened with a start, sweating, knowing she had dreamed but unable to remember. Each time she added wood to the fire and drank water from the stream.

Esau was sleeping soundly. His strength was building. They would be able to continue their journey in the morning.

Mahalath slept longer than she expected. She awoke to Esau's gentle shaking of her shoulder.

"Mahalath, wake up. It's time to go."

Her mind was barely awake as she looked up into his eyes. This time she saw a hardness, a determination. So. He had made a decision. Evidently they were still going to Haran to complete the mysterious mission. But he said nothing more.

Once again traveling over rugged terrain was difficult. Late that afternoon they came out of the hills and turned away from the Jabbok River, now just a small stream. The trail they followed led to a broad road, trampled by many caravans, armies, and migrations. She guessed it was the so-called King's

Highway, which ran north toward Haran and south to Egypt. The southern route passed very close to Punon, her home.

And Esau turned to the right. South.

She gasped. A warm feeling flooded her breast, seeping down into her stomach. It awoke a tingling inside her, that old, familiar sensation. Suddenly the world around her became alive.

She looked around. On her right — west — were hills, forested with oaks and terebinth and balsam and pines. On her left — east — was a barren plain, desert, mile after mile of sand and rocks and emptiness. At this moment the sun was shining, although clouds in the west promised rain.

She took a deep breath. The world was lovely. Esau was a marvelous master. God was good.

Best of all, she was going home!

14

Before nightfall, they came to a small village. Actually it could hardly be called a village; only three tents clung to the side of a hill around a well. A small herd of goats grazed in a nearby pasture.

A man stood by the largest tent, staring at them. His linen cloak of Egyptian weave was worn over a plain woolen robe, probably to impress his guests. His headpiece was also for dress and show. But his ragged beard, uncombed hair, and dirty feet showed him to be a peasant in noble's clothing.

As Esau and Mahalath approached, the man bowed low, speaking an unfamiliar language.

Esau spoke softly. "Talk to him. Maybe he speaks Egyptian."

Mahalath turned to the man. "Sir, my husband asks if you can speak Egyptian?"

The man grinned, revealing rotten teeth. "Yes, lady. I speak Egypt good. My name Jogbehah, a son of Ammon. I buy, I sell. Much business."

Mahalath turned to Esau. "He says his name is Jogbehah. He's an Ammonite. A trader."

Esau nodded. "I have some silver. Maybe you can buy some food."

"My husband wants to know if you have food."

"Yes, lady. Much food. Every kind."

"Lentils? Barley meal? Dates?"

The Ammonite nodded to each of the requests.

"We'll buy some of each, if your food is not infested or rotten, and if the price is low enough."

Jogbehah nodded enthusiastically. "Food good, very cheap. We make deal, I charge nothing, you come to my bed tonight. Yes?"

Mahalath shuddered. The man was vile. "If I translated that, my husband would kill you."

The dark eyes narrowed, glancing nervously at Esau. "No tell. Make another deal. Maybe husband tired of you. I give him boy for tonight. My son —"

"No. Silver. Nothing else. My husband is a fierce man, well known for slitting throats of people he doesn't like. Just last month he cut off a man's ear, just because I asked him to. Now, show me your food."

Jogbehah stared open-mouthed at Esau. He scurried into the tent. They heard a garbled conversation with someone; a moment later the Ammonite reappeared with three bags. Mahalath examined each one. Lentils, dates, and barley meal. Not good quality but free of maggots at least. They would do.

"How much?"

"What kind of coin?"

She had to ask Esau. He produced a shekel, minted in Hazor.

Jogbehah took it and bit solidly. He nodded. "Coin good. Three shekels, one for each bag."

"No. One shekel. That's a fair price."

"Two shekels. I have family; need money."

"One shekel. And I will tell my husband not to cut off your ear."

The Ammonite gulped. "One shekel. Please tell him, lady."

She was afraid she would giggle.

Fortunately, Esau interrupted. "Does he have any arrows?"

When this was translated the man nodded. "Much arrows. Good quality. Used by Egypt soldiers." He waddled into the tent, and came out with ten arrows.

When Esau saw them, he snorted. "Child's toys!" he roared. "Have you any good arrows?"

Jogbehah cringed, thinking about his ears, no doubt. "But your worship," he fawned, "these traded to me by Egypt soldier. He used them in battle, he say."

When this was translated, Esau spat at the man's feet. "These are pine. They are not cedar. No tips. Inferior fetching. Warped. Nocks worn. How can they go straight?"

The trembling man scarcely heard Mahalath's translation. His words were jumbled, stuttered. "Please, your worship. Take them. N-no charge. T-They are yours. Just don't — don't —"

This time Mahalath couldn't repress her laugh. "It's all he has, my lord. He gives them to you. Just don't cut off his ears!"

Esau looked at her. "You told him that?"

"Yes."

"What else did you tell him?"

"That you are my husband. He's an evil man."

Esau's scowl made him look ferocious. "Why that —"

"My lord, he's not worth dirtying your blade. But we should sleep lightly tonight."

Esau snatched the arrows from the trader's trembling hands. "Let's get out of here," he growled.

She picked up the sacks of food and followed him. On impulse, she turned and spoke sharply to Jogbehah.

"My husband says, if he sees you again,

he'll cut off your ears, and maybe your nose too!"

"What did you say to him?" asked Esau when they were out of hearing.

Mahalath smiled. "Just a little threat. I don't think he'll bother us tonight."

"Wants to keep his ears, does he?"

Mahalath nodded. "And his nose, too."

Esau threw back his head and laughed. This was the first time Mahalath had heard him laugh. She liked its hearty if loud tone. And in that moment she didn't feel at all like a slave.

About a mile south of Jogbehah's tent, Esau selected a small grove of oak trees for a campsite. The darkening skies promised rain. They looked for fuel. A flock of sheep had pastured here recently. They gathered dry chips and piled them under an oak, whose gnarled branches reached out over the bare ground. Esau cut wood from under the bark of a rotten tree stump for tinder. Soon a small fire pushed the darkness away from their camp.

Mahalath made barley cakes. They feasted on the cakes, strips of dried meat, and dates. She soaked lentils in Esau's clay cup, intending to cook them in the morning.

Under the broad branch of the oak tree, with a cheerful fire in spite of its smoke, Mahalath relaxed. She felt at home. She won-

161

dered about this feeling; her home was in Punon. No, that wasn't exactly right. Her home was with Esau.

Mahalath was tired. Her legs tingled, as though they were still walking while the rest of her body rested. The arches of her feet ached. She smiled; once she had thought riding an ass was uncomfortable!

Esau was watching her. She lay against the trunk of the old oak tree, the blanket wrapped securely around her. She wondered if Esau were still in a cheerful mood. Their experience with the trader had been a shared adventure; she was sure he had enjoyed it as much as she.

"Mahalath," said Esau with unaccustomed softness, "how did you become a slave?"

Mahalath took a deep breath. Her mind had been shutting out the memories of those horrid days, but she knew she would have to tell someone. And she could think of nobody she wanted to tell more than Esau.

"Less than a year ago," she began, "I was working in the fields. Suddenly a man leaped from behind a bush and grabbed me. I screamed, but he dragged me away before help could come."

"Who was it? One man alone?"

"No. They were Horites. A band of raiders scavenging the country for anything they could steal. There were six of them. And when they brought me to their camp they —"

"They raped you?"

She dropped her eyes. "No. Their leader said something I couldn't understand, but I guessed he told them to leave my virginity intact. I would have a higher market value."

She felt Esau's eyes on her, but she couldn't meet them. Was he relieved that she was still a virgin? Or did he already know? This might explain why he hadn't taken her to his bed; he respected her virginity.

She assumed it was the same among Esau's people as hers — a woman's virginity belonged to her husband. Promiscuity was severely punished. Even a woman who was raped lost value in the eyes of her husband. Many times a marriage contract was broken because the husband, on the day after the bridal night, claimed his wife was not pure.

Esau's gentle voice broke into the silence of her thoughts. "Tell me more about your captivity. How did the Horites treat you?"

Mahalath clenched her jaw as she remembered. How could she tell him of the horrors of those three days in the Horite camp? They had torn her clothes off and poked at her body, snickering and pointing. During the day, she was forced to carry their packs, and because she had to hold them with her hands, her torn clothing kept dropping down from her shoulders, exposing her breasts. Those disgusting men constantly stared at her, eyes filled with lust.

They took her to Jericho, the largest city she had ever seen. There they sold her in the slave market — an experience as horrifying as her first night of captivity. She was forced to stand naked on the slave block, while lewd men did revolting things. It was a relief when Sakkara bought her.

She couldn't tell this to Esau. She couldn't tell anyone. She had tried to drive those memories out of her mind. What she said to Esau was, "They sold me to Sakkara the slave trader."

Esau nodded sympathetically. He had been watching her face as she relived in a few seconds those unspeakable few days. But she knew he would not insist she talk about it.

"Tell me about your life with Sakkara."

She had no hesitation in speaking of that, for it was a reasonably pleasant experience. Becoming Sakkara's slave was actually a welcome change after the Horites.

"He treated me well — not because he was by nature kind, but because it was good business to treat his slaves that way. Recognizing my market value as a young virgin, he pampered me."

"Yes, I saw how well he treated you. You didn't do any of the women's work in camp, did you?"

"Not only that, my lord. I slept in Sakkara's tent, I ate his food, and I rode an ass when we traveled. My value increased when he found out I could play the harp and sing."

"How did he learn that?"

"One of the Egyptian slaves played the harp, although rather poorly. One evening in Sakkara's tent, I asked to play for him. I couldn't speak Egyptian then, but they understood my motions. And they liked my singing and playing, even if they couldn't understand my words. That increased my market value."

Esau grunted. "I don't understand how anyone could think of you as just a valuable piece of property." He paused, while appreciation for his comment made her smile warmly. But Esau had another question. "You speak Egyptian fluently. How did you learn so quickly?"

"Sakkara assigned an Egyptian slave to teach me. She was my constant companion day and night. It wasn't too difficult. I'm glad I did; it helped us deal with that Ammonite trader!"

Esau grinned, remembering their adventure. "Yes, Mahalath. You are a valuable slave to *me* now. You have a very high market value!"

Mahalath laughed. She knew he was only teasing. Her fatigue drained from her body. She was more than just a slave to him. Knowing it, she slept soundly that night.

15

The next day, traveling on the King's Highway south, Mahalath found the walking easier. The road crossed a broad plain. About noon they saw a town in the distance.

As they approached, Esau dug into his pack for his mantle, which he handed to Mahalath. "Wear this," he said.

Mahalath nodded. Esau didn't want anybody looking at her. Her tattered linen dress was torn, shrunken, and came only to her knees. It fit tightly. No, Esau would not want strangers to see her like that. The mantle was large and hot. The hem dragged on the ground, and the shoulders sagged around her body.

Nevertheless, as they drew near the town, she pulled the hood over her head and fastened the sagging sides around her face like a veil. She wondered what she looked like. Would the townspeople think Esau was leading an old lady? Well, why not? She bent over and plodded. Let them think that.

The town was small, but permanent. Twenty squat mud-brick houses were scattered haphazardly along the road — traders' houses, the front part set up as stalls for displaying wares. It must be busy when a caravan passed through, but now only a few people stood outside. They stared with sleepy curiosity at the big red man and his shapeless old follower.

"Speak to them, Mahalath," said Esau.

Mahalath turned to a man who seemed a little more alert than the rest. He was short and stooped, as though an ancient injury had crippled him. His woolen robe, though tattered, had once been a glossy black.

"May your god smile on you," said Mahalath in Egyptian, speaking through the veil of her hood. "My master would like to know what town this is," she added.

The man squinted at her. His short bushy beard and crag-like eyebrows seemed to be constantly moving.

"Jazer." He spoke quickly, as though nervous. "We children of Ammon. You buy something from us?"

Mahalath turned to Esau. "This is Jazer, an Ammonite village. He wants to know if we want to buy anything."

Esau nodded. "Two things: some decent arrows, and a suitable dress for yourself."

The second request startled her, but she understood. They were on a well-traveled road, and her clothing was not only indecent but provocative. And they were going to her home. Esau would not want her to appear before her people dressed in tattered linen rags, nor an oversize woolen mantle.

There were no arrows to be found in Jazer. But she did purchase a plain woolen dress, fastened around the waist with a sash, and a headpiece with veil. Esau paid for it with a Hazorian shekel.

Esau would not stop in Jazer but hurried through the town and continued south on the King's Highway. The road entered the mountains but was still easy walking. At last Esau stopped by a grove of oak trees.

"Change clothes here," he muttered, and turned his back.

Quickly Mahalath put on her dress, and they continued their journey. But an itch developed on her back, and then another on her thighs.

"My lord," said Mahalath, "I'm afraid these fine clothes are infested. May we find a place to wash them?"

Esau grunted. Maybe little intruders on his body meant nothing to him, but Mahalath was accustomed to more cleanliness than her master. She was forced to endure the tiny pests for another hour.

They crossed a tiny mountain stream. It dropped from the hill to their left, then trickled down a valley to their right, making its way to the Jordan River.

Esau stopped. "Wash your dress here," he said gruffly.

Mahalath looked at the tiny stream. If she stood in it the water would barely cover her feet. She wanted to take a bath, but that was impossible.

Esau watched her. Would he stare at her while she undressed and washed her clothes? He had a right to do whatever he wanted. But she rebelled at the idea of displaying her body, as she had been forced to do with the Horites and on the Jericho slave block.

"My lord," she said firmly, "I plan to take off my robe and wash it. Will you please go away and not look?"

She looked into Esau's eyes. What she saw startled her. Pure lust. When she told him she would take off her clothes, his eyes lit up like a brush fire. She watched the struggle in his face for a minute before he turned and climbed the trail, turned into a cleft of rocks, and disappeared.

Quickly she took off her dress and sat in the stream. The water was icy cold, but it felt good as she splashed it on her bites. She soaked the robe in the water and scrubbed it with sand. As she drew the wet cloth around her body, she shivered. At least the fleas would be frozen to death, she thought grimly.

Mahalath followed Esau up the trail to the cleft where he had disappeared and called to him. When he came out, he stared at her, lust still in his eyes. Would he wait until she got home? He wanted to bring her to her family as a virgin, but could he discipline himself?

They made camp that night by another small mountain stream. Mahalath again cooked barley cakes which they ate with dried meat and dates. She soaked lentils for breakfast.

Usually Mahalath enjoyed these cozy evenings by the fire with Esau. Often they sat in silence; Esau was never a talkative man. Tonight, she noticed, he seemed to be brooding.

When he finally spoke, his voice was gruff. "Tell me about your family, Mahalath."

Mahalath stared into the dying fire. What would he want to know? Names, families, occupations — any background which would help him keep all her relatives straight.

"My father, Ishmael," she began slowly, "is an old man. He has hunted all the way from Havilah to Shur. He's too old to hunt now. My mother's dead and Ishmael had no other wife."

She had already told him this much. She went on. "I have twelve brothers. Nebaioth, the oldest, is married to Atarah the Moabite. They have three sons: Jetur, Naphish, and Kedemah. Nebaioth is a hunter like father. His sons — my nephews — are more inclined to be shepherds."

Esau's fixed gaze caused her to drop her eyes. "You are Ishmael's youngest?" he asked.

"Yes, my lord. A child of Ishmael's old age. The youngest of Ishmael's twelve sons is now twenty-five; I am ten years younger. All twelve of my brothers are married and have children."

"Who takes care of your father now?"

"Probably Nebaioth. Ishmael and I lived alone before I was captured. I suppose he moved in with my brother."

Atarah, Nebaioth's wife, wouldn't like that. She could picture that household — three growing boys, who spent their time in the sheep field; a husband who was away hunting most of the time; and an old man who loved to talk about the past.

She glanced at Esau. He was still staring at her. What was he thinking? She looked deeply into his eyes, but all she could see in their depths was lust.

"Mahalath." He spoke her name softly and hesitantly. But then he paused for a long time,

172

so long that she began to feel that strange tingling sensation deep inside her.

Finally he continued, and his voice almost broke. "Mahalath, if you . . . had a choice, would you stay with your father?"

There it was, the question she had been waiting for. The catch in his voice told her how much her answer meant to him.

And what did it mean to her? She thought about her father. Would he need her? He would probably arrange a suitable marriage for her with one of the Moabite men in the village of Punon. Probably that wealthy goatherd who already had two wives. Esau would go his way . . . alone.

When she answered her voice was firm. "No, my lord Esau. If I had a choice, I would continue to be your slave." Then boldness surged up within her, and she spoke words which surprised even her. "Or your concubine, if you wish."

She saw Esau's eyes widen. He licked his lips. But he said nothing. For a long time there was silence.

At last Esau spoke, softly, almost whispering. "Mahalath, when we get to your home, I shall ask Ishmael for permission to marry you."

She gasped. Marriage to Esau! But she was his slave!

"My lord, there is no need. I am your slave, your rightful handmaiden! You don't need to honor me with marriage! I would be grateful if you —"

"No! You were *never* my slave! I will marry you, and let there be no more said about it!" He wrapped himself in his mantle and rolled over, his back to her.

That night, as Mahalath lay huddled in her blanket, she listened to the soft sighing of the wind as it plucked at the branches of the pine trees on the hillsides. Moonlight filtered through the branches. She realized that the flickering was not the dying fire but the shadows cast by the swaying branches. That should be lulling her to sleep but sleep would not come.

God had been good to her.

She wrinkled her brow and curled up inside the blanket. She couldn't understand the meaning of God. Her father believed in God, but spoke very little about him. The religious beliefs of their clan were actually the product of Grandmother Hagar's faith. She had spoken of God often as someone who had watched over her all her life.

When they moved to Punon, they began calling God "Qaus," which was the Moabite name for God. Yet Ishmael refused to make any graven image of Qaus as the Moabites did. God was always the invisible being, an eternal presence.

Even here? So far from home? She had never experienced this presence, yet she could say God was good to her. Maybe Esau's God was helping them. Yet Esau would worship the same God, since Abraham was their common ancestor. But Esau had never spoken of his faith.

It was all very confusing. She felt vaguely that a benevolent Providence watched over them, but she didn't know who or what. God? Qaus? Luck?

She shrugged and closed her eyes. Maybe Esau would explain. Some day. Some day. And sleep claimed her, as the wind sighed in the trees and traced moving shadows on the rocky hillside around her.

The days which followed were for Mahalath some of the most pleasant of her life. The weather moderated; as they drew closer to the Salt Sea, the rainfall was not as frequent as in the north. During *stav* the days were not too hot, though the nights were cool.

Best of all, she was with Esau.

He still did not say much. She accepted his natural reserve, even preferred it to the shallow babbling talk of many people she had known. Just being near him was enough. And to know that she was more than a slave to him.

Most of the country they crossed was mountainous, but traveling the King's Highway was not hard. They would soon be in the broad fertile basin of the Salt Sea, with its trees and good pasturage and plains of grass, inhabited by the gentle Moabite shepherds.

But first, they must pass through country inhabited mostly by Ammonites. Mahalath knew little about the Ammonites, but she did know they were hostile to everyone. They didn't hesitate to steal, vandalize, or kill anyone or anything they came across. Esau, evidently aware of this, became increasingly vigilant.

When they came to a hilltop, Esau would stand for many minutes searching the country for any signs of people. When they approached a narrow canyon, he would scout cautiously before motioning Mahalath to come ahead. At night he chose his campsites carefully, back from the road, usually in a thick copse of trees. He built small fires, only under a tree so the branches could filter the smoke. And always his bow was ready.

His vigilance was rewarded. Several times he spotted a band of men, armed with clubs, staves and slingshots, either approaching or waiting in ambush for unwary travelers. Esau avoided them, sometimes taking a circuitous route. He avoided a caravan coming north, probably bound for Damascus.

Mostly they bypassed the towns. Twice they entered villages to buy food, and each time Esau asked for arrows. In a town called Abel-Keramim, he bought enough well-made cedar arrows to fill his quiver. He immediately discarded the arrows he had bought from Jogbehah.

Only once were they surprised and forced to fight. They approached a village located on a broad stream. Since they didn't need supplies, they climbed the hillside. Using the forest of pines as their cover, they skirted the western edge of the town. There was no path, and the going was slow. They crossed a ravine filled with rocks, evidently a gully for water runoff when it rained.

At the far side of the gully, Esau reached down to help Mahalath up. He used his right hand, since his left hand held his bow. She slipped on the steep bank but scrambled to the top and stood beside him. That was when the attack came.

A band of Ammonites — Mahalath had no time to see how many — came rushing out of the trees, screaming and shouting their war cries. They were only fifty feet away.

"Hide!" hissed Esau. He pushed her back into the gully.

She tumbled down the steep slope, crawled under a bush, and flattened herself against the ground. Her actions were spontaneous; her only thought was to obey Esau.

Above her, she heard the shouts and war cries turn to screams. It lasted only a few seconds. Then there was silence.

It was broken only by Esau's voice. "Come out, Mahalath. It's safe now."

She crawled out from under the bush, bruised and dirty from her attempts to hide. Esau stood at the top of the ravine, reaching down his right hand for her, as he had a few minutes before.

"Esau!" she gasped. "Are you . . . are you . . . all right?"

He grinned. "I am," he replied. "But they aren't."

She saw them then. They were sprawled on the ground in bloody pools, their bodies grotesque, their eyes open and staring. One arrow protruded from each man.

There were only four, poorly armed, carrying clubs and knives. Three had an arrow in the chest; the other had an arrow in his back. It wasn't hard to reconstruct the brief battle.

Trembling, she went to Esau, putting her

head on his broad chest. Esau put a protective arm around her.

Again, the thought occurred to her: *God is good to us. God — and Esau's skill with the bow.* She wondered if her brother would be able to do what Esau just did. Killing a helpless animal was one thing, but facing charging men intent on killing you was something else.

Gently Esau pushed her away. "Keep watch," he muttered. "There may be others." Then he drew his knife and began the grisly job of cutting out the arrows.

Mahalath was still trembling as she looked around. No one was in sight. She took deep breaths, trying to control herself. Her legs felt weak.

Mahalath would not look at the lifeless forms on the ground. Once they had been men . . . dangerous enemies. Now they were twisted masses of blood and flesh. She shuddered. It was not good to think about that.

As she followed Esau through the forest on the side of the hill, she forced her mind to think of something more pleasant. Her thoughts went back to the moment just after she had climbed to the top of the ravine, when Esau had held her in his arms.

That was the first time. Since she had known him, he had never held her. Because of the excitement and fear and shock of that moment, she had not been able to enjoy it. But now as she remembered, she tried to pick out details of that experience. The strong arms. The corded muscles. The shaggy beard. The gamy smell. She couldn't remember any of these things. All she could recall was the terror, the shock, and the weakening relief.

16

Four days later, a deep ravine forced the King's Highway to turn east. They came to Iye-abarim, a Moabite city, where the road forded a stream. This stream, which the Moabites called the Brook Zered, tumbled down toward the Salt Sea.

Mahalath knew where they were now. Her breath came in gasps as she realized how close to home they were. The King's Highway followed a ridge of a long mountain range just to the west of the Arabah. Through the trees she caught glimpses of the familiar panorama below and to her right. The Arabah!

The vast plain of the Arabah stretched from the southern tip of the Salt Sea to the mysterious gulf to the south. The barren salty soil, unable to support crops or pasturage, reflected the sunlight like a body of water. Only on the near slope was there fertile land, fed by countless springs from the mountains and ravines. The Moabites planted barley and tended olive groves and vineyards. Shepherding was limited because of space limitations, with the arid desert to the west and to the east the rugged mountains covered with oaks, juniper, and hawthorne trees.

The major occupation of the area was copper mining. The ore was mined and refined. Then it was worked by metalsmiths into cooking vessels, weapons, even jewelry. Punon was well known throughout the world for its mines and metal trade. Four of her twelve brothers were miners. Occasionally Mahalath glimpsed the rich red clay for which the area was sometimes called — Edom, the Red Lands.

As they neared Punon, her home, the King's Highway followed the ridge. A large rift ran through the mountain range, dipping into the valley far below. She indicated to Esau the trail led to Punon.

And there was Punon! A sleepy town on the hillside, it consisted of mud brick houses, set apart on an offshoot of the mountain, where several springs provided fresh water for the village. And the wall — some people called it a fortress.

The closer they came, the more she smiled as questions danced in her head. Was her father now entertaining his listeners at the city gates? Would Nebaioth be home or out hunting? Had his wife Atarah become distraught by her father-in-law's constant talking? Were her three nephews — Jetur, Naphish, and Kedemah — still tending the sheep?

More practical questions crowded in. What about Ishmael's house? Would he have gone to live with Nebaioth after Mahalath's abduction? Where would she and Esau stay for the night? Would Ishmael be glad to see her? Would he permit Esau's marriage request? What bride-price would he demand? These questions made a frown displace her smile as she followed Esau down the trail along the giant rift toward Punon.

They climbed a hillside toward the main gate. The wall towered above them. Made of bricks, it was solid and sturdy. The city, they claimed, was impregnable. Yet no one watched from the walls or the gate tower. Even the gates were wide open.

Then she remembered the outposts, strategically located on the hilltops overlooking the city. Signal fires were ready to warn of an approaching enemy. An army would have to be very clever to surprise Punon.

The path — now a broad road — led up to the small saddle on which the city was built. They entered the gates silently, preoccupied with their own thoughts. Mahalath looked for her father — and there he was, seated in his usual place on a bench. A group of old men and boys was around him. He was, of course, talking.

His resonant voice, cultured by many years of storytelling, sounded clearly as they entered the gate. He was lecturing on how to track a gazelle. No wonder parents permitted their children to idly pass a working day listening to the old man at the gate; this was a hunting school.

His bench was about thirty yards inside the gate. The dirt courtyard was filled with eager listeners. Esau and Mahalath, standing just inside the gates, were behind the crowd facing him. He looked just the same — short and fat, his white beard long and oiled, his faded headpiece pulled down over his bald head to protect it from the sun's glare. His bright eyes flashed in the excitement of his story.

Ishmael then caught sight of Mahalath, who stood at the outer edge of his audience. His voice stopped in mid-sentence. Even this far away, Mahalath heard his gasp.

The people turned to see what had disrupted Ishmael's story.

"Mahalath!" Her name was spoken by her nephew Jetur, Nebaioth's eighteen-year-old son, a shepherd. Why was he attending his grandfather's storytelling session?

Jetur was on his feet, running toward Mahalath. His broad grin pushed back the short black beard under the hawk nose. Older than Mahalath, he had shown interest in claiming her as his bride, even if she were his aunt.

Jetur stopped as he came face to face with Esau. The young man's grin disappeared. His eyebrows first went up, then down. He didn't know what to make of Mahalath's fierce-looking companion. As he stood open-mouthed, Mahalath pushed past.

She strode through the crowd toward her father. They parted for her in silence. At last she stood before the old man. His face was impassive, staring at her.

Finally he spoke. "Mahalath. You have come home."

"Yes, father." Her first impulse was to throw herself into his arms and kiss his wrinkled face. His impassivity stopped her. She stood there, embarrassed, staring at him.

The silence accused her. Had she done something wrong? This was more than shock at her sudden appearance.

Then she knew. The last anyone had seen Mahalath, she was being dragged away by a Horite savage. They assumed she had been cruelly raped, her precious virginity destroyed, death would have been accepted more easily than the ultimate insult to her usefulness as a woman.

"Father," she said quickly. "I am still an unspoiled woman. I am a slave. My master Esau has protected my virginity, so that I may return to you whole."

She watched Ishmael as he listened to her words. He took a deep breath, his eyes widening. Then he heaved his heavy frame to his feet and opened her arms to her. There was a slight catch in her throat, and her eyes were wet on his robe.

"My daughter!" Ishmael turned her face to him and kissed the wet cheeks.

Ishmael gently pushed his daughter away from him. "Esau, you said?" Then he projected his voice. "Esau, my friend, come."

Esau strode forward through the widening lane as the men and boys stepped back to give him room. His broad shoulders, matted red hair and beard, and large bow must have been a fearsome sight to the people of Punon.

Ishmael reached out to Esau, grasped his shoulders, and kissed his cheek. Then his deep bass voice proclaimed the ritual welcome. "Welcome to our home, my friend. My house is your house, my family is your family, and all my possessions are your possessions. You are welcome here for a lifetime!"

Mahalath's eyes strayed to Jetur, who stood at the edge of the crowd now. He was frown-

186

ing. Ishmael's welcome used the word "lifetime" instead of the usual two nights and a day between, or the month allotted to a special guest. Ishmael meant "join our family." Jetur and everyone else would understand that. And Jetur wouldn't like it.

"Thank you, Father Ishmael." Esau's voice was loud because of natural energy, rather than through the cultivated resonance of Ishmael the storyteller. "May God richly bless your flocks and vines!"

He used the word "El" for God, not realizing that the Moabites used the word "Qaus." To them, "El" meant one of the false gods of unenlightened people. Mahalath, however, knew that Esau's God was not an idol, but the same as "Qaus."

"Jetur!" Ishmael's voice rang with authority. "Run to Atarah, and tell her we have guests. Tell her to prepare a meal. Also open my own house. I will move immediately."

As Jetur moved to do his grandfather's bidding, Ishmael chuckled. "She'll be glad to hear that, I'm sure. But come, my friend. Come to my house. We have much to talk about!"

Putting his arm around Esau's shoulder, he led him down the street. Mahalath followed. So did the townspeople. They went along the broad street through the town center, then turned left on a side street leading to Nebaioth's home.

All the time, Ishmael was talking. ". . . and when the women reported Mahalath's capture by a barbarian Horite, we concluded she was lost. Nevertheless, we made a search. . . ."

The voice went on and on, never stopping. His left arm was around Esau's shoulder; his right hand gesturing to illustrate his story. And the story went on and on.

Mahalath frowned. How would Esau feel about this? His taciturnity and Ishmael's garrulity were in stark contrast. How long before — but no, it would never come to that. She was home. And with Esau. She forced herself to think about that, while her father's deep voice droned on.

When they arrived at Nebaioth's house, Atarah was frantic. The only woman in the household, she now had to cook a meal for guests as well as prepare Ishmael's house. She gave Mahalath a brief greeting before putting her to work. Ishmael took Esau to the roof, the best place to entertain a guest.

"I'll cook," said Atarah. Her spare frame seemed unable to support the large quantity of energy she exuded. "But I can't prepare Father Ishmael's house. You'll have to do that."

"Yes, Atarah." Mahalath was glad to get

away from the bustle and bossiness of her sister-in-law.

As she walked the half-block to her father's home, she was joined by Jetur. But he should be on the roof entertaining Esau. As the oldest son in Nebaioth's absence, he was the official host. Ishmael himself was little more than a guest.

"I'll help you, Mahalath," he said.

Small help he'll be! thought Mahalath. Cleaning house was women's work, and Jetur would do nothing to assist her. What did he want? Was he still interested in marrying her? Or was he merely curious about her captivity — and Esau?

"Where's Nebaioth?" she asked. "Hunting?"

He spat. Fortunately they were still on the street outside the house. He would have spat on the floor had they been inside, and she would have had to clean it up.

"Father doesn't hunt any more. He's at the copper mine."

Mahalath stopped outside the door of her house. She looked at Jetur in surprise. "The copper mine?"

"Yes." Jetur's voice contained a sneer. "He went into partnership with his brothers in the mining business. He has his mind on *darics* and *shekels* now, not meat and hides."

There *was* more profit in mining. Mahalath

thrust aside the deerskin door. But what would the family do for fresh meat? Become vegetarians like many of her neighbors?

The house was musty and filled with dust. She snatched the broom in the corner and began sweeping.

The house had only one room and a courtyard, with a small room on the roof. Ishmael wasn't wealthy like a miner or an owner of a large flock. The large room downstairs was divided into two unequal parts. The upper half, the "shelf," was where the family slept. The lower half was where the women cooked and wove and ground their meal. The floor was flagstone; right now it was dirty.

Jetur seated himself in the doorway. "Not only that, but Father decided *I* will be the hunter now. Bah!"

This time he spat on the floor. *I'll clean that up last,* she thought. *He'll surely spit some more.*

"I'm surprised," she told him. "I thought you'd rather be a shepherd." Shepherding was not a strong man's job; hunting was. She wondered if he caught her slight sarcasm.

"I never did want to be a shepherd," said Jetur fiercely. "I want to be a warrior!"

Mahalath remembered Jetur expressing this desire several times as he was growing up. Ordinarily the father chose the occupation of his sons. She had always assumed her three nephews would be shepherds and nothing else.

"But I didn't come here to talk about that," Jetur said. "Tell me about Esau. I assume you were lying to Father Ishmael when you told him you're still a virgin."

Mahalath stopped sweeping, her hands cold on the broom. "I told the truth," she said softly.

Again he spat on the floor. "That's hard to believe. How long have you been with that savage?"

"He's not a savage! He's more civilized than you are."

In one lithe motion, Jetur leaped to his feet and slapped her face with his open hand. The force of the blow sent her reeling back to the wall. "Don't talk to me like that, woman! Somebody forgot to beat you while you were a slave!"

Mahalath leaned against the wall, breathing heavily. She had forgotten Jetur's violence. Several times in the past he had slapped her. No one had ever reprimanded him. It was the accepted thing to do when a woman forgot her place. She had not experienced such treatment all during her captivity. Not even the Horites had beaten her. She thanked God Esau came from a culture where a woman's dignity was respected.

But there was more to Jetur's violence. She looked in his eyes as he stood before her, poised for perhaps yet another blow. Jetur enjoyed it. He liked hurting others.

There was only one way she could avoid a severe beating now, and she didn't hesitate. "You're right, Jetur." She bowed her head. "I had no right to speak to you like that. I'm sorry."

Her words fed his starved ego. He would not need to torment her physically now. He could make her grovel. To him, this was better than a beating.

She glanced at him as he resumed his seat by the doorway. An idea was forcing itself into her thoughts. An answer to a troubling question which had occurred to her on the road with Esau. Jetur just might provide the solution.

"Jetur," she said gently. "You will make a fine soldier. You have all the right qualities."

He smiled. He liked her tone of voice.

"I would be the best. I could become an officer in the Egyptian army if I had the chance." His smile changed to a frown. "But I won't have the chance. I have to be a hunter."

"Esau can do the hunting. If he were properly asked, he could be the family hunter. Then you would be free to be a warrior."

"Esau!" Again he spat on the floor. She

would have to scrub it now. "What does that savage know about hunting?"

He wanted her to react again to his insult to their guest. But she was in control now. "Esau is an excellent hunter," she replied. "As good as Father Ishmael. Each man in our family has something he excels at, and Esau's strength is in hunting. Yours is in soldiering. But how else would you become a warrior, unless Esau takes your place hunting?"

She reached her broom for cobwebs which had formed on the low ceiling. The broom was heavy, unlike the light-weight Egyptian brooms. Jetur was silent for a moment, absorbing her words. When he finally spoke, his voice was soft, almost as though he were speaking to himself.

"As the oldest son, I have the right to sit in the family discussions. Maybe if I spoke at the right time. . . ." He fell silent, thinking.

Mahalath nodded and continued working. She had planted the seed; now it was taking root in Jetur's small mind. He would think this was his original plan.

Jetur stood. "I'll go talk to this savage," he said. Without another word, he walked out.

As soon as he left, Mahalath became aware of the tingling feeling inside her. She frowned. What did it mean? This was not the beginning of that feeling. She realized it had been there since the moment she stepped inside the gates of the city. What was her gift telling her? That there was danger in Punon? Or was it a warning about an individual? Ishmael? Jetur? Or this plan of hers, to use Jetur's vanity for her own benefit?

Mahalath picked up the water jar to go to the well in the center of town. At least her plan was succeeding.

Ishmael would demand a large bride-price for his daughter's wedding. Esau had no money. But he had hunting skills, and the family needed a hunter. How long would Ishmael demand that Esau hunt for the family? Seven years? That was the usual term of service for a poor man's dowry.

And Esau would like it. The wild country was filled with all kinds of game. His skills would be tested, and he would find respect and status among her people.

Best of all, it would prevent his going to Haran and completing his mysterious business. She didn't know how she knew, but all her instincts told her that this "business" was evil and destructive. She must find ways to keep Esau away from Haran. And at home. Home, in Punon. She would give him children, and love, and respect. He would sit in the gates with the elders and tell hunting tales, perhaps eventually taking Ishmael's place.

And Esau would always be with her.

That tingling sensation was still there. Warning her. Something was going to happen, or somebody posed a threat to her. But she pushed the feeling aside. Everything was going well. She decided to ignore the warning and put on a cheerful face.

Mahalath smiled as she filled her water jug at the community well. She lifted it to her head for the walk home. And she continued to smile as she scrubbed the floor by the door of the house.

Soon Esau and Ishmael would be coming home, and she had to have the house ready. She would find her *mahalath,* tune it, and entertain her family tonight. As she worked, she reviewed in her mind an old song she would sing to them — a song about love and home.

Later that night, after they returned from Nebaioth's home, she had a chance to sing for the two men she loved. They sat on the ledge in the darkened room, eyes on her, quietly waiting. Her fingers gently stroked the familiar seven-stringed instrument for which she was named.

The small fire in the brazier had become coals exuding a warm glow in the chilly room. A small flame danced on the oil lamp hanging from the low ceiling. Outside the wind whistled; inside it was warm and cozy.

Night has fallen; the hunter is home.
Meat is hanging from the rafters;
Another week of feasting awaits them.
The night air is chill, but the fire is
    warm,
And the hunter is home with his family.

Mahalath wondered what they had discussed at Nebaioth's house. The wedding? And after Jetur joined them, Esau's hunting? The bride-price? Ishmael, of course, had done almost all the talking.

Tomorrow is another day, a day to hunt!
The plump gazelle waits in the forest,
Taking a long drink at the flowing
    stream.
Drink well, swift deer; graze well
    tonight,
For tomorrow, tomorrow, the hunter
    will come.

The song she had rehearsed that afternoon flowed from her fingers and lips. Her voice was soft, since the song was wistful and melancholy. It wasn't a song about hunting as much as home.

The owl sits quietly in its tree.
The night hawk soars aloft, seeking prey.

The lion prowls through shadowed
   darkness,
But the hunter is home, home with his
   family.

The song described the peace of the restful
scene: smoke filling the room, the smell of
fresh meat recently cooked, the occasional
pop as a small piece of firewood would fall
into the fire. All these Mahalath sang about as
her father and future husband silently absorbed the mood.

And now it is time to sleep.
The hunter lays aside his bow.
He will sleep, and dream of tomorrow,
Of the sunrises, the sunsets, and the
   hunt.

The last soft chord was struck and hung in
the stillness. For a brief moment there was silence in the dark room. Again Mahalath was
conscious of the rising wind outside. *Tomorrow will be cold,* she thought.

"I've missed you, Mahalath." Ishmael's
voice was husky. "Your harp has been silent
too long in this house."

"It won't be silent again," whispered
Mahalath.

Esau said nothing, but she felt his eyes

upon her. The intensity of his gaze was disturbing.

Ishmael cleared his throat. "Mahalath." He fidgeted with his hands for a moment. "My child."

He's at a loss for words, marveled Mahalath. She knew what was coming.

"My daughter, it is time for you to marry. You have been the child of my house for fourteen years, from the time your mother gave birth to a scrawny little baby."

Ishmael's resonant voice gathered momentum as he told of Mahalath's birth and childhood. The words were for Esau, even though addressed to her. Ishmael would broach the subject of marriage in his own way, and that way was filled with words. "And so I have chosen a husband worthy of you. As an obedient daughter, I'm sure you will concur."

"Yes, Father."

"You shall marry Esau *ben* Isaac of Beersheba. He will bring me many grandchildren to comfort my old age. There is nothing like grandchildren, when a person has reached that time of life. . . ."

Mahalath glanced at Esau. He seemed to be listening, but that was merely a respectful pose. Ishmael's unending monologue would surely be tiring, even boring, to such a man.

When Ishmael had rambled on for some

time about grandchildren, then family responsibilities, the opportunity arose for Esau
to break in. "My father," said Esau, as
Ishmael paused for breath.

"Yes, my son?" Even Ishmael was caught
off balance. He hadn't expected another voice
in the discussion.

"I wish to begin my duties tomorrow."

"Tomorrow? Isn't it cold for hunting?" The
old man turned to his future son-in-law. "You
only arrived today. You have not met
Nebaioth, nor my other sons. Nebaioth is still
at the copper mines, and Kedar —"

Again Esau interrupted. "Father, you will
need meat for the wedding. There's only a
week."

"But Nebaioth —"

"*I* will bring in the meat."

The sentence was spoken quietly, but with
authority. Ishmael was momentarily silenced.
Mahalath recognized the beginnings of a
power struggle here. Ishmael would seek to
control Esau by the sheer power of words.
Esau would insist on going his own way. She
smiled to herself. Nobody controls Esau.

But there was something else, something
deeper in the statement by her future husband that he will bring in the meat. No, two
things. If the wedding were only a week away,
Esau would need something to do. Some-

thing other than listening to Ishmael, meeting future relatives, and . . . controlling his lust for his future wife. He had done so now for almost two weeks, while they were alone together on the road. But they had been traveling, with Esau preoccupied with the problem of slipping through a hostile country without detection.

Now they were home. Everything was peaceful, relaxed. There was little to do. Yes, Esau would definitely need to get away, to hunt, to occupy his mind with something other than his desire for her.

The other reason for Esau's eagerness to hunt was even more disturbing. Esau wanted to get away from his father-in-law. He would surely be troubled by the prospect of a life listening to Ishmael's constant monologue. What did that mean for the future? Would Esau want to stay at home?

"All right, my son." Ishmael's voice reflected his resignation. "I only wish I could go with you. I would like to show you the game runs, the water holes, the —"

"Father, I hunt alone. Just designate a meeting place where I can bring my kills. There someone from the family can find it and bring it to the village."

"Yes, my son. There is a place. If you go south on the King's Highway to the first peak on the east. . . ."

What did her father think about this brash newcomer to the family, who didn't hesitate to interrupt the venerable patriarch? Ishmael — consciously or unconsciously — dominated his conversations to the point where his listeners were dulled to passivity. But Esau was different. He cut into the long-winded dissertations and went straight to the point.

The future would be interesting, as the power struggle developed — Ishmael's wordiness against Esau's boldness. Mahalath smiled as she put away the harp to prepare for sleep. *Yes,* she mused. *It will be very interesting.*

17

Mahalath awoke the next morning to the sound of her father's voice. "When will you be back?" Ishmael asked.

"In three days," Esau replied. "Before the wedding."

With a guilty start, Mahalath pushed aside the blanket and got to her feet. The room was dark; the sun was a long way from sending shafts of light into the house. Esau was ready to leave for the hunt, and she had not even prepared food and water for him.

"My lord Esau," she said softly, "let me fill your pouch with food, and your bottle with water."

"I've already done it, girl. Go back to sleep."

"But Esau —"

"Hush, child."

He was standing near her, his bulk barely visible in the glow of the small fire. She was aware of his smell, however — that familiar gamy odor of unwashed body and clothing.

She would have to ask Ishmael to talk to him before the wedding, asking him to bathe.

Suddenly he caught her in his arms and held her tight. She gasped. The embrace was unexpected and . . . delightful. She turned her face upward.

But he didn't kiss her. Instead he mumbled, "Take care, Mahalath. When the time comes —"

She knew what he wanted to say, and a warm feeling coursed through her body. He released her as abruptly as he had grasped her. He shouldered his pack and quiver, picked up his bow, and left hurriedly.

She knew her father, a poor sleeper, was awake, but he said nothing. Slowly she returned to her pallet, wondering how near dawn was. The room was silent, almost bare now that Esau was gone. The wind had died down but it was cold.

She was still tingling from the ardor of his embrace. Tingling. She caught her breath. The feeling was not what she had thought. It was not warm love for Esau which moved inside her, but her gift. And today it was very strong.

She sat up and pushed the blanket aside, in spite of the coolness of the morning. Should she run after Esau and warn him? Perhaps even ask him not to go? She bit her lip. He would only laugh at her. Tell her she was being silly. What could she say? That her gift warned her of danger?

The small fire was beginning to shed more light and a little heat into the room. Evidently Esau had placed a few sticks of wood on it before she woke. She pulled her blanket around her and lay back, watching shadows dance on the raftered ceiling.

If only Hagar were still alive! She would understand. She would know what to do. Hagar was the wisest person Mahalath had ever known. She remembered Hagar's dying words to her about her gift: "Use it only for good." Mahalath shut her eyes. She still didn't know what that meant.

Later that day, she was completing her work of cleaning the house. There was still much to do at her own house in preparation for a wedding just five days away.

She raised the heavy broom and destroyed a spider web. The spider fell to the floor and tried to escape, but she stamped out its life under her sandal. Poor spider! She hoped no one would stamp out her home and family like that.

Then the tingling feeling struck her, stabbed into her breast and her stomach. Sharply now. Something was happening — now! The time had come!

She whirled to find Jetur in the doorway. The broom fell from her hands as she backed away against the wall. Jetur! She didn't know how she knew, but Jetur was the one her gift was warning her about. And he was here — menacing, dangerous!

Jetur smiled. "Qaus be with you, Mahalath," he said. She shuddered. He stepped into the room out of the sunlit courtyard. Something in his eyes. . . . Something sinister.

"What do you want?"

"Mahalath." His voice was husky. "Esau has gone. I know you're not a virgin. I have come to lie with you."

She knew she must remain calm. This was not a total surprise to her; her gift had been warning her for the last two days. But she knew she was in grave danger.

"Please, Jetur. You mustn't. I'm a virgin. I *am*. Please believe me!"

Jetur snorted. "You've been alone with that savage for several weeks. Don't tell me he didn't touch you! Huh! I'll bet he did more than touch you! By now, you're probably experienced; I'll bet you love it!"

A small dribble of saliva dripped from the corner of his mouth as he stepped toward her. She tried to back up but was already against the wall.

"Jetur, please! Esau will kill you!"

"He won't believe you! You'd look silly telling him I lay with you. He'd probably drag you out for stoning!"

"Not Esau! He'd believe me!" Her words were useless. Jetur would believe what most men of her culture believed: in a case of adultery, the woman was always at fault.

Jetur reached out and grasped her wrist. She twisted away, but he pulled her close. She struggled against him, hitting his face with her free hand, clenching her teeth to keep from screaming.

"So you want to play games, eh?" Without releasing her wrist, Jetur swung his free hand and slapped her hard in the face. The force of the blow snapped her head back. She yelped with surprise and pain.

Jetur's voice was harsh. "You need a little reminder of your place. This ought to do it!"

This time his hand was a fist, and it smashed into her jaw. He let her go, and she fell to the floor. His foot caught her in the stomach, and she rolled away from him, gasping. He kept coming toward her, and she kept rolling.

Something was underneath her. The broom. She grasped its heavy handle and leaped to her feet.

"Please, Jetur —" She grasped the broom

in both hands and raised it.

He laughed. "Put that down, girl. Now you've earned a *real* beating!"

He stepped forward. She swung the broom, but he pushed it aside and reached for her. With a strength she didn't know she had, she twisted away from him, swinging all the way around, the broom making a wide arc.

Crack!

The heavy broom handle caught him on the wrist and he jerked back, a startled look on his face.

"Agghh! You bitch! You —" He looked from his wrist to her face, then back to his wrist again.

"I — I think it's broken!"

"I'm sorry," she said, lowering the broom.

Instantly she knew it was a mistake. Begging for forgiveness would only feed his need to hurt her. His eyes narrowed; despite his pain he came at her again.

She backed up. What should she do? Hit him again? The first blow was a lucky one; she didn't have the strength to win in a combat such as this. Something else must be done. Suddenly she knew what.

She threw the broom to the floor in front of him and held up her hand. *"Stop!"*

He stopped. His face showed surprise at her sudden command.

Then she knew what to say. *"Thus says Qaus!"* The words were spoken slowly, calmly, in a deep voice. *"Behold, the oldest son of Nebaioth has arrived at a crossroad in his life. He can continue to harm the daughter of Ishmael, or he can leave now, go to Egypt, and become a soldier."*

Her words startled her almost as much as him. Jetur's eyes were wide and his mouth gaped.

Again the words tumbled from her. *"Behold, if the son of Nebaioth becomes an Egyptian soldier, long life and glory shall come to him. But if he harms the daughter of Ishmael, he will die before the sun has set on this day! Qaus has spoken!"*

Jetur continued to gape at her. He blinked his eyes. He gulped. Then without a word, he turned and ran.

Mahalath leaned back against the wall. Her knees felt weak, and she slid to the floor. She trembled and began to sob.

What had happened? Had God really spoken through her? Was this the fulfillment of her gift?

The trembling suddenly left her; she felt a strange calm. Something had happened to her; something vague which she only partly understood — but it *had* happened. She was a new person. A person . . . *through whom God spoke!*

208

Again she recalled Hagar's words about her gift. "Use it only for good." Yes, she must do that now. In the past, she had always been aware of her gift when something was happening — or about to happen — concerning her. No more. From now on, she must use the gift only to help others.

She rose, still feeling a little weak. But she was not the same person she had been a few moments ago. She would never be that person again.

The Ishmaelite clan gathered in Punon for the wedding. Only two men were absent. One was Mishma the Trader, known as "The Ishmaelite," who traveled, supervising his caravan of trade goods and slaves between Babylon, Hazor, and Egypt. His wife and sons were present, but the Ishmaelite was not expected for six more months.

The other absent family member was Jetur. He had disappeared. His shepherd brothers, Naphish and Kedemah, wondered if he had run off to join the Egyptian army. For years he had boasted of doing just that. But why now? Nobody knew, but as in all family gatherings, there was an abundance of opinions, speculations, and questions.

There was plenty of food for the celebration. The family granary was full, and dates, figs, and nuts were always abundant. Jars of wine and beer were constantly on Moabite tables. But there was also a plentiful supply of meat. Speculation about Jetur's whereabouts took second place to celebration of the marvelous hunting skills of the groom, which seemed to surpass even Ishmael and Nebaioth. Yes, they said, nodding wisely, Nebaioth could retire and become a miner of copper, insuring he would become a wealthy man like several of his brothers. He would no longer be needed as the hunter of the family.

As Mahalath moved around the family, listening to the gossip and news, she was surprised to find no discussion of Esau's origins. Surely Esau had told Ishmael he was a son of Isaac and grandson of Abraham. All the Ishmaelites knew the story of Hagar's expulsion from that family. And although they revered their ancestor Abraham, they held his descendants in low esteem. They must not know who Esau was, she concluded. Her father, wisely, must not have mentioned it.

The women were fascinated by Mahalath's adventures following her captivity almost a year ago. She told them some of it, omitting parts she would like to forget. But she told glowing accounts of Esau, and his daring rescue of her, and his surpassing hunting skills.

Esau, through all of this, said little. The men tried to make him talk. What would be more natural than for a stranger to boast about his exploits as Mahalath's rescuer, or impress on his listeners his knowledge of hunting? That was what Ishmael would have done — had been doing for years. Nebaioth too, to a lesser extent. But not Esau. He lumbered about from one group to another, saying little. He listened politely, answered questions briefly, but remained the mysterious stranger of unknown past, exceptional skill, and taciturn manner.

Mahalath was the only one who knew how uncomfortable her future husband was. Several times she had seen him, while listening courteously to a garrulous in-law, lift his eyes to the range of hills to the east. His eyes held a longing to be away, to be alone, to follow the spoor of an elusive game animal. He seemed to yearn to be anywhere but here, shackled by the chains of a family whose many words warmed air chilled by *stav* winds from the north.

She wanted to go to him, comfort him, or just sit with him silently while he refreshed himself with solitude. But this was her wedding day. Custom dictated that she not speak to him but remain isolated from him until the final ceremony. She moved among her guests, chatting gaily with them, but when she saw Esau, she avoided him. He understood this, but once she caught his gaze above the crowd. She read in his eyes the loneliness, the discomfort, the sexual hunger, and something else — love.

Esau. Mahalath promised herself to be his devoted wife. To give him the depth of love he needed. To provide a home for him, to make and mend his clothing, to cook, to be willing and passionate in his bed. He might not be home much, but she vowed never to complain.

There was something else Mahalath promised herself. She recalled her newly discovered vocation — to use her gift in the service of others. She would begin with Esau. She would use her gift for his benefit as much as possible. Opportunities to help others would come to her — would seek her out — but with Esau, she would make a special effort. She sensed something within him, some deep need, which only she could fulfill.

The hours seemed to drag. Finally it was time for the ceremony. The sun had just set; daylight lingered after the sun had sunk behind the peaks. Long shadows stretched across the town square where all the family, and many Moabites of Punon, had gathered for the wedding.

Ishmael presided. He enjoyed the ceremony and would prolong it as long as he could. "Mahalath, my daughter." He had already talked for a long time about the joys of marriage, the responsibilities of the husband and wife, the importance of sons.

Now he reluctantly came to the most important part of the ceremony: the joining of two people in wedlock. "You are flesh of my flesh, bone of my bone. You are my beloved daughter. You are a virgin. I certify this by the Holy One who is Creator of all."

The sonorous voice paused, then with dramatic skill he turned to the groom. "Esau, my son. You are a man of honor, a man without home and family. Therefore you are my son, my family. And I give my daughter, Mahalath, to you."

Mahalath breathed a sigh of relief. At this point it was customary to recite the family origins of the groom. Ishmael's silence was either because of ignorance or wisdom. She suspected wisdom.

"Give me your hand."

Mahalath, heavily veiled, reached out from the folds of her clothing with her right hand. Esau, scrubbed clean and wearing a new robe, held out his. The hand which reached for hers was covered with red hair.

Ishmael took both hands in his own and joined them together. He then took the *migdol* he wore around his head and bound the two

213

hands gently with the brown cloth. "You are one. May Qaus bless you forever. May you have sons, many sons. May good health and prosperity be yours. And may your sons rise up and call you blessed."

The ritual blessing was over, but Ishmael continued. "May you find wisdom and happiness in the conjugal bed." The words went on and on. Unnecessary words.

Esau frowned; the crowd grew restless. Then at a moment when Ishmael came to the end of a sentence and drew a breath for the next verbal assault, Esau spoke. "Here ends the ceremony," he proclaimed in a booming voice. "I accept my bride. We will now retire."

There was a gasp from the crowd. Nothing like this had occurred in a marriage ceremony before. Did this show disrespect for an elder — the clan patriarch — to interrupt him and conclude the ceremony? Or was this an attempt by the newest family member to assert his independence? Mahalath was suddenly proud of her husband.

Her husband! She was no longer a single girl, daughter of the clan patriarch. She was the husband of the hunter, the stranger — the man she loved.

As he gently led her away through the crowd toward her house, his arm around her shoulder, he whispered to her. "I'm tired of all this talk. Hurry, wife!"

She giggled. And she hurried.

18

The night was cold, bitterly cold, with wind whistling around the small room on the rooftop where Esau and Mahalath were spending their bridal night. Downstairs was warmer, but Ishmael was there. The lovers wanted to be alone.

Mahalath stirred in Esau's arms. With the heavy blanket wrapped securely around them, she was not cold. On the contrary, she felt cozy and comfortable.

Esau had said nothing during their lovemaking. He was gentle, mindful of her virginity and considerate of her inexperience. She had given herself completely to him.

Now as she lay in his arms, she was aware of a fundamental need within her. She needed the security of married life, the protection of a strong man, the knowledge that the future contained happiness and companionship — together.

For the first time since they wrapped themselves together in the blanket, Esau spoke.

"Thank you, Mahalath." His voice was husky.

Those simple, formal words sent a warm glow flooding through her. She knew what he meant. He was thanking her, not just for surrendering her virginity, but also for giving herself completely to him. She was his totally, now. As a slave, she had belonged to him before this. But he had never accepted her as his slave; he wanted her as his wife. This was the surrender for which he was trying to express his gratitude.

Mahalath snuggled closer to her husband, running her fingers through the matted hair on his chest. This was so soothing, so relaxing.

But something was wrong; she couldn't ignore the seething and boiling inside her. It had something to do with Esau. She recalled her resolve to use her gift to help others, beginning with her husband. Now was the time. She had to speak, to say the words which she knew would reach the terrible, dark secret he carried in his soul.

"Esau, my love," she whispered. "This is the time to share our secrets. Tell me yours."

He tensed. Had she gone too far? Perhaps the euphoric mood would break, and she might never again feel this peace and contentment. But it would be selfish to ignore Esau's burden just for her own personal peace. If she really surrendered to her husband, she must travel this road. Now.

A long agonizing moment passed before Esau spoke. When he did, his voice was a whisper. "I have another wife."

She caught her breath. His words shocked her. She hadn't expected this. She was not repulsed at not being his first sexual experience; she had expected that. Nor was it that he waited until after their marriage to tell her about another wife. Multiple marriages were common; in fact, many women preferred polygamy.

No. What disturbed her was something else . . . something she couldn't define. "Tell me about her," she finally said.

He took a deep breath. "Her name is Basemath, a Hittite. I left her in Beersheba. At first she was only a concubine, but before I left, I claimed her as my wife." He paused, then added, "I don't expect to see her again."

"Is she alone?"

"No. She's with my mother, Rebekah. They are well provided for."

Then Mahalath's gift prompted a question. "Does she have an heir?"

"No."

In the silence Mahalath could hear the wind whistling around the small room. She wanted to drop the subject. But her instinct said to go on. "Then you must produce an heir — for your mother's sake."

She heard his barely perceptible intake of breath. This was the right road to follow; she was boring to the heart of his problem. A small part of her mind marveled at her gift's guidance.

When he finally spoke, his voice was bitter. "An heir. There already is an heir."

Would he talk about it? Would he dredge up his painful secret which was buried inside him so deeply?

"Who?"

This time the silence stretched out for so long she thought he was retreating into the depths of loneliness and isolation.

At last he sighed. "Jacob."

"Who is Jacob?"

"My brother." His snorted. "My *younger* brother."

Inside Mahalath was boiling, seething, a fury of turmoil. She was close to the truth about Esau, close to discovering the hatred and bitterness which soiled his soul.

She sensed how painful this was to Esau, but she pressed on. "And where is Jacob now? In Beersheba?"

"No." With that whispered word he became silent.

Now truth flashed into Mahalath's brain like lightning. "In Haran," she said quietly.

He said nothing.

She went on, ruthlessly. "And you were going there to find him."

Again he was silent.

"To kill him." This time the silence was a heavy weight. Outside, the wind rose to a screech, seeking to reach through the cracks and crevices of the small room to grasp them with its icy fingers.

At last he spoke. "Now you know." But his voice was soft and gentle. He bore no resentment at her probing until his terrible secret was revealed.

Had she pressed him any other time, she sensed, he would have reacted differently. But she had just given herself to him in total surrender; he could do no less for her.

She nestled closer to him, and her lips caressed his hairy cheek. "Esau, my love," she whispered. "Let me help you. Please . . . stay with me. Don't go to Haran. Please!"

He said nothing, but his strong arms pressed her close to him. Was this his answer? Was he surrendering himself to her? No, there was something more. Something which tugged at him from two directions. His love for her — against his relentless compulsion for vengeance.

Suddenly she became aware of the awesome responsibility she had just taken on herself. She — and she only — stood between Esau and the long journey to Haran. In her total surrender to him, she had placed her frail life between Esau and his own self-destruction.

Then abruptly the warm feelings of peace returned to her body. She accepted the responsibility. She had promised to use her gift only in the service of others. And that service began here.

She smiled in the darkness. The burden might be heavy, but it was Esau's load she bore. By carrying it, she could save his life and his soul. This she would do gladly.

"Thank you, Esau," she whispered, aware she was echoing the words he had spoken to her moments before when she had surrendered herself to him.

As she said the words, she felt the tenseness leave his body and desire return. He still had a need. A need she now shared.

The wind continued to whistle ominously outside, but inside it was warm and cozy. Within the cocoon of the heavy blanket, the young lovers continued to give themselves to each other.

Part IV

Adah
bath *Elon*

19

Adah lay on her back, naked, her hands and feet tied securely to pegs in the ground. Dawn was near; the stars paled in the east. She shivered; the night had been cold. The sweat and blood on her exposed body had caused her much suffering through the long night. At least the men had left her alone while they slept.

Death was near. When those men woke this morning they would surely kill her, but death would be a relief. Adah sighed. The pain was not as sharp as it had been last night when they raped her. Four men had taken turns ravaging her helpless body. When she had fought so viciously against the first one, they had tied her wrists to pegs on the ground. Her struggles had merely excited the four men; she learned that lying passively without movement made them less eager.

She didn't know if they would continue their torment this morning, or just kill her. She hoped they'd kill her. Then she thought of a way to force them to do just that: she emptied her bowels and bladder. When they came to her this morning, they wouldn't want to rape her. Small revenge for what they had done to her, but it was all she could do. She hoped they would be angry enough to kill her quickly.

During the night she had thought about her past life. Three years ago, when she was eleven, that wild man destroyed her family. The big red giant had stood at the edge of the clearing, shouting obscenities, firing his arrows at the huddled mass of women and children in her clan. Adah's mother had thrown herself across Adah's body, taking the arrow meant for her. After a night of lonely terror, she found in dawn's light the grisly carnage around her.

After that, survival had been her only thought. She had scavenged as much as she could from her family's camp. She would have died had she not discovered the cave in the rocks. That had been her home for three years.

Adah recalled some of her first triumphs — kindling a fire with her flint rocks; catching fish in the stream with her bare hands; learning to make a delicious stew of bugs and lizards and snakes. Her most triumphant recollection was the time she had caught a hare in her clumsy trap. Her worst memory was when she was attacked by a lion. Although she killed it with her knife, the wounds from its fangs and claws festered and caused her several days of fever and agony.

No, that wasn't her worst memory — yesterday was. Those dirty men had captured her, leaping at her as she bent over the stream to catch a fish. They had dragged her to their camp. She shuddered at the memory.

Now it was over. They would kill her this morning. Soon. The light in the east was expanding, and the sun would be up shortly. The sooner, the better.

She shivered as another spasm of chill shook her body. She sneezed. It wakened one of the men. He grinned foolishly, then came to her.

Now he'll see what I've done to spoil his fun. Well, I've got one more surprise for him. She worked her mouth to gather enough saliva for one last defiant spit in his face.

The man stopped abruptly two feet from her, his eyebrows raised in shock as he stared at her. He grunted, then frowned, saying something in that unintelligible gibberish, which they spoke. He drew a knife from his belt. He was going to kill her. Now all she had to do was spit in his face.

But the knife fell from his hand. The man's

mouth gaped in surprise. Something protruded from his chest — an arrow! He gasped, then screamed as he tried to pull it from his body. His eyes went blank and he collapsed.

The other three men leaped to their feet. Adah heard a whirring noise, and she watched, fascinated, as feathered shafts embedded themselves in the bodies of the three men. They too began to scream and writhe.

"Stinking Horites!"

The voice of the intruder startled her, and she saw him for the first time. He stepped from behind a tree and strode toward the men he had just shot. Adah gasped as she recognized him — the giant madman who had killed her family three years ago!

His hair and beard were red, tangled and dirty. His eyes blazed. His short leather robe was stained and torn. The hand holding the bow was covered with red hair.

The red giant strode to where the three men had fallen under his arrows. One was still alive, writhing and screaming. When he looked up and saw his executioner standing above him, he became still and silent. Then he began to speak his gibberish, probably begging for mercy.

The red-bearded madman had a knife in his hand. "Die, you Horite pig!" he said, and with a deft motion slit the man's throat.

The dying man's scream turned into a croak, then a gurgle and whistle as blood gushed out of the wound. Adah watched horrified as the big man looked around. He would surely see her next. Would he rape her? Or just kill her? Probably slit her throat as he had done to her former captor. Well, she was prepared for death anyway. But she would spit in his face as her final act.

The madman spotted her lying on the ground, and walked slowly toward her. He gasped as he looked down on her. His eyes were wide; to Adah they seemed wild. Out of his mind. Like the last time when she saw him, three years ago — that killer glaze in his eyes.

He still had the bloody knife in his hand. He dropped to his knees beside her and slowly brought up the knife. Gathering all her strength, she spat. The spittle struck him squarely in the face.

He grunted. His eyes opened even wider, and his mouth formed a circle inside his hairy red face. That would be Adah's final sight in this life; she shut her eyes and tensed her body in preparation for the knife on her throat.

What she felt instead was a loosening in her arms and legs. They were free. Something had cut the thongs which held her to the pegs. Was this what death felt like? She opened her eyes. The big man had turned his back and was walking toward one of the fallen men.

"I'll get you some clothes," he said.

This was her chance! Without thinking, she rolled over and scrambled to her feet. Her knees were weak, but she stumbled off into the bushes. She ran as fast as her wobbly legs could carry her.

Behind her the madman shouted, "Come back, girl! I won't hurt you!"

She wasn't fooled. Desperately dodging trees and rocks and bushes, she staggered through the forest until she came to the stream where she had fished yesterday. She splashed across it and scrambled up the hillside among the trees and rocks. Would he follow? No. Impossible. But just to be sure, she took a roundabout path to her cave.

Just below the cave, a spring bubbled from the rocks. This had given her an unfailing supply of clear cold water for the last three years. Now it would do something more for her. She sat down in the pool she had created just below the spring.

The cold water felt good on her damaged body. She wiped away the filth and blood as best she could. The cold numbed her, and she felt a lassitude stealing up her body. Now all she wanted to do was sleep.

She staggered up the hill to the bushes

which masked the entrance to her cave. On hands and knees she crawled through the small opening into the room inside. The fire was out, but the room was still warm from its heat. She wrapped herself in the tattered blanket and rolled onto her couch of pine needles. She drew her knees to her chest and put her thumb in her mouth. Exhaustion claimed her then, and she slept.

Dreams troubled her sleep, that old familiar dream of the red madman killing her family. But it was mingled with his arrows flying to the bodies of her tormentors. Then her dream was filled with pain as those filthy men lay on her and —

She awoke, sweating and panting. The dream had been so real that the pain was still there. Then the dream faded into the place where all dreams die, but the pain didn't go with it. She would have to sit in the cold spring again and soak until the pain went away.

She tried to get up but was shocked to realize how weak she was. At least she was alive! A soak in the stream, a few nuts and figs from her store of food, and she would be all right. But she would stay in the cave most of the day; that red-bearded madman might still be searching for her.

As she crawled toward the mouth of her

cave, she froze. A voice was calling to her from outside.

"Come out, child! I want to help you."

The madman! He was here! But how had he tracked her? He couldn't possibly have followed her trail. Could he? Yes, she would have dripped blood all the way. A skilled woodsman could find it and come after her.

Now she was trapped. She would die. The giant who killed her family would kill her too. And she had just begun to have thoughts of living when this happened!

Well, she would sell her life dearly. She grasped the spear she had salvaged from her family's camp, a spear she had never used. Until now. Now she would use it to kill her red-bearded tormentor. Maybe he'd kill her, but if she were lucky — and quick enough — she could stab him first.

She crawled through the opening of the cave, spear in hand. He was standing in the late afternoon sunlight, bow in hand, holding aside the bushes which hid the cave. Waiting to kill her. But she had a surprise for him!

She charged. But her weakness caused her to stumble. The big man dropped his bow and the bushes to grasp the spear and wrest it from her. She fell trembling at his feet.

Now he'll kill me. And I can't even spit in his face this time! Her mouth was dry; the weakness in her body made her powerless to move. She had begun to bleed again.

She felt his hands on her shoulders. Gentle hands. *Is he going to strangle me? Or just pull my bones apart?*

He picked her up and carried her to the spring. There he bathed her wounded loins and gently put clothes on her. The clothes, she guessed, were from one of the men he had killed yesterday. They were too big for her and were infested with little pests which bit. But she had endured bites before, and she was too weak to care anyway.

The man held a cup of water to her lips. "Drink this," he said softly.

Poison? She drank eagerly, hoping it would bring a quick death. The cold liquid felt good on her parched throat, and spread through her stomach like a healing balm.

"Now chew on this," he said.

He put in her mouth a small piece of dried meat. Venison! It was a taste she vaguely remembered from childhood, and it was good. Again, was it poisoned? She chewed and swallowed; he gave her a few more sips of water.

"Now I'll take you home," he muttered. "Mahalath will know what to do with you."

He picked her up as though she were a feather. She settled into his arms and shut her eyes. She was too weak to care what he did with her next.

Just before she went to sleep, she had one indistinct thought. *Mahalath? That's a musical instrument. What does a mahalath have to do with knowing what to do with me?* But the thought was erased by the comforting darkness of sleep. She had just enough strength to thrust her thumb into her mouth as she bounced along in his arms on her way to being taken care of by a *mahalath.*

20

Adah was only vaguely aware of brief moments of consciousness during the days which followed. Each time she opened her eyes she saw a beautiful young woman, who smiled and talked soothingly to her. The woman forced her to eat a broth which spread warmth through her body. The love and concern she saw in the woman's eyes restored in her the fierce will to survive.

Once Adah opened her eyes to see the red madman looking down at her. She shrieked and turned away, trying to get to her feet and run. But the woman was there, holding her, comforting her, coaxing her back to sleep. After that, Adah never saw her giant enemy in her brief waking moments.

One day she felt a little stronger. When her nurse lifted her head for a spoonful of broth, Adah watched her carefully. She noted the brown wavy hair, oiled and coiffed; the long eyelashes surrounding wise brown eyes; a short stubby nose and small chin. The woman's ready smile revealed straight teeth and two dimples on her cheeks. She was always smiling.

"Who are you?" Adah whispered weakly.

The smile broadened on the young lady's face. "Mahalath," she replied. "Rest now. You're going to be all right."

So this is the mahalath. No wonder she's called "Mahalath." She makes music in everything she does.

There was another man in the house, an old man with bald head and deep voice who talked a lot. He slept on a bed beside Adah at night. Once Adah awakened, frightened, and called for Mahalath. The old man got up; a moment later, Mahalath came. She held Adah in her arms, speaking soothing words, until Adah was again lost in the oblivion of sleep.

One morning when Adah woke she was hungry. When Mahalath came to her with some broth, she managed to whisper, "May I please have something else?"

"Of course!" Her smiling nurse laid aside the broth and came back in a moment with a barley cake, which she fed to Adah. Mahalath propped her up on a pillow.

"I'm glad you're feeling better. What should I call you?"

"I am Adah," she said, attempting to smile.

"Adah. Tell me, Adah, who is your family?"

Adah felt she could trust this person who was so good to her. "I have no family," she replied.

The beautiful nurse took Adah's hand. "You do now," she said softly. "My husband, Esau, and I will care for you."

"Esau. . . . Is he that old man with the bald head?"

Mahalath's tinkling laugh sounded like the harp she was named for. "No, child. That's my father, Ishmael. My husband's not home now."

"He must be very nice, to have a wife like you."

"But, Adah, you've met him. He's the man who brought you here."

Adah gasped, her eyes wide. "Him? That monster?"

Again, that musical laugh. "He's no monster, dear. Esau is a gentle and loving man. He saved your life."

Adah shook her head. This couldn't be. Mahalath, the only person to give her love and tenderness since her mother died — married to the madman who had killed her family.

But when Mahalath looked into her eyes and smiled, Adah felt safe. Mahalath's words reassured her: "Have no fear of Esau, dear.

He won't harm you. Never. I promise!"

Adah relaxed. She could believe Mahalath. She would protect Adah from that madman. He could not kill her as long as Mahalath stood guard. Adah closed her eyes and slept.

Voices wakened her. Adah looked around. In the dim lamplight she saw three people sitting on the floor: her beautiful young friend, the old man — and the madman!

Would he kill her? No; she was safe as long as Mahalath was there. Nevertheless, Adah trembled at the sight of him.

He was fierce-looking. His bulk was muscular and lithe; his red-tinted skin was burnt almost brown by constant exposure to the sun. The red beard and hair were matted and wild. And his eyes were blazing — that madman look.

He sat on a mat on the floor, a bowl of steaming stew in his hand. The old man was doing most of the talking, with the giant grunting an occasional answer. Mahalath suddenly rose and came to Adah. It was as though she knew Adah was awake.

"How are you feeling, Adah? Well enough to talk to Esau?"

"Please, Mahalath! Don't let him come near me!"

"All right, Adah." She took Adah's hand.

"But look at him. Does he look dangerous to you now?"

Adah stared at Esau, recalling the first time she saw him. She didn't know his name then. He stood at the edge of the clearing, shouting angry obscenities, firing his death-arrows, a wild maniacal look in his eyes. The next time she saw him, he looked much the same as when he killed those vile men who had raped her. And there he was now, sitting not twenty feet from her, staring at her. Their eyes met; Adah trembled.

"Esau," said Mahalath gently, "speak to Adah."

Esau nodded his shaggy red head. "Greetings, Adah. Welcome to our home. I mean you no harm."

Adah gripped Mahalath's hand tighter. She wasn't fooled by the giant's smooth words. When the time came, when Mahalath wasn't there to protect her, Esau would kill her.

Mahalath propped Adah up on a pillow. "I'll get you some of the stew we're eating, child. I'll be right back." She walked to where the large kettle was suspended over the brazier of coals and dipped out a bowl of the steaming stew.

Adah didn't relax until Mahalath returned to her side. She felt strong enough to feed herself, so she took the bowl from Mahalath's hands and raised it to her mouth. It was hot but tasty, and it spread warmth inside her.

"It's good, Mahalath. Thank you."

Then the old man — Ishmael — spoke. "Tell us who you are, child. We know your name is Adah, but that's all we know."

"Yes," said Mahalath gently. "Please tell us."

Looking into Mahalath's loving eyes, Adah felt a little confidence returning. She *should* tell them. Mahalath had been so good to her, she at least owed her that.

"I am Adah," she said softly. "Daughter of Elon the Hittite —"

Esau gasped. He leaped to his feet. "Elon the Hittite!" he roared. "Your father? Then you must be —"

Adah cringed, but Mahalath's arm was around her. "It's all right, Adah. He won't hurt you." She turned to Esau, her voice firm. "You're scaring the child. Please sit down. Speak softly. What do you know about her family?"

Esau did not sit down; he stood staring at Adah. She recognized the glazed look in his eyes — the stare of a madman. But when he finally spoke, his voice was considerably softer.

"I understand," he said. "I know why she's so frightened of me. She has every right to be." He looked at the floor. "I . . . I killed her family."

Adah was aware of Mahalath's sharp intake of breath. "But why?" Mahalath asked. "I know you had a reason."

"Yes," said Ishmael, "tell us your story."

But even Adah could see Esau was not a storyteller. "Because of Judith," was all he said.

Now it was Adah who gasped. "Judith? My sister? But she died as a sacrifice to Moloch!"

That was another bad memory which Adah had tried for years to block. The fire, the screams, the smell — it all came back. She shuddered. Mahalath held her tighter.

"Moloch's fire didn't kill Judith," said Esau. "I did."

"You!" Ishmael's voice was as loud as Esau's. "In the name of Qaus, man, tell us your story!"

In the center of the dark room, dimly lit by the oil lamp and the coals from the brazier, Esau stood silently. To Adah, his eyes were flashing insanity.

"No!" he said. Then reaching for his mantle, he strode toward the door and went out into the night.

Adah breathed a sigh of relief. The crazed giant was gone. Only Mahalath and the talk-

241

ative old man were left, and she feared neither of them.

"I'll . . . tell what little I know, Mahalath," she said.

"Are you sure you want to?" asked Mahalath gently.

"Yes. I need to tell it." When Mahalath nodded, she continued. "Judith, my sister, was away, living in someone's tent as his concubine, I never knew who it was. Then one day, I don't know why, my father brought her home. He sacrificed her to Moloch — through the fire. We had to watch."

She shuddered, recalling Judith's screams. But Mahalath's comforting presence encouraged her to continue. "We left Judith's body by the altar and went back to our camp. That night, Esau came and killed everyone. I alone escaped, only because Mother protected me with her body."

Adah sobbed. Mahalath pressed her head to her breast and spoke soothing words. But Adah had spent all her energies in telling this wrenching story. All she could do was put her thumb in her mouth and drift into the dark land of slumber, protected from Esau and her dreams by Mahalath's comforting arms.

When she awoke next morning, Adah felt much better. The steady diet of nourishing broths, the sleep, and above all the love which

Mahalath had lavished upon her, combined to restore her body and mind to health. She was still weak, but when Mahalath offered to help her up to sit on the ledge in the middle of room, Adah gladly accepted.

"Where is he?" Adah asked, looking furtively around.

Mahalath's tinkling laugh reassured her. "If you mean Esau, he's hunting. If you mean my father, he went to the city gates to tell his stories. There's no one here but us."

Adah breathed easier as she looked around. The room was cozy; the brazier in the center, which was used for cooking, kept the morning chill outside. There was no furniture; everyone sat on mats on the tile floor, or on the ledge as she was doing. Small high windows let out the smoke and let in light. The mud-and-brick walls were covered with cooking utensils, tools, weapons, and even a few pegs on which clothing was draped. It was neat and well organized, so domestic, so comfortable. Adah recalled the portable tents of her childhood, and their nomadic life. She looked at Mahalath, envying the settled comfort of her home.

Mahalath was watching her as she looked around the room. Almost as though she knew what Adah was thinking. Mahalath said, "This is *your* home now, Adah. *We* want you in our family."

Tears clouded Adah's eyes. She had never had a home before. She remembered family, but there was not a great deal of love in her childhood. And for three years she had been starved for love in her solitary struggle for survival.

"Mahalath," she whispered, "you can't know how much that means to me."

Mahalath sat on the ledge beside her and took her hand. "I know, child. Please think of us now as your family."

"But . . . but —" Adah grasped Mahalath's hand tightly. "I don't know how to say this —"

"You're worried about Esau, aren't you? You still think he's a monster who killed your family. And he intends to kill you."

Adah gaped at her. "How did you know?"

Again Mahalath's tinkling laugh set her at ease. "Adah, Esau is no monster. Believe me, I know. You're too easily fooled by outward appearance. Look inside the man. Look deeply. You'll see him as he really is."

"But I saw him kill my family. He was insane!"

Mahalath turned to her and looked directly into her eyes. "Yes, child. He was insane — temporarily. I asked him last night why he killed your parents. He only vaguely recalls doing it. What he remembers most was Judith's death."

"Judith's death? But she died in Moloch's fire."

"No, she didn't, Adah."

"But . . . I saw her! Her body —"

"She was still alive when you left her by Moloch's altar. That's where Esau found her."

"Then Esau was —"

"Yes, child. Esau was Judith's lover. And Esau's seed was in her body. That's why she was sacrificed to Moloch."

"But I thought the sacrifice was to curse someone."

"The curse was on Esau. But it didn't work. Moloch's fire did not kill Judith."

"But how —" Adah gasped, as the truth hit her like a blow from a club. "Esau —"

Mahalath put her arm around Adah. "Yes, my dear. Esau killed her. It was an act of kindness; she was suffering so much. But you can imagine what this did to Esau."

Adah nodded. She recalled the vivid picture which had returned so often to haunt her dreams — the picture of Esau she had harbored in her mind for three years.

But there was another picture in Adah's mind also. "Mahalath, I saw him again, when he killed those men. He was the same madman I had seen before. He shot them like they were wild animals, and he had that same look in his eyes."

"Maybe he was saving your life. You *were* their prisoner."

"But . . . he didn't even see me until after he had killed them! He wasn't rescuing me. He was just killing them!"

"What did these men look like, Adah?"

"Short. Black beards, straight hair, worn very long. Dirty. They wore skins and wrapped their legs in woolen leggings."

Mahalath frowned. "They might have been Horites."

"Horites?" That was familiar. "Yes, that's what Esau called them. 'Stinking Horites!' he said."

"Ah! Of course!" Mahalath's mouth was a tight line. "I wish Esau wouldn't hate them so. I don't. But he seems determined to kill any Horite he meets."

"But . . . why?"

Mahalath turned her face to Adah and smiled. "Because, child, some Horites captured me once."

Adah gasped.

Mahalath continued hastily. "Oh, they didn't treat me as they did you. They spared my virginity. My price would be higher in the slave market if I remained a virgin."

Adah stared open-mouthed at her friend. Mahalath looked so innocent, so pure, so protected! She was so cheerful, so loving, how could she have had such awful experiences in the past?

"Tell me more, Mahalath."

"All right, Adah." Mahalath began her story.

Adah sat, wide-eyed and open-mouthed, as the drama unfolded. Then Mahalath described Esau. His rescue. His gentleness. His thoughtfulness. Taking her home. Marrying his slave.

Adah swallowed. This was not the picture of a madman. Could she have been wrong about Esau?

21

As the days passed, Adah grew stronger. She began to feel more and more at home in her new family. One day, when the sun had climbed to the center of the sky, Ishmael came home for a midday meal and rest.

At Ishmael's insistence, they ate together, sharing the meal of venison stew, figs, and barley cakes while seated on mats on the floor. Ishmael turned to Adah.

"My child, while I was seated at the gates today, I heard disturbing words from the good people of our city. Many were there today. The usual old men, the boys who wanted to learn the art of hunting. They were all there, and among them was one of the elders of the city of Punon, Manarkan, son of Debulon, who lives on the west —"

"Please, Father!" Mahalath's words interrupted him. "What disturbing words?"

Ishmael paused, frowning, almost as though he didn't know what to say. He looked at Adah. Then slowly he continued.

"There is some concern about our guest. They wonder what a girl of marriageable age is doing in this house."

Mahalath's eyes widened, then she frowned. "I see. Does it matter what some people with small minds think?"

Ishmael nodded. "Do you remember Menorah?"

Mahalath gasped. "No!" she whispered. "They wouldn't —"

Adah could keep quiet no longer. "What is it, Mahalath? Who was Menorah? And what does all this mean?"

Both Ishmael and Mahalath were silent for a moment. Then unexpectedly, Mahalath laughed, her tinkling peal of laughter out of place in the tense situation.

"Father," she said between giggles, "let's have another wedding!"

Ishmael frowned, then slowly a smile fluttered across his lips. "Yes, daughter. It would certainly solve the dilemma. Are you sure it would be all right with you? And with Esau? Of course, when I was a young man —"

"Father, please!" Mahalath's audacity in interrupting her father was a source of wonder to Adah. "Why don't you lie down for a few minutes, while I talk to Adah. Poor dear, she doesn't understand what we're talking about."

Mahalath helped her father to his feet. Together they hobbled to the ledge. He was still muttering softly when he lay down on his bed and covered his face with one arm. He was soon snoring softly. It was a comforting sound, which Adah had grown accustomed to during the nights.

Mahalath resumed her seat on the mat beside Adah. "Now we can talk. I have some explaining to do."

"Yes, please, Mahalath. I don't understand."

Mahalath drew a deep breath and looked into Adah's eyes. "First, you must understand something about the people of Punon. They are good people, but . . . well, they have a tendency to resent the ways of strangers."

"You sound like you're not one of them."

"In a way we aren't." Mahalath smiled. "Our family moved here about fifty years ago. We're newcomers!"

Her soft laughter had a musical quality in the quiet room. Then she became serious again as she turned to Adah.

"My dear, here is the situation. When a city elder thinks there is an improper situation in the community, he can take steps to remedy it."

"Improper situation? You mean . . . my being here?"

"Exactly. You are an embarrassment to the town. A young girl of marriageable age, living in our family — well, they could easily accuse us of harboring a prostitute."

"What! Me? But you don't think that, do you?"

Mahalath smiled. "Of course not, child. But sometimes the people of this village don't think the same as we do. And they have power of life and death in their hands."

"Life and death? What do you mean?"

Mahalath moved closer to Adah and spoke softly. "Some years ago, a similar situation arose. The girl's name was Menorah. Accusing her of adultery, they stoned her to death."

"Oh!"

"Yes, Adah. It could happen. No girl of marriageable age should live without the protection of a family. Otherwise, she's a prostitute. That's the thinking of this small-minded town."

"Oh, Mahalath! What should I do?"

"There's a convenient solution. Marriage. We will find you a husband."

"A husband? For me? But . . . but where. . . ."

Mahalath smiled. "Yes, child. A husband for you. And that husband is . . . Esau."

"Esau!" Into Adah's mind popped the image of the wild madman, his red hair askew, eyes blazing, firing arrows into her family. "Oh, no! I couldn't!"

Mahalath took Adah's hand and held it gently. "Yes, Adah. You could. You would belong in our family then. You and I would be forever linked with family ties to the same husband. Nothing could separate us!"

Suddenly it was too much for Adah — her weakness following her illness, her fear of Esau, the long morning conversation which tired her. She flung herself into Mahalath's arms, sobbing.

And Mahalath comforted her, as she had so often in the past few days. She spoke soft words, soothing words, words which fought to drive away the terror and meaninglessness that seemed to press in on her. Adah's thumb sought her mouth, and in a few moments her sobs subsided. She slept.

Adah slept poorly that night. Several times she awoke, whimpering, crying softly. Once Ishmael asked, "Do you want me to call Mahalath?"

"No, Father Ishmael." After that she tried to lie quietly.

By the time daylight outlined the features of the room, she had made a decision. She would marry Esau. She had considered many alternatives. If she ran away, she would be lost in an unfamiliar world, and there were a lot of people like the Horites out there. If she refused to marry Esau, the townspeople would kill her. Death was not unattractive.

Killing herself was an alternative. Was there a way to do it? Adah sucked furiously on her thumb, considering the possibilities. She could cut her wrists with one of Mahalath's knives. She could wait until Mahalath was at the well or some other errand away from home, then hang herself from the rafters. Either way, Mahalath would find her when she returned. Mahalath would be upset. She would cry. Adah could not do that to Mahalath.

The only other possibility was to marry Esau.

Esau. Monster. Killer of her family. Madman whose very appearance spoke of insanity and cruelty. Her husband?

She thought of all the men she had known in her life. She had never felt affection for her father, who was indifferent to her mother and cruel to his children. All the men she knew were that way. And the Horites — she shuddered. That was what a man did to the woman he married. That was what Esau would do to her. Degradation. Beating. Making her do abominable things.

What could she do? Was there nothing but

marriage to Esau in her future? Must she always suffer?

She drew her knees up to her chest, biting her thumb to keep from crying. She saw no happiness in her future. The only alternative would bring pain to either herself or Mahalath. And she would rather endure the pain herself than cause anguish for Mahalath.

So . . . she would marry Esau.

Then she recalled something Mahalath had said: *Nothing can separate us. We'll be linked together by the same husband.* This was the only good thing in a marriage with Esau. She and Mahalath would always be together. Esau was away during the day; only at night would she have to endure him. But her days would belong to Mahalath.

With this thought, she was able to sleep. Her dreams were confused — Esau raping her; Mahalath comforting her afterward. Suffering and love. One made the other endurable.

When she awoke, the day was well advanced; everyone was gone. Adah rose from her bed, still feeling shaky but tired of lying in her blankets. She wanted something to do. She was also hungry, but she didn't know where to find anything to eat. She didn't even try to look for food, thinking it might displease Mahalath.

She wanted to do some work in the room to please Mahalath, but as she looked around, she had no idea what to do. During her childhood she had done only what her mother had told her. The past three years she was occupied with survival in a situation far different from a civilized home such as this. She simply didn't know what to do. So she just sat on the ledge, sucking her thumb, waiting. A long time later Mahalath came in, carrying a basket of grapes.

Adah was so glad to see her, she jumped down from the ledge and hurried across the room. Mahalath laid aside the basket and opened her arms. Adah buried her head in Mahalath's chest and sobbed.

"It's all right, child." Mahalath's soft voice was soothing. "I'm here. I'll never leave you. Sometimes I'm gone for a short time, but I'll always come back to you. We'll always be together. Nothing can separate us."

Adah's sobs subsided. Mahalath always knew what to say. Her words were like healing balm to her troubled mind.

Mahalath's next words were also welcome. "Adah, you need something to do. Would you help me make wine today?"

"Oh, yes!" Adah stepped back from Mahalath and smiled. She wiped her tear-streaked face. "But . . . I don't know how."

Mahalath's lilting laughter warmed her. "I'll tell you what to do. You'll enjoy it. First, we need to spread out these fresh grapes on the roof. Then we'll take a basket of the ones already bleached to the wine vats." Mahalath paused, a small frown touching her forehead. "But first, dear, we'll find something for you to eat!"

Mahalath was right, the day was filled with laughter and companionship. Adah forgot her dread of Esau as she tramped barefoot on the grapes in the upper wine vat, squashing the warm liquid between her toes, watching it flow into the lower vat. Mahalath sang as they marched around inside the vat, dancing to the rhythm of the song.

Some of the townspeople came to the wine vats to watch and make their own wine. At first Adah was afraid of them. She wondered if they were condemning her for living in Esau's house, and were even now thinking about killing her. But the women and small children were cheerful and friendly. Everyone loved Mahalath. They begged her to sing for them.

But Mahalath said no. "We have work to do," she said, her voice filled with laughter. "We can't sit here all day, tramping grapes and singing and wasting our time. Do you want your men to beat you?"

The words were ominous to Adah, who assumed men beat women all the time. But Mahalath's voice belied the words, and the women laughed when she spoke. How could they joke about things like that?

Finally Mahalath dipped the wine into her jar. Then with Adah close to her, she made her way through the confusing city streets to the sanctuary of their home. Although the day was warm and pleasant, it was good to be inside the safe walls, away from the threat of other people. And be with Mahalath.

Later that afternoon, Mahalath made Adah sit on the ledge with her. Adah knew by Mahalath's serious face that she was about to open an important discussion.

"Adah." Mahalath's hand sought Adah's. "Tell me. How do you feel about marrying Esau?"

Adah met her eyes. She had already settled this in her own mind. "I'll marry him, Mahalath. That's what you want."

"I do want it, dear. I want you with me always."

Adah could feel a warmth in her breast. Her hand tightened on Mahalath's. "And I want to be with you, always. But . . . what did Esau say when you asked him?"

Mahalath's smile was reassuring. "He was pleased. He said it was an excellent solution to the problem."

"And — how do you feel about . . . sharing Esau with me?"

Mahalath nodded. "It's a good thing for a man to have more than one wife. Good not only for him, but for his wives — *if* they get along all right. And we will."

"Yes, yes, Mahalath. Of course we will."

Mahalath's smile faded. "Tell me what's troubling you, Adah. I know you're worried about this marriage."

"Oh, no, Mahalath. It's all right. Really."

"No, it isn't, child. You're afraid. I can see it in your eyes. If you won't tell me, I'll tell you. You're afraid of Esau, and what he'll do to you after the wedding. You think he'll be like those Horites."

Adah pulled her hand away and turned her face. But she said nothing.

"Adah, listen. You will not share Esau's bed for a while. You're not ready. Esau will respect that. He'll wait until you honestly want to be in his bed. Do you understand?"

Slowly Adah turned to look into Mahalath's eyes. "But . . . but Esau will. . . ." She didn't even know how to say it.

"Esau will respect your wishes, Adah. Believe me. If you can't believe that about Esau, believe it about me. I will not let Esau take you to his bed until you're ready."

Adah wanted desperately to believe her.

She took a deep breath. "Mahalath, I love you. I trust you. Whatever you want, I'll do. If you say go to Esau's bed, I will do it. I'll do anything for you — as long as you stay with me!"

"I'll always be with you, dear. Always. There's so much you don't understand. But trust me. You'll see."

"I do trust you, Mahalath."

"Good." The smile which created the dimples creased Mahalath's face. "Now we can plan a wedding. It will be simple. Father will conduct the ceremony at the city gates. All Punon will see that you are a married woman and belong in this house."

It was done, then. Sealed. Adah was promised in marriage to the man she feared and despised.

At least during the days she could continue to do things like make wine with Mahalath. The days would be good. The nights. . . . She looked at Mahalath, who smiled reassuringly. Mahalath had said she would not share Esau's bed until she was ready. No. That couldn't be. Esau would take her, and Mahalath would be unable to stop him.

So be it. She would endure. That would be her gift to Mahalath.

22

The wedding took place the next day. This was not a gala celebration like Mahalath's wedding, since its purpose was merely public proclamation of marriage. Nevertheless, the town square was crowded with people from the village, curious about this stranger in Esau's home.

The entire event was a nightmare to Adah, since Mahalath could not be present at the all-male gathering. As Adah walked to the square beside Ishmael, she cringed from the gathering crowd of men. Staring. Thinking vile thoughts about her. They were men, and men were cruel. The only one to protect her was Father Ishmael, an old man.

Esau was there, looking as fierce and insane as ever. Even washing his face and combing and oiling his beard — at Mahalath's insistence — could not cover that maniacal look. When he brought her home — she fled from the thought. Mahalath would try to stop him, but how do you stop a madman?

Adah stood on Esau's left. Despite his bath, Esau smelled of animals and lust. She knew the smell; it was etched in her memory. It was the smell of the Horites — the odor of rutting beasts.

Adah could not concentrate on Ishmael's words. The deep voice droned on and on. Finally he took a cord from his headpiece and bound it around the hands of the bride and groom. Adah shuddered, feeling the hairy red hand she was bound to.

"They are now one flesh!" Ishmael's ominous words now bound them together — as binding as the symbolic cord around their hands. "Esau my son; Adah my daughter. You are one."

"I accept my bride." Esau's voice was guttural and harsh with lust. "I will take her now to my home."

The crowd murmured. A frown fluttered on Ishmael's face. Adah wondered why. Was it because Esau referred to their house as "my" home? Or was there something else — some unspoken subtle struggle between Esau and Ishmael?

Then Esau put his left arm around her and led her through the parting crowd. "We'll go home now, child," he said softly. "Mahalath will be waiting."

This puzzled Adah. They weren't going

261

home to Mahalath; they were going to that upstairs room where he would do things to her. Her pace slowed, and Esau hurried her along. Was he that eager to vent his lust?

Mahalath stood in the courtyard waiting. Adah started to go to her, but the cord still bound her to Esau's hand. She bit her lip. No, she didn't want to cry. Not in front of Mahalath.

Then Mahalath came to her, smiling. "Now we are both Esau's wives." She untied the loose knot which bound her wrist.

The next minute Adah flung herself into Mahalath's arms. In spite of her resolve, she burst into tears.

"It's all right, child. You're safe now."

Mahalath's soothing words only frightened Adah more. Any minute now, Esau would snatch his new bride away from his wife and drag her upstairs. Mahalath might try to stop him, but she would only be hurt. Adah couldn't stand that. Better to let Esau do those terrible things to her.

But Mahalath only led into the house. "You will sleep in your usual bed tonight, dear. Esau and I will go upstairs. Don't be afraid. You won't be bothered tonight."

Adah's knees trembled as Mahalath led her to her bed. When the blanket was wrapped around her, she drew her knees up to her chest and put her thumb in her mouth. Mahalath knelt beside her and tenderly kissed her cheek.

"Sleep well, Adah," she whispered. "And please try not to worry. Esau and I will be upstairs all night."

Then she was gone. The room was in deep shadows as only light from the stars and a half-moon filtered through the high windows. But Esau would come for her soon.

When she heard a noise at the door, she jerked her body and cringed. But it was only Ishmael, coming to his bed for the night. Soon his snores were the only sounds in the room. Esau might come later, but he would come. She only hoped Mahalath would not be hurt trying to stop him.

When a cricket chirped somewhere in the courtyard, she began to relax. Not even her fear could overcome the exhaustion and weakness in her body, and soon she slept. Once she awakened, thinking Esau had come for her. But the only sounds in the room were Ishmael's snores and the cricket in the courtyard. She could see nothing but the moonlit patches on the floor. Then, sucking her thumb, she closed her eyes.

When she woke next morning, Esau and Ishmael were gone. Mahalath sat on the ledge near her mending a sandal. The heavy awl in her hand poked through the thick leather strap, causing the frown of concentration on Mahalath's forehead.

"Mahalath," whispered Adah, "where's Esau?"

Mahalath quickly put aside the sandal and turned to her. "Greetings, Adah. How do you feel this morning?"

Adah stared at the broadening smile on Mahalath's face, watching the movement of the dimples. She couldn't put into words the questions which disturbed her.

Mahalath's smile faded; she pursed her lips. "I know, dear. You don't understand why Esau didn't come to you last night. You still think he's a beast who will treat you as the Horites did."

Adah sat up in bed. She reached a hand to Mahalath, needing the touch of those fingers. Mahalath scrambled across the few feet which separated them. She put her arms around Adah.

Adah's face went down on Mahalath's breast, and tears squeezed from her eyes. Mahalath's hand stroked her hair.

"Dear, dear child. You have so much to learn. We must begin to teach you. First, you must trust me. Remember that I love you, and would never do anything to harm you. That's why we wanted this marriage, so you'll be safe."

Adah nodded. Mahalath's calm voice and healing hands spoke to her as much as the words. But the words penetrated the haze of her mind. She felt a warm glow as she absorbed the truth that she was safe in Mahalath's arms, and safe from the townspeople in her marriage to Esau.

"The second lesson." Mahalath's voice became serious and urgent. "Believe me when I tell you this — Esau loves you too. He is kind and would *never* hurt you."

Mahalath was mistaken. Esau was a monster, ruled like all men by lust. Sooner or later he would begin his degradation and torture of his new wife. Not even Mahalath could stop him.

But Mahalath said this wasn't so. Did she know something Adah didn't? She seemed so sure. And she *did* trust Mahalath. Adah lifted her head and looked into Mahalath's now serious eyes. She couldn't put into words what she felt; all she could do was shake her head.

Then Mahalath spoke. Her voice was strong and demanding. "Trust me, Adah. Believe me. Esau is good and kind. In time, you will grow to love him, as I do."

More than the meaning of the words, the personality and power of her friend penetrated Adah's confused awareness. *It can't be. But if Mahalath says so. . . .*

"I say so, Adah. I, who love you, ask that you trust me. Lean on me. And take a good look at Esau. Look at him as he really is. Put aside your fear, your bad memories, your revulsion. Look at him through *my* eyes. Look at Esau. And — *love him!*" The last words were spoken forcefully.

Adah shook her head. But she couldn't pull her eyes away from Mahalath's. She shuddered. Then Mahalath's arms enfolded her, and she put her head on her friend's breast. The gentle hand stroked the back of her head.

"You will learn to love him, as I did. It will take time, but time is what we have. Years and years and years. Time for you and me to live together, to grow and explore the true nature of our husband. We will do this together."

Together. With Mahalath. No other words could bring as much harmony and peace to Adah's troubled soul. A soothing balm had been applied to a painful sore.

Adah nodded. "All right, Mahalath," she whispered. "I'll try. But help me . . . please!"

23

The beginning of *stav* brought some changes to the household. The cold winds came early this year, and Esau and Mahalath moved their bed downstairs for warmth.

Adah and Ishmael now slept on one side of the ledge, with Esau and Mahalath on the other side. Adah could hear them in the night. Esau was doing . . . *that* to Mahalath. What confused Adah was the occasional muffled giggle from the other end of the ledge. Did Mahalath enjoy it — or was she just pretending to?

In the morning, Esau went hunting. He seemed to find new vigor and energy in cold weather. Ishmael, in his heavy mantle, went to the city gates. For Mahalath and Adah, it was another routine day of work and pleasure.

Today, they went to the village washbasin, not far from the well. After drawing water from the well, they filled the basin to the stained half-way mark and dipped the clothes in the tub. The tub was set into the ground, lined with clay, and the two women knelt at the edge to scrub their clothes. They used flails to beat the cloth and drive away any evil which might cling to it. Mahalath sang while she worked.

> Fly, fly, fair flail;
> Chase away the dirt!
> Evil spirits, fly away,
> You must not give us hurt!

Mahalath was scornful of the odd superstition that evil spirits clung to the clothing and must be driven out. "I can't tell the difference between dirt and evil spirits," Mahalath had said once, laughing.

Many of Mahalath's songs spoke of love, and she revised them so they spoke about Esau and his gentle affection for her — for both his wives. Did Mahalath really believe this? She must. She always spoke the truth. The songs as much as any of Mahalath's statements about Esau had a profound impact on Adah's growing understanding of her husband.

She listened again as Mahalath sang.

> Esau's love is a gentle love,
> So pure, so tender, and mild.
> He lies with me, makes love to me,

Even now, I carry his child!

Adah gasped as she heard this new variation of an old love song. "Mahalath! What are you saying? Are you — ?"

Mahalath nodded and continued her song.

Esau's child is in my womb,
He grows within me now!
The seed's a boy, and that I know,
But please don't ask me how!

Adah clapped her hands and shouted, "Wonderful! At last, we'll have a child to love!"

Suddenly Mahalath frowned and clutched her stomach. She looked thoughtfully at Adah. "When happiness comes, can tragedy be far behind?"

Was this an old proverb, or did Mahalath make it up just now? And she wondered about Mahalath's words — she almost seemed to know exactly what the future would bring.

"What tragedy can there be in the birth of a male child — an heir for Esau?" asked Adah.

Mahalath just shook her head. For a long moment she said nothing, the flail in her hand forgotten. Then as abruptly as the frown had come, it fled. "Let's not be so gloomy." She smiled; the laughter was back in her voice.

"We have some planning to do. The boy will be born in *aviv* when the weather is warm."

That afternoon Ishmael came home early from the city gates, complaining of a sore throat. Mahalath insisted he lie down. She fixed a broth for him, but he could not eat.

From that moment, Adah detected a change in Mahalath. Sometimes she saw her looking furtively at Ishmael, and occasionally her eyes were red from crying. She clutched her stomach as though she had an inner pain. She refused to allow Ishmael to go to the city gates next day. He was only too happy to remain at home.

The next day Mahalath sent Esau to Bozrah where a famous *rophe* lived. Adah was mildly surprised that Esau went so willingly on this apparently needless errand, but Esau didn't even question her.

The *rophe* arrived next day and examined Ishmael's throat, now swollen and painful. The gentle fingers of the healer touched the neck while he said mystic words, calling to Qaus to heal. Then he showed Esau where to find a certain root which could be ground and mixed with water. The medicine would not cure the throat, he said, but would at least ease the pain.

Ishmael grew worse. Mahalath mixed the vile-smelling medicine for gargling. But he could not eat. Even worse, he could not speak. That great voice was silenced.

Esau stayed home now, and his tenderness to Ishmael surprised Adah. He looked so wild and spoke so loudly; his gentleness seemed uncharacteristic of a madman. Often Adah knelt beside Esau at Ishmael's pallet, helping her husband as they held up the old man's head to gargle. And at this unaccustomed closeness, she had no fear of Esau.

On the fifth day after the illness began, Mahalath took her harp and began to sing. All day she sang, songs of the hunt, of family, of good times. Adah marveled that she could do so while Ishmael lay dying, but she knew it was what Ishmael wanted. It would ease his dying hours.

As the afternoon sun disappeared from the windows, Mahalath laid aside her harp and went to her father. She knelt beside the pallet and whispered in his ear. When she rose, there were tears in her eyes.

She turned to Esau and Adah. "Say good-bye to him now."

Esau went first. His gentle embrace and soft words brought tears to Adah's eyes.

Then it was Adah's turn. She knelt beside the old man. "Ishmael, my father —" But she could say no more.

The dying man looked into her eyes and

nodded. She kissed his cheek and stepped back, unable to hide the tears.

Mahalath began to sing again, forcing her voice to be untouched by the turmoil within her.

The hunt is over, the meat is secure;
The hunter is home with his wife.
The fire is warm and the children in bed.
And he laughs as he thinks of his life!

The song continued to speak of the joy of a life well lived. Ishmael's death-song. His time was at hand.

The hunt is over, the meat is secure,
Soon death will come to this place.
Rejoice, oh, hunter, your hunt has
   begun,
It is time to begin a new chase!

The final dramatic chord, and Mahalath laid aside the harp. She burst into tears, wailing, "Oh Ishmael, my father, my father!" Esau tore his robe and groaned. Adah too began to cry and moan as was the custom among Mahalath's people.

Adah looked at the still form on the bed, eyes closed, mouth open. She expected to hear that gentle snore she had heard so often in the night. She would hear it no more. Then with a start she recalled Mahalath's comment a few days ago: "When happiness comes, can tragedy be far behind?"

Through her tears, Adah looked at Mahalath. She had known! She had known he would die, and even exactly when. She knew the baby inside her was a boy. She knew this. *She knows all things!*

As the neighbors pushed their way into the house to comfort the family and bewail the passing of the patriarch, Adah drew into a corner, confused. For now there were conflicting emotions struggling within her: love, sorrow — and awe. Not fear. She did not fear Mahalath and her amazing powers. Nor did she fear Esau — not any more. That in itself was a startling discovery.

In the midst of these emotions, she made a decision. She would go to Esau's bed. First she'd go to Mahalath, after the customary week of mourning, and ask her permission. Now that Mahalath was with child, ancient prohibitions demanded that she not lie with her husband during her pregnancy.

Adah didn't know why she had made this decision to take Mahalath's place in Esau's bed. Perhaps the mixed emotions had confused her and clouded her thinking. But she would do it. She might not like it, but she would do it. Willingly. For Mahalath.

The Ishmaelites, as the people of Moab called them, gathered at Punon for the funeral of their patriarch. Adah was amazed at how many there were. Ishmael's twelve sons had produced large families. Though scattered far and wide in Moab, they were a close-knit clan. Many were wealthy. Nebaioth, Mishma, and Duma mined copper in Punon and sold metalworks to caravans traveling the King's Highway. Meassah and Tema were shepherds, with flocks throughout the Arabah. Even Kedar came to the funeral. Known all over the world as "The Ishmaelite," his caravans traded goods in Egypt, Babylonia, and the ancient Hittite empire.

Only one of Ishmael's descendants was missing — Jetur, Nebaioth's son. There were rumors of his military exploits in the Egyptian army. Kedar — The Ishmaelite — claimed he'd talked to an officer who served with Jetur on the Nubian front, where Jetur had distinguished himself for bravery. He was a *kepesh*, a swordsman of renown, honored by Pharaoh.

Adah noticed that Mahalath listened attentively to Kedar's story about Jetur. She smiled, as though she wished him well. Adah wondered how well Mahalath had known that mysterious young man, but she didn't ask.

The women of the clan were fascinated

with Adah. They bombarded her with questions, which Adah shyly answered. Mahalath tried to stand between her and the curious family, for Adah was uncomfortable with all this attention.

Adah continued to be surprised by Esau. He had hunted for two days, sending back a large supply of meat for the gathering of guests. Then he had stayed home for the last three days of mourning. He seemed especially tender with Mahalath.

This only strengthened Adah's resolve to go to his bed. She could hardly believe her decision. Why should she do this? What compelled her? She owed Esau nothing. Or did she? Esau had saved her from the Horites, brought her to Mahalath, and married her to protect her from the townspeople. And despite his obvious hunger for women, he had respected Adah's hesitancy. Maybe she did owe him something.

But mostly she would go to his bed for Mahalath's sake. Esau needed a woman. Adah would take Mahalath's place. She knew a pregnant wife must be separated from her husband, so as not to mix the seeds in her body. Adah would not only protect Mahalath but also the child during the pregnancy.

On the last day of the week of mourning, Ishmael's body, freshly anointed with spices and wrapped in a linen shroud, was carried by the men to the *mishor*. There morning sun would light the cave, and evening shadows would bring peace. Here, surrounded by hills and forests and much game, Ishmael had spent many happy hours on the hunt. In the shallow cave, his body would rest undisturbed by the family who respected the sanctity of the place, hidden from any who might desecrate it.

The women remained behind as the men marched off with the funeral bier. The wailing and moaning stopped; the traditional day of silence prevailed. This silence oppressed Adah, lightened only by an occasional touch or smile from Mahalath, who seemed to sense Adah's uneasiness.

The next day, when the guests had gone, Esau stayed home. Although she didn't fear Esau now — especially with Mahalath there — Adah didn't want to talk to Mahalath with him present.

Once Mahalath startled her by whispering, "Tomorrow, when Esau has gone hunting, we'll talk."

She knew, then! She knew everything! But Adah did not feel threatened. She trusted Mahalath, even with Adah's thoughts. Tomorrow, then, she would find the courage to talk to Mahalath.

24

"Adah, wake up, sleepyhead! Do you want the wolf to find you in bed?"

Adah sat up with a start. She had slept poorly during the night, worried about her discussion with Mahalath and the ordeal of going to Esau's bed.

The patches of sunlight were well advanced along the floor. Adah shoved aside the blanket and crawled to the ledge, where she sat and watched Mahalath sweep the floor.

"I'm sorry, Mahalath. I guess I'm just lazy."

Mahalath's laughter filled the room, the first time that lilting laughter had been heard for many days.

"You're not lazy, dear. Just worried. Esau has gone. There's no one but us. We have the whole day to talk."

But Adah wasn't ready to talk yet. She took the water bottle and poured herself a drink. Her sips were slow and deliberate, wanting to postpone the moment.

Mahalath came over and sat beside her, laying the heavy broom against the ledge. She took Adah's hand and looked into her eyes. "Don't put it off, Adah. Say it quickly. It will be easier."

Adah laid aside the cup. She stared at the floor.

"Don't you know?"

Mahalath's soft laughter was warm and reassuring. "No child. I don't know. I can't tell what you're thinking."

Adah shook her head. "I thought you . . . knew everything."

Mahalath squeezed Adah's hand, and her face became serious. "I do know more than people realize, but I can't tell what you're thinking. I sense that you have something important you want to say to me today. Now say it quickly!"

"I want to go to Esau's bed!" Adah said breathlessly.

"Ah!" Mahalath's sharp intake of breath was followed by a broad smile. "At last! This is good. You have come a long way from the silly child scared of the monster who brought you here. What caused this change?"

Adah bit her lip. "I'm not as scared of Esau as I once was. And . . . and I want to protect your baby."

Mahalath's eyes opened wide. "What do you mean?"

"Please, Mahalath. You must not lie with Esau until after the child is born! You'll mix the seed, and he might turn out to be a dog or sheep or . . . something."

Adah was afraid Mahalath would laugh at her. But she didn't. She spoke softly. "Where did you get that idea?"

"I . . . don't know. I thought everybody knew that."

"It isn't true, dear. Don't worry. Our child will be a whole, healthy boy."

Adah sighed, still not convinced. "I suppose this means you don't want me to take your place in Esau's bed."

Mahalath's tinkling laugh filled the room. "On the contrary, Adah dear. I want very much for you to go to his bed. For your sake. To heal the hurt festering inside you. To change your mind about the cruelty of men. I have been waiting for you to come to this decision. So has Esau. Now we're happy for you!"

"You truly don't object?"

Impulsively, Mahalath kissed her on the cheek. "Object? I'm delighted! Why not tonight?"

"Tonight?"

"Yes, tonight. He'll be home early today,

and I'll tell him about it. He'll be glad you've finally agreed."

"Will he?"

"Yes, Adah. He will."

Adah turned her head away. "Why?"

Gently, Mahalath's fingers turned Adah's face back until she was looking into her friend's eyes.

"Because, Adah, Esau cares about you. He loves you, in his own way. He wants you to have his child."

Adah slowly shook her head. "Why?"

Mahalath frowned. "Don't you know? You really don't know? Really? No, of course you don't. How could you?"

"Know what, Mahalath?"

"How important it is to give your husband sons. How important to you as well as to him. They will bring joy to you as you grow older. They will be your security in your old age. You will be respected by the townspeople. A barren wife is like an empty water jar in the desert."

"But Mahalath, your son should be the heir. Not mine."

The smile returned to Mahalath's face, chasing the dimples across her cheeks. "It doesn't matter which one of us is the mother of the heir. It only matters that Esau has a son."

Again Adah turned her face away. She would like to give Esau a child. What worried her was not giving birth to children; it was the idea of conceiving a child in a man's bed. She recalled again the Horites.

Would it be like that again tonight?

Esau did come home early that day. Mahalath went to the courtyard to speak to him. Adah gripped the large wooden spoon tightly as she stirred the pot of lentil stew on the brazier. She could hear their muffled voices.

A moment later, Mahalath came in. "He's delighted, Adah. He has gone to the stream to bathe."

Adah stared into the pot of lentils, watching it bubble and boil. Steam from the hot stew rose into her face; she smelled the venison as it cooked in the thick mixture. This should make her hungry; instead it almost nauseated her.

Then Mahalath's arm was around her shoulder. "It's all right, dear. Don't be afraid."

When Esau came in, face scrubbed and hair and beard oiled, he didn't look as wild as usual. He put his hand on Adah's shoulder as she stared into the cook pot, still stirring the stew.

"Thank you, Adah," he said gently.

Adah nodded. "I'll try to . . . give you pleasure tonight, my lord." But her voice trembled.

They ate dinner together in the lamplight. Esau did not follow the custom of men eating first.

"No songs tonight, Adah," said Mahalath. "We'll clean the bowls, then go right to bed."

The words, spoken cheerfully, sounded ominous to Adah. When she gathered up the bowls to wash, she moved slowly.

Mahalath laughed softly. "Move along, child. Esau's waiting!"

The moment could not be put off. Esau already lay on the shadowed pallet in the corner. Mahalath held the lamp which gave a tiny brave light to the house. Even the brazier fire was covered for the night.

Mahalath kissed Adah. "Go to him now, dear," she whispered. "And give yourself to him, completely!"

Mahalath blew out the lamp and left her alone. She stumbled in the darkness but managed to crawl toward Esau. She heard him breathing in the darkness.

He put his hand on her arm. Gently. "Adah, my love," he whispered.

She shuddered at his touch but lay still. Esau put both arms around her and pulled her to him. His movements were slow and gentle, as though he were taming a wild animal.

It wasn't at all like her experience with the Horites. There was no pain, no abusive language, no degradation. She began to relax as his tenderness reassured her. When it was over, he kissed her gently and said, "Thank you, Adah."

His arms were around her as he went to sleep. She lay warm and relaxed in his embrace, relieved yet confused. There was a warm feeling inside her, as though she had done something not only good and right, but . . . enjoyable. Impossible! Making love to a man was enjoyable to the man only. The woman was supposed to endure it — endure the pain, grunting, slobbering, abuse — just to give her man pleasure. This was the price a woman paid for a baby. Then why didn't it hurt? Why did she feel so good about it?

She closed her eyes. A lassitude crept over her. It felt so warm and comfortable here in Esau's arms. She had done her duty. Maybe Esau's seed was now planted in her body. Maybe she and Mahalath would have their babies together.

Adah awoke several times during the night, startled to find a hairy male body beside her. Once her fingers touched his face, and she almost cried out before realizing who it was.

Her husband! Perhaps in time she would grow accustomed to this intrusion into her lonely bed. She was surprised at her feelings about Esau. She didn't resent him.

When Esau rose shortly before dawn, Adah wakened. She offered to prepare food for him, but he said no. "Go back to sleep, dear wife," he whispered. "Come to my bed again tonight. And thank you for last night."

When he was gone, Adah lay sleepless on the bed. She still had that good feeling inside her. She couldn't understand it. His gentleness and consideration was totally unexpected. He was nothing at all like the Horites!

Tonight, she vowed, she would go to his bed eagerly. She would give herself to him, perhaps even find new ways to give him pleasure. Now that she knew she had nothing to fear, she might even go against all tradition and find ways to enjoy the experience herself.

Without Esau in her bed, Adah was cold. She had never realized the value of sharing a bed with someone. Not only was there warmth on a cold night, there was also inner warmth and peace in the companionship of a shared life.

Light was seeping into the room as she lay in Esau's bed, thinking about her husband. Right now he was in the wilderness, alone, cold. This was the coldest part of *stav,* yet

Esau preferred to be out there rather than here, in a warm house with his two wives. What drove this mysterious man to solitude? She would ask Mahalath in the morning.

But it was already morning. Adah pushed aside the blanket. The room was not as cold as the bitter outdoors; Esau had put more wood on the brazier before leaving. Nevertheless, she put on her heavy mantle, shuddering as she thought about the work she and Mahalath would do outside.

Adah began the tedious process of starting a fire in the smoke oven. At least the oven would keep them warm as they worked in the courtyard, butchering the gazelle Esau had brought home yesterday. The wind reached into the open space just outside their house with its icy fingers. Even the heavy woolen mantle she wore could not keep her warm.

She thought of Esau, out there on the mountain. *He must be freezing! But he'll have a warm home to greet him tonight, and a warm meal, and a warm bed . . . and two warm wives!*

Then Mahalath stepped out of the door, shivering in her heavy mantel. Together they worked on the gazelle, peeling the skin back from the flesh, cutting the meat from the bones in strips which they hung from the rods in the smoke oven. It took them most of the morning, but as the weak sun reached the highest point in the sky, there was nothing left but a pile of bones, a skin stretched on a rack, and a two-week supply of meat in the hot smokehouse.

Next Mahalath and Adah fled to the warm interior of the house, where they refreshed themselves with beer and bread. Tonight the stew would be enriched by fresh chunks of meat.

Then Mahalath asked the question which Adah had been expecting. "How was it last night, Adah?"

Adah smiled. "Not as hard as I expected. It was almost pleasant. You were right about Esau; no one could be more gentle."

Mahalath nodded. "And did the experience convince you that not all men are like the Horites?"

"Yes." Adah's smile turned to a frown. "Mahalath, tell me something. How can the Esau I first met — the madman who killed those Horites — be the person who was so considerate last night? How can he so love you and me, and so hate them?"

Mahalath slowly shook her head. "I don't know, Adah. Esau is complex. There are two forces inside him — hate and love. He hates the Horites because of what they did to me — and yes, to you. When Esau hates, he becomes a beast. Think of it this way, Adah. He has us to love every day. The Horites he has met only once in his lifetime. If we fill his days with love, he may not have much room left in him to hate."

Adah stared at the glowing brazier, her cup of beer on the floor untouched. Finally she spoke. "I think I *can* love him now, Mahalath. Because of you. But . . . it's so hard to forget what he did to my family."

Mahalath's voice was gentle. "I know, dear. That was when Esau was mad with hatred, because of what they did to Judith. But you have turned that hatred around; now he loves the only surviving member of your family."

"Will he hate again, Mahalath? Will he turn into a madman? What if he meets more Horites while he's hunting?"

Mahalath was silent for a while. When she spoke there was a catch in her voice. "Esau still has a lot of hate within him, dear. Deep inside. There is another hate, a hate which festers and threatens to destroy him. Only our love can save him, Adah. Only our love."

Adah could see tears on Mahalath's cheeks. She went to her friend and took her hand. "Then, dear Mahalath, it's up to us to give him that love. Both of us. We'll fight as hard as we can to kill the hate!"

Mahalath looked into Adah's eyes and

smiled. "We'll do it, Adah. Together."

A tear ran into Mahalath's dimple and paused a moment before falling to the floor.

25

Mahalath's child was a girl. Only Adah knew the shock and disappointment to the child's mother. She had been so sure it would be a boy — Esau's firstborn, his heir. She had predicted it. Adah too was shocked, not because the baby was female, but because the all-knowing Mahalath had been wrong.

Nevertheless, Mahalath's natural cheerfulness reasserted itself. Soon the house was filled with lullabies and laughter. They named the child Hagar, for Mahalath's grandmother. Adah felt very close to this child, even though her own would be born very soon.

Adah hoped her baby would be a girl too, for Mahalath's sake. But Mahalath insisted the child in Adah's body was a boy. Adah questioned this, knowing now Mahalath's fallibility.

Mahalath was adamant. "My gift," she said, "only speaks to me when someone else is involved. I can't use it for selfish purpose, such as forecasting the sex of my own child."

Adah's baby, born a month after Mahalath's, *was* a boy. Mahalath showed no resentment. Her songs and laughter were louder and brighter than the occasional cry of an infant.

Since Esau's first child was a girl, he allowed his wives to select the name. The second baby, the boy, he named himself. Mahalath and Adah accepted this. In both their families, the father named the sons.

The name Esau chose for his firstborn son surprised his wives. Eliphaz. Like many names in their family, the first part, *El,* meant God. The second part was not easy to understand. It slurred the word for "fine gold" and "crush." Esau refused to explain his meaning. Was it "God is fine gold?" or "God crushes?"

"Surely it means 'God is fine gold,' " said Adah. "Esau is so kind, so loving. It's hard to believe he would want his child to grow up to be God's fist to crush anybody."

The two mothers were suckling their babies on the rooftop to catch the cool breeze. It was hot, but they had wrapped the infants in linen to protect them from dust in the air.

Mahalath smiled. "Last year you couldn't say that. Esau's love for you has changed your understanding of him."

"That's why I think Eliphaz means 'God is fine gold.' "

Mahalath's dimples disappeared as a frown

creased her forehead. "I wish I could be sure. I just don't know. . . ."

"But he seems so loving, so gentle. Surely there's no more hate inside him now?"

"There's hate in all of us, Adah. We control it with love. But it's there. Sometimes even our love isn't strong enough to push it away."

"Is there still a chance he might go to Haran?"

Mahalath had told Adah the full story of Esau, his hate for his brother and his vow of revenge.

"I don't know. I only wish my gift would tell me something about this . . . and what to do about it."

Adah's son had gone to sleep at her breast. She gently disengaged the tiny mouth and raised the child to her shoulder.

"You'll know, Mahalath, when the time comes. Your gift will tell you."

"But my gift's been wrong before."

"Not this time, because it doesn't concern you. You'll find a way to save Esau."

Mahalath shook her head. "I wish I could be sure."

Hagar continued to suckle noisily at her breast. Mahalath's dimples returned. "Look at this child, will you? Always hungry! Why can't she sleep like your son? That boy needs to stay awake and eat, to grow up strong like his father."

As if to answer Mahalath's accusation, Eliphaz emitted a sleepy burp. The two mothers laughed.

"Adah," said Mahalath between giggles, "you'd better wake that child and make him eat more. Remember, he's the heir."

Adah pressed her baby to her breast; soon the sleepy mouth began a lazy suckling. Adah looked at Mahalath, who was watching them. The dimples were showing.

She's always laughing. She never shows any jealousy. Adah lifted her eyes to the clear blue sky. *Maybe that God of theirs — Qaus or whatever his name is — sent me to them. If that's true — if he really is stronger than Moloch — then maybe he'll take all the hate out of Esau.*

There were no clouds in the sky; only the hot blinding sun. Adah glanced at Mahalath. Her dimples were gone now as she studied Adah thoughtfully. Adah closed her eyes, wondering if Mahalath sensed her sudden chill of fear. Fear for Eliphaz, Hagar, Mahalath — and most of all, for Esau, her beloved husband.

Esau seemed to accept his responsibility as father of a rapidly growing family. His hunting income was meager, but he was still able to build a new house. Nebaioth, whose copper business was prospering, sent skilled servants to help. A large house soon rose on a wooded hillside near enough to town to be safe. To the east towered Moabite hills. Here they would be comfortable.

Adah had no more children, but Mahalath did. After seven years of marriage she had three girls — Hagar, Rebekah, and Timna. The large house was filled with children's laughter as well as Mahalath's songs.

So the years passed. Esau had apparently forgotten his vow of vengeance and had settled down with a growing family in a spacious home. Adah breathed easier, but Mahalath still worried.

"His hate is still there," she confided to Adah one day. "We have almost smothered it with our love. There are a lot of us to love him now. But it's still there."

Adah shook her head. "I wish we could be sure. Why doesn't he tell us what he feels? He never tells us anything."

"It's not Esau's way," replied Mahalath. "But something's going to happen . . . soon. I feel it."

Adah looked at her friend in awe. Many times since she had come to live in Esau's house, she had observed Mahalath's strange gift at work. She had come to trust Mahalath's powers.

What happened then was as startling to Mahalath as to Adah. One day Esau brought home a homeless girl.

"Her name is Oholibamah," said Esau. "Tomorrow I will take her to the city gates and proclaim her my wife."

Adah and Mahalath stood in the courtyard gaping at him. Even the children were hushed. The two older children, Hagar and Eliphaz, both seven, stood in the doorway. They stared at the tall beautiful girl standing beside Esau.

She *was* beautiful. Long black hair fell straight down to her waist. Her smooth features were dark, and bushy brows creased a mysterious cave for sunken black eyes. Hollow cheeks highlighted a wide mouth, and the small chin crowned a long regal neck. Her young body showed promise of becoming voluptuous.

Mahalath recovered first. She smiled, went to the new girl with hands outstretched, and said, "Welcome, Oholibamah, to your new home. Don't be afraid."

The obvious friendliness in Mahalath's greeting brought a hesitant smile to the young girl's face.

"You'll have to teach her our language," said Esau. "She's a Horite."

Adah gasped. An enemy! Esau had sworn

to kill Horites on sight. Yet here one was, about to become Esau's third wife!

Questions crowded Adah's mind. Another person for their impoverished household to support! How could they communicate with her if she spoke that heathen gibberish? And how could Adah reconcile herself to live with a Horite?

Mahalath's ready acceptance and offers of friendship caused Adah to push aside her questions. She sucked in her breath. She should have gone to welcome her, as Mahalath had. But she couldn't. Adah's feet seemed heavy, chained to the flagstone courtyard floor. Her breath came in short gasps; she clenched her fists.

A Horite! Of all people for Esau to bring home. Into Adah's mind there flashed the scene she had almost forgotten: her naked body on the ground, four dirty men violating her. She had felt no remorse when Esau's arrows brought a violent end to their lives. *May all Horites end that way!*

And this Horite was to be Esau's third wife! Adah stared at her, marveling at her dark beauty. *She could well become Esau's favorite! Will he want me in his bed anymore?*

"Adah!" Mahalath's voice was stern, and she frowned as she looked at Adah. "Put aside your fears. We must accept Oholibamah as one of us. *Do you understand?*"

The last words were spoken with such vehemence that Adah was shaken from her frozen reverie. She looked at Mahalath. "Didn't you hear Esau? She's a *Horite!*"

"Of course she's a Horite," said Mahalath, smiling. "Poor dear! We must make her feel welcome. Please, Adah!"

"But —"

"Adah, prepare a bed for our newest family member. I will introduce her to our family."

With this curt dismissal, Adah fled into the house. *A bed for the newest family member indeed! She deserves a bed of thorns.*

And Esau! How could he?

He had sworn death to all Horites for what they had done to her and Mahalath. Now he had brought one home for his wife. Why? How could he forget so easily?

Adah's head jerked up with a shocking thought. *Hate!* She, not Esau, still held hatred in her heart. Not Esau? He had brought home a Horite wife, whom he intended to give an honored place in his home. What had happened to all his hate?

Adah shook her head in bewilderment. She and she only retained a residue of hate. Ugly, soul-wrenching hate. Deep down. And she knew she must dredge it up and destroy it before it ruined her. Only then could she continue to live in this family.

She looked around the large familiar room. Sounds of voices came from the courtyard, laughter blending with excited welcomes as the children met the newcomer. *So much love in this family! And Mahalath says that only love can conquer hate.*

Adah swallowed hard. *Love!* Love had conquered hate in both Mahalath and Esau! Could it do the same for her?

Later that night, after they had finished eating and the children were in bed, Esau told them his story. "I came on the band of Horites in the wilderness west of the Arabah." His blunt words went to the point, scorning oratory. "About twenty of them. Zibeon, their leader, calls himself king of the Horites."

"You could have killed them," said Mahalath softly.

"What for? I felt sorry for them. So I made peace with them. They seemed afraid of me."

Little wonder, thought Adah. By now Esau would be a legend among them. Mothers probably frightened their children at night: *Esau will get you if you don't behave!*

Mahalath's question was practical. "How could you talk with them?"

"Zibeon could speak our language. He seemed glad to make peace with me."

Adah smiled in the darkness of the room. She didn't doubt that a bit.

"He offered his granddaughter Oholibamah to me. At first I refused, but he insisted. I could see that I must either accept her or fight them. So I agreed."

Now Adah spoke, trying to hide the bitterness in her voice. "A hostage."

"A wife." Esau's words were firm.

"She is welcome here," said Mahalath hastily. She glanced at Adah. In the lamplight a warning glint flashed in her eyes.

Adah was silent.

Esau glared at Adah. "She will bear my children," he said softly. "And there will be no trouble in my family."

Adah lowered her eyes. "Yes, my husband," she said.

She would have to accept this Horite girl who would share Esau's bed. As Mahalath and Esau did. Adah glanced at the dark figure of the newcomer seated on the mat near her. Her mysterious beauty was enhanced by the flickering lamplight. The questing eyes darted from one person to another as she attempted to understand the emotions which were passed among the members of her new family. *Love and hate*, thought Adah. *Emotions I must learn to control.*

The next day Mahalath confronted Adah.

"Your battle is not with Oholibamah but yourself."

Esau had taken the Horite girl to the town square to proclaim his marriage. The children played noisily in the courtyard while the two wives worked in the house.

"You're wrong, Mahalath." Adah laid aside the heavy broom and began stoking the fire in the brazier. "It's because she's a Horite. I can't believe Esau would take a wife from those people after what they did to us."

Mahalath had gathered the pine straws in the mattresses. She planned to replace them with fresh straws. "Adah, be honest with yourself. For one thing, you're jealous of her. Esau will take her to bed tonight. Now there are three of us for him to share."

Adah sighed. "You're an Ishmaelite and I'm a Hittite. I can't stomach the thought that he'll be with a Horite."

Mahalath headed toward the door, her arms filled with the old pine straw. "Think about it, Adah. Think about your hate. And remember the love you have found in Esau's house. Love big enough to include even the Horites." Then she was gone.

Adah stared into the coals on the brazier. Absently she pushed the poker into them and watched as sparks flew and blue and yellow flames flared briefly. She sighed. *Love!* She had certainly known love during the past nine years. First when she was befriended by Mahalath. This love had healed her. Healed her of hate and fear for Esau. Now she could love Esau, whom she had once detested.

She had seen what love had done for Esau. His deep hatred for Horites had vanished. His vow of revenge to his brother had seemingly gone, although Mahalath said it was still there, smoldering. Love had made the difference.

Adah frowned. Why did she still hate? Why not just accept this Horite wife as Esau and Mahalath had? Was she jealous, as Mahalath said? She found comfort and fulfillment in Esau's arms at night, but did not begrudge the sharing of his bed with Mahalath. But with a Horite?

Adah scooped the lentils which had soaked overnight into the large stew pot on the brazier. She'd have to accept Esau's Horite. Swallow her hate. Love her. As Mahalath had done for her twelve years ago. She sighed. Mahalath was right. Her battle was not with Oholibamah. It was with herself.

26

That night, Esau took his new wife to his bed. She went eagerly. Adah lay in her own bed, tense and restless, while from the corner of the room came not just giggles but loud laughter, moans, sighs, and unintelligible words whose meanings were clear enough. *This slut likes it, even on her first night!*

In the days that followed, the children began to teach Oholibamah their language. They discovered their new family member was a delightful companion. She enjoyed children and seemed to be one herself. Their laughter filled the house. Soon Oholibamah could converse in halting, stumbling speech.

When she announced that she was pregnant — only a month later! — Adah was appalled. And when Mahalath predicted a boy, she was devastated. The girl continued to monopolize Esau's bed, and Adah smiled grimly. Maybe the seed would be mixed, and the baby to be born would be a dog — better yet, a pig! What would Esau think of that?

When the child was born — a beautiful, healthy boy — the children were thrilled.

"Mother!" cried Hagar. "May I hold the baby?"

"But it's my turn!" shouted Eliphaz.

Even four-year-old Rebekah wanted a turn. They teased the baby until he laughed, then rocked him until he slept. Never had so much love been showered on a child of Esau's household.

The name Esau selected for the boy — Jeush — meant "God help." Although Esau offered no explanation, Adah suspected it meant Esau was grateful for God's help in giving him such a loving family. Or could it mean that Esau still needed God's help to overcome his hatred for Jacob?

As the baby grew, Adah struggled with her hate, trying honestly to love the new child and his mother. The battle grew harder when Oholibamah announced that once again she carried Esau's child, and again Mahalath predicted a boy.

On the second day after the birth, Esau held the child on his knees. "What shall I name this boy?" he asked.

Adah wondered if Esau had already chosen the name, but was teasing the children. He had grown mellow lately, often playing games and joking with them. The children loved him.

Several suggestions were offered by Eliphaz and Hagar. Even Rebekah, now six, joined in. Then Timna, age five, said solemnly, "Just call him 'Young Man.' "

Esau looked from his youngest daughter to his new son. "Young Man," he said softly. "*Jalam*. Yes. His name is Jalam!"

When Oholibamah's third son was born a year later, Esau followed the same procedure. This time the name suggested by the children was "Korah," meaning "the bald one." This child, unlike the others, had no hair on his head.

Adah wondered about Esau's casual methods of naming his children. Most parents put a lot of thought into a baby's name, believing a child would grow into it and take its character. Often the name reflected how the father felt at the time, describing something he was struggling with. Or the name might be temporary, the parents intending to rename him later. Surely such was the case with Jalam — "young man," — and Korah — "bald one." Both would grow out of these names quickly.

With the growing family, the large hilltop house suddenly became too small. The main room alone was larger than the old house in the village, and the courtyard extended to the edge of the clearing. But with a large man, three wives, and seven children, it was extremely crowded.

Esau planned an expansion. Two spacious rooms were added, plus another courtyard on the west overlooking the Arabah valley. Another room was built on the roof. Nebaioth's carpenters labored many days to complete the structure, but when finished, all agreed it was adequate.

Esau now worked part-time for Nebaioth, training a small army of bowmen. Nebaioth's thriving copper business, his trading ventures, and marketing of copper wares, brought the need for bodyguards. In gratitude, the Ishmaelite patriarch gave Esau a young Moabite couple to be his household servants. The young man, Marduk, tended the livestock which Esau owned. Because he was a trained archer, he also was assigned the task of guarding the family while Esau was away on hunting trips. His wife, Keth-morah, did gardening, gathered wood for fuel, and brought water from the nearby village well.

As the years passed, Adah's hostility toward Oholibamah subsided. There was just too much love in the family for her to be filled with hate. Her son was now thirteen, a fine boy. Although he showed no interest in following his father's profession as a hunter, he exhibited a shrewd head for business.

When streaks of white appeared in Mahalath's hair, Adah was unperturbed. Age was stealing in upon them all, but it was good. This was the way life should be spent — in a large loving family, watching the children grow up, soon to marry. Then there would be grandchildren, and after that, old age and death. This was the cycle of life, and Adah was content.

She was unprepared, therefore, when tragedy struck.

They were skinning and smoking an ibex on the western courtyard. Hagar skillfully sliced the skin from the flesh, while Rebekah gently pulled the hide away. Timna and her mother were kindling the fire in the smoke house.

Timna screamed.

Instantly all work ceased. Everyone rushed to the smokehouse. Adah and Oholibamah, who were inside the house, were the last to come out. They found Mahalath doubled over, holding her stomach.

Adah ran to her. "Mahalath, what is it? Are you ill?"

Mahalath gasped. "No. It's just . . . oh, Adah! The time has come!"

"What? What's the matter?"

"My gift! It's speaking to me!"

Adah took a deep breath. Mahalath's problem was not physical, then. It was that tingling feeling inside her, only this time, it was obviously more than just tingling.

"What is it, Mahalath? What does it mean?"

Mahalath was still doubled over, holding her stomach. She looked up into Adah's eyes. Tears overflowed and ran down her cheeks.

"Esau!" She began to pant. "He's — oh, Adah!" She threw her arms around Adah and sobbed on her shoulder.

Adah's stomach churned. "Is Esau hurt? Should I send Marduk to find him? He was to hunt today —"

"No. He's all right. But . . . his old curse — his hate —"

"What curse?" demanded Oholibamah. No one but Adah and Mahalath knew Esau's secret.

Adah and Mahalath ignored her. They looked into each other's eyes. Adah felt her throat tighten as she realized what Mahalath meant.

"Someone's coming!" gasped Mahalath. "Someone who will bring Esau trouble. Oh, Adah, what can we do?"

"Shall I call Marduk? He can kill whoever's coming. Tell me what to do."

"No, we can't do anything, but Esau will be in great danger."

Adah looked from Mahalath's tearstained face to the bewildered faces of her large family around her. They didn't understand. They still thought Mahalath was ill.

But Adah knew. The years of peace, of love, of contentment — they were coming to an end.

And there was nothing she could do to stop it.

27

"We must prepare to entertain guests," said Mahalath, as calmly as she would announce a visit of the neighbors.

She went to the water bottle near the door of the house. While her family watched, she poured some on her hands and wiped her face. When she turned around, she was smiling.

"Marduk," Mahalath said to the servant who had just stepped out of the house. "Go to the east courtyard and welcome our visitors. Adah, will you serve them wine and prepare a meal for them? I myself shall wash their feet."

As she went to prepare the meal, Adah shook her head. Mahalath! Would she ever understand her? Sinister visitors approached the house, and Mahalath acted as though nothing important was happening. She should have told Marduk to get his bow and arrows and kill these men, whoever they were.

Two men entered the house, or rather a man and a boy. The man was about thirty years old, with curly brown hair and beard. The boy was no more than sixteen, tall, beardless, and muscular. His strong face was set in a hard frown.

Adah looked again at the boy as she served him a goblet of wine. There was something familiar about him. Had she seen him before? No. But he looked like someone she knew.

Mahalath was a charming hostess. "Welcome, sirs. Esau will be home soon. Until then, eat and drink and be at ease." She knelt before them, removed their sandals, and wiped their dusty feet with a damp cloth.

The man nodded. "Thank you, Mother," he said, using the term of respect common to all people of the region. "We have come a long way to see Esau. We will wait."

"We are preparing a meal. We will serve you soon."

A little later, she set before the guests a platter of meat, lentils, and bread. The man said, "Thank you, Mother. You are very kind. I am Markesh *ben* Jubal. This is Reuel."

Adah and Mahalath left the room then. Entertaining visitors was men's work; women could only cook and serve the food. As they came out into the west courtyard, Hagar and Rebekah dropped their skinning knives and ran to them.

"Mother, who are they? What do they want?"

"Mother, are you all right?"

"Why are they here?"

Mahalath's tinkling laugh rang out. "Go back to work, you chirping curlews! They're just two men who want to talk to your father. What? You haven't stretched the skin yet? You should use your hands more than your tongues!"

She was so cheerful and natural, the girls relaxed. Adah followed Mahalath into the smokehouse, marveling at Mahalath's composure and wondering what the next few hours would bring.

Esau came home before sunset. When he entered the house, Mahalath and Adah stood near the door.

"Greetings, my friends, and welcome," he said. (Marduk had told him guests awaited in the house.) "I am Esau *ben* Isaac. I trust your needs and comforts have been taken care of."

The two visitors rose. Although the boy just stared at his host, the man bowed deeply. "Thank you, my lord. Your family has been most gracious. You have not changed much since I last saw you seventeen years ago. I am Markesh *ben* Jubal of Beersheba."

"Markesh!" Esau held out his hands and Markesh grasped them warmly. "*You* have changed. You were a beardless boy when I saw you last!"

"We have all changed, my lord," Markesh said solemnly.

Esau frowned. "And how is . . . my family?"

Markesh spoke frankly. "Your mother died, my lord, within the past month. Her last request was to find you."

"Dead." Esau's face was impassive. "Was she contented until her death?"

"She was quite content, my lord," Markesh answered. "The latter years of her life were peaceful and in good health."

"God is good." The formula response was muttered. Esau seemed to fumble for his next words. "And how are . . . the rest of the people? Your father?"

"Jubal is well, his stewardship prosperous. Your mother said you may inherit all the flocks and herds if you wish."

"I'm not the heir." Esau's voice was bitter.

"Your brother Jacob is in Haran. He's a wealthy man. I'm told his flocks and herds are huge. He doesn't need more."

"Nor do I." Esau's shoulders squared and his red-bearded chin lifted slightly. "Who else is there to inherit?"

Markesh paused. "Your wife, my lord."

"Basemath?"

"Yes, Basemath."

"Is she well?"

"Quite well, my lord. She sends her greetings."

Esau frowned. "I see."

Markesh took a deep breath. "There is more. The lady Basemath also sends you your son. This is Reuel."

He turned to the beardless boy beside him. The youth glared at Esau, frowning, his mouth a tight line.

Esau gasped. "My son?"

"Yes, Esau. Your son. He was born to Basemath shortly after you left. He is your firstborn, your heir."

Adah, standing in the corner with Mahalath, caught her breath. She was hardly aware that her own son, Eliphaz, had joined them and was standing beside her.

Yes, the boy could well be Esau's son. He had the same facial features, but not the red hair. The tall rangy body was powerful. Adah realized then who the boy looked like: Eliphaz. They could have been brothers. In fact, they were.

Then the impact of what had just been said struck her. *Firstborn! Heir!* She looked at Eliphaz. His jaw had dropped.

"No!" Adah's words caused the men to turn around. She had no right to speak; this

was men's business. She spoke anyway. "Esau, my husband! Eliphaz is your son! He's your firstborn, your heir! You must not —"

"Quiet, woman!" Esau barked. "The first-born is always heir! *Always!* No child of mine shall be cheated out of his birthright!"

Tears welled up inside Adah. She felt Mahalath's arm around her shoulder. She wondered why Esau felt this way. Why was the birthright so sacred to him?

The boy — Reuel — had been quiet. Now he turned to Esau. For the first time he spoke. "I want no part of you or your cursed birth-right!" There was a sneer in his voice. "I want you to know this: I have come here to kill you. I have sworn an oath to do so."

"What?" Esau's eyes opened wide.

Markesh shifted his feet uneasily. "What he says is true, my lord. Several years ago, he proclaimed his hatred for you, and swore a sa-cred oath to kill you. Neither his mother nor his grandmother could persuade him to re-nounce his foolish vow. That is why we have come to you."

Esau looked from one to the other. "I don't understand."

"Your mother's last request was to bring the boy to you. She felt that only you could persuade him otherwise."

"I see."

Although Reuel's back was to Adah, she could feel the intensity of the young man's animosity.

When the boy spoke, his words were barely controlled. "Now you are stronger than I. But I will grow. Someday I will kill you."

Esau stared at his son. "But . . . why?"

"Because you are not fit to live."

Markesh spoke hastily. "He feels, my lord, that you have wronged your brother, whom he admires. You sent him into exile, away from his mother. You covet his birthright, which Reuel feels rightfully belongs to Jacob. You threatened his life. Your son feels he can protect his uncle by taking your life."

"Who taught you to hate, boy? Was it your grandmother? Or your mother?"

"Grandmother Rebekah was very kind to me. She never had hate in her heart for anybody, even you. As to my mother, that pig cares nothing about anybody —"

Esau's open hand slapped Reuel's face with a *thwack!* The powerful blow sent the boy tumbling backward to the floor. Esau took a step toward him, but Markesh stepped between them.

"Please, my lord. Forgive him. He's impulsive and young. Don't beat him."

Esau glared at the prostrate form of his son. "No son of mine shall speak that way of his mother!" he roared.

Beside her, Adah heard Eliphaz gasp. He had never seen his father strike anyone or seen on his father's face such mad rage.

Reuel sat up, holding his face. "When Jacob comes home, he will kill you! And I want to be there when it happens. In fact, I would like to be the one who puts an arrow into you!"

Esau stared down at the boy. "When Jacob comes home? Do you know something? Is he coming?"

"Yes! Even now he comes! Soon your bones will rot on a deserted hillside. Not even jackals will want to eat your flesh —"

Markesh cut him off. "Quiet, Reuel. You've said enough."

Esau pursed his lips. "So my brother is coming home. And he is wealthy, probably with many servants. All right. The time has come. I will go to meet him."

Markesh placed his hand on Esau's shoulder. "Peace, my lord. The lady Rebekah asked me to say to you, 'Make peace with your brother, Esau. If not, God will curse you!' "

Mahalath's hand sought Adah's. She was trembling and clutching her stomach. Adah too shivered as she turned to look at her husband.

Esau's voice was cold. "I too have sworn a vow. And the time has come to settle everything. I will go to meet Jacob. And you —" He stared down at Reuel, still seated on the floor. "You shall come with me. When we meet my brother, we shall all learn what is God's will in this affair."

As he said these words, Adah had a clear view of his face. She didn't need to have Mahalath's gift to know what was in her husband's soul. His lips were pressed tightly together, his forehead creased in a frown. His eyes blazed. What Adah saw in them could not be denied.

It was hate.

28

When Esau explained his plans to Nebaioth, the Ishmaelite patriarch put all of his resources at Esau's disposal. Esau chose fifty men, archers he himself had trained. He asked Nebaioth to set adrift a rumor along the caravan routes that he was coming north with four hundred men.

Esau's household frantically prepared for the departure. Large quantities of game were brought in. The women spent hours butchering, cutting meat into strips, smoking it, and wrapping it in individual portions to last a month.

For Adah, the most difficult time came when Esau told her Eliphaz would accompany him.

"But, Esau," she protested, "he's only a child. And Reuel will be going. What if he decides to harm Eliphaz?"

Esau snorted. "You can't hide the boy in a cave forever! He's a man, almost fourteen. Time he found out what that means!"

Markesh and Reuel had agreed to go with Esau. Each stated his own reasons. "I want to be there when the brothers meet," said Reuel. "I plan to fight on Jacob's side. I only hope I will have a chance to fulfill my vow!"

"I promised my father, Jubal, I would look after Reuel," said Markesh. "Where he goes, I go."

When Esau heard this, he went to where the two were encamped on the hillside east of Punon and confronted Markesh. "I charge you with the protection of both my sons," he said gruffly. "If Reuel tries to harm Eliphaz, I'll kill you!"

"Yes, my lord," replied Markesh.

During the month of preparations, Mahalath's laughter and songs kept the family and servants in good humor. Was it a mask, Adah wondered, or did Mahalath know something? "Tell me, Mahalath," she asked, "is there danger?"

Mahalath smiled. "Of course there's danger. There's always —" Suddenly her smile faded, and she burst into tears. "Oh Adah, I can't pretend with you! I just don't know!"

"But you're supposed to know everything!"

"I don't! I just don't! Oh, why doesn't God speak to me?"

Adah felt a constriction in her throat. "Mahalath, you're the only one God speaks to. You've got to do something!"

"But I can't!" She clasped Adah's hands tightly. "God hasn't spoken to me! I don't feel anything! Will God ever speak again?"

Adah took a deep breath. It was her turn to wear a mask.

"He will, dear. He will. When the time comes, you'll know."

"Thank you, Adah. You're so strong! You must help me."

Adah nodded. "God will help you, Mahalath. Wait and see."

But she didn't feel the conviction of her words. If she were in her own family now, they would pass one of the children through the fire as an offering to Moloch. She shuddered. How much better was Esau's God than Moloch!

When she married Esau, she had adopted the religion of her husband. This unseen God was hard to understand, but Adah believed he spoke to Mahalath. If this God suddenly withdrew her gift, they were lost. Adah sighed. She hoped her confident words to Mahalath would come true.

The day to leave finally came. The army waited on the slope of the trail leading to the King's Highway while Esau and Eliphaz went to the house to say good-bye. The family gathered in the east courtyard. Eliphaz was a warrior now, and he wouldn't allow the women to say their tearful farewells to him. A brief embrace and a kiss were all he would permit.

Then Esau tenderly hugged his children and kissed them fondly. He turned to his wives.

"Oholibamah, come here."

Eagerly she came to his arms, and he kissed her loudly. "Keep my bed warm for me, dear wife," he said.

Oholibamah tried to match his cheerfulness. "I will, my husband. But come back soon. I hate lying in a cold bed alone."

When he released her, he turned to Adah. She came to him, and felt the strong arms around her and smelled his familiar smell. She could not be cheerful like Oholibamah; she sobbed.

"Please come back, my love!" she pleaded.

"Dear sweet Adah! I have loved you ever since you spit in my face on the first day we met. Of course, I'll come back to you." He kissed her and squeezed her, then released her.

"Mahalath," he said. "Come to me."

"No."

Adah gasped, as did everyone in the courtyard. Esau's mouth formed a small circle, and his bushy eyebrows raised.

"What — ?"

Mahalath frowned. "I have something to say first."

Silence settled on the assembled family. They didn't know as much as Adah did about Mahalath's mysterious powers, but they knew enough to expect something. Esau gaped at her.

"God will bless your journey," she said, her voice low-pitched and authoritative.

Adah caught her breath. At last! God was speaking to her!

"God will bless your journey only if you obey him."

Esau's voice was low, almost trembling. "What shall I do?"

"Go to the ford of the Jabbok!"

"The ford of the Jabbok? What do you mean?"

Mahalath shook her head. Her shoulders slumped. "I don't know. I just feel the Jabbok River ford is where you must go."

"But the Jabbok has many fords. Which ford?"

"I don't know, Esau. Maybe it means that place where we spent three nights. Do you remember that ledge of rock?"

Esau nodded. "All right, Mahalath. I'll go there first."

"Oh, Esau!" Mahalath ran to him, and he embraced her. His kiss was long and tender. Abruptly he released her, then turned and walked out, Eliphaz following.

There was a silent tension in the courtyard after they left. Adah felt an emptiness, as though the house were deserted with Esau gone. Did everyone else feel it too?

The silence was dissolved by Mahalath's ringing voice. "To the rooftop, all of you! Get a white cloth and wave it to our departing men. Show them we care!"

Her words broke the spell and sent the women and children scurrying toward the stairs leading to the roof.

Adah stood staring at Mahalath, who hadn't moved from the courtyard. She went to her friend.

"Mahalath! God spoke to you! What does it mean?"

Mahalath turned to Adah, a frown on her forehead. "I don't know, Adah. I don't understand. I felt so strongly the need to say, *the ford of the Jabbok*. Do you think they were God's words?"

"They must have been! Now that he's speaking to you, tell me — will Esau and Eliphaz be all right? What will happen?"

Mahalath continued to frown. Her hands went out; Adah grasped them.

"I don't know, Adah. I feel . . . I can't explain what I feel. I think my gift has gone."

"Gone?"

"Gone. Forever. It's as though God says to me: *I gave you the gift for a purpose. Now the purpose is fulfilled, and you won't need the gift anymore.*"

"But Mahalath . . . God is so real to you! He's — oh, Mahalath, what will you do without your gift?"

Mahalath smiled, her face as bright as the morning sun. "I think I'll be happier. I feel relieved!"

"But Mahalath, if your gift is gone, how will you know Eliphaz will be all right? If Reuel —"

Mahalath touched Adah's hand. "Well, there's nothing we can do." Abruptly her mood changed. Her laugh rang so loudly that several of the children leaned over the rooftop to look down on them. "I know what *I'm* going to do. I'll sing a song tonight at supper. I know one about men going to war, and the women who wait for them. The way I'll sing it, it will be a happy song!"

Adah glanced up at the family on the rooftop, still waving their white cloths even though the men were almost out of sight. Would Esau and Eliphaz come back?

Right now, they were climbing the trail to the King's Highway, which led to Haran, to Jacob, and to the ford of the Jabbok River. And . . . to death?

Part V

Esau ben *Isaac*

29

"I am Esau *ben* Isaac, Hunter of Edom! The Lord has delivered you into my hands."

The ritual words were spoken mechanically, for he had said them hundreds of times in the past. The dead gazelle was sprawled on the ground before him, an arrow in its heart.

A fine animal. Proud. Healthy. Until a few moments ago, filled with the joy of living. The Hunter of Edom had slain his forest brother to provide meat for his men.

Esau had long ago grown accustomed to the conflicting emotions within him. He had killed, the primordial instinct of the hunter. He was proud of his skill, exulting in the climax of the hunt. At the same time he was sad, sad that so noble a beast must be conquered by a man, even though a man was a "little less than God" as his father had once said.

His ambivalent feelings were intensified today. He had killed because he was the hunter, and killing was his profession. Yet he did not need to kill today. There was enough dried venison in the men's pouches for another week. And tomorrow, they would meet Jacob.

His men were waiting for him to return from the hunt. Their camp was about four miles from Mahanaim, where scouts had reported Jacob's large household was encamped. He could have confronted Jacob today. Instead, he had gone hunting.

Esau shook his head to rid himself of these unpleasant thoughts. He drew his knife, knelt by his prey and quickly cut out the arrow from the heart, cleaned it and thrust it into his quiver. Then he made short, jerky slashes in the belly, cutting around the genitals, and scooped out the warm entrails. With a practiced motion, he sliced off the poison sacs on the hind legs, then wiped his knife on the dry grass.

He glanced at the sky. There they were, hovering, waiting for him to finish. They knew; they always knew. For many years, Esau had provided them with a fresh kill.

It was always the same. The long walk, the sign, the stalking, the waiting, the sighting of game, the kill, the gutting of the beast, and the waiting vultures. He sighed as he swung the carcass onto his shoulders. Always the game. Until now, always a thrill. Today he felt only emptiness.

The way to his camp was downhill. He

wanted to be in camp before dark. The cooking fires would be ready, for the men knew he would bring in fresh meat.

The path home. The familiar burden on his back. The end of the hunt. Why did it not feel the same this time?

He knew why.

Esau squared his shoulders under his burden. He hated this ambivalence within him. He was putting off the inevitable. Tomorrow he would meet Jacob.

No. Tomorrow, he would go to the ford of the Jabbok. He had promised Mahalath. He should have gone today, but he had been compelled to go hunting. The hunt had restored his perspective; now he would do what he had been postponing.

At the edge of the clearing his men were encamped. He paused to survey the scene. This was a pleasant valley, where the Jabbok flowed in a small swift stream. Behind him, to the west, was a waterfall where the small river dropped from a shelf of limestone rock. The valley was surrounded by a forest of balsam and fir, whose fragrance brought an aura of peace to the meadow, carpeted with splashes of red, yellow, and blue flowers. The men had indeed kindled fires, knowing he would bring in game.

Reluctant to leave the comforting haven of

the forest, Esau watched his encampment. To the east and south, facing Jacob's camp, guards had been placed. Beyond the Jabbok on the north, a steep cliff rose into the graying sky. Just a mile upstream the trail forded the Jabbok. The ledge was there; the cave where he and Mahalath had spent three days. Three golden days. Esau sighed and eased the burden on his back. He would go there tomorrow.

Reuel and Eliphaz were arguing again. This was the only sound from the quiet camp.

"He is not!" That was Eliphaz's voice.

"He is!" Reuel's voice was deeper, more mature. He was sixteen, two years older than Eliphaz. "We should have met Jacob today! But no, Esau went hunting!"

"Stop it, you two!" Markesh thrust himself between the young men. Esau nodded approvingly. The servant spoke with authority to the boys in his charge. Was it because of Esau's threat to kill Markesh if Reuel harmed Eliphaz?

Reuel and Eliphaz glared at each other for a moment, then the younger man turned and stalked away. Esau chewed on his mustache. Something would have to be done about those two boys. They knew about his threat to Markesh and he was sure they wouldn't harm each other, but he was thinking of the long future. They would need to live together peacefully if they were to be in the same family. He smiled grimly. If there was a future for his family.

Tomorrow would change everything. No, not tomorrow. He'd have to go to the ford of the Jabbok first.

Esau took a deep breath, disgusted with himself for his indecision, his ambivalence. He'd go to the ford of the Jabbok tomorrow and be done with it. Then whatever God planned for him, no matter what, would happen.

God. He shook his head, for this was an old unresolved question. Did this God of Isaac really exist? Had he really spoken to Mahalath? He could not dispute Mahalath's powers, but he had no personal experience with Isaac's God. To Esau, God was an enigma, a mystery for others to wrestle with. He was not a theologian; he was the Hunter of Edom.

He shrugged, stepped from behind the tree, and strode into the clearing. The hunt was over now. His day of grace was done.

Esau's men were Moabites, who considered skinning a carcass and cooking it women's work. They might have done it if Esau ordered them, but they would have butchered it badly. Esau would do it himself.

Skinning a carcass was something one person could do slowly, two faster, and three most efficiently. Esau called Eliphaz. In his household, it was not a disgrace for a man to learn the art of preparing food. The women always did it, but the men learned how and helped when necessary.

Eliphaz came willingly. Esau smiled at him. His son was pleasant company, always willing to do his share of work.

"Hold the skin, son," Esau said. He drew his knife.

Eliphaz knelt at the back of the gazelle, ready to grasp the skin when the sharp knife made a handhold. They must work quickly, for the light was almost gone. Then to Esau's surprise, Markesh knelt beside him.

"I'll help," he said.

Esau nodded. He recalled Markesh, the eager boy at Beersheba, who never hesitated to do a man's job. He would be a worthy successor to Jubal, Isaac's faithful steward. During the past few weeks, Esau had been impressed with Markesh. He said very little, but his intelligence and industry reminded Esau of Jubal.

Suddenly Markesh stood. "Reuel," he said sharply. "Take over here. I'll prepare the cooking fires."

Esau's oldest son was standing at the edge

of the crowd of men, watching. He hesitated only a second, then stepped forward and knelt beside Eliphaz.

Esau grunted as he made the first slash on the back of the animal's head. This small incident told him two things. First, Reuel had been trained in the tradition of Esau's family; he did not hesitate to do "women's work" and could do it skillfully. Second, Markesh was shrewd enough to place the young man in a position where he and Eliphaz would be working together, supervised by their father.

The skinning went quickly. Reuel indeed knew what to do, and with three people working, the meat was quickly quartered, deboned, and ready for cooking. No words were spoken, but Eliphaz and Reuel shared the task of peeling the skin as though they had done it together all their lives. Markesh came with sharpened sticks for spitting the meat. In a few minutes it was sputtering on the fire, while the hungry Moabites watched and waited for the fresh meat.

Under Markesh's watchful eye, the venison was soon cooked and ready to eat. Markesh himself distributed it in equal portions to the fifty men in the war party.

It was growing dark rapidly. Esau stood and faced the men. "We will not meet Jacob tomorrow," he said. "Instead, you will wait here in camp another day. I have something to do, and our battle can wait."

Although unexpected, the men accepted this in silence. They wouldn't know the real reason for the postponement. But they knew Esau well enough to know it wasn't fear.

Esau watched their faces in the firelight. He had chosen them well. These were older men, in their twenties and early thirties, with families, the more responsible citizens of Moab. Esau had trained them as bowmen, and Nebaioth had given them jobs as guards in the copper mines. They would know how to handle themselves tomorrow. Their leader was Manu-baal. He came from Tamar in the Salt Plain.

Esau spoke to him now. "Manu-baal, send scouts tomorrow to watch Jacob's camp."

"It shall be done, Esau." The warrior wrinkled his brow. "Where will you be, sir?"

"I'll spend the day at the ford of the Jabbok."

Esau looked around at the faces of his men. They would think it strange, his wandering off alone for no apparent reason on the day before the battle. Just as they thought it strange for him to leave them today to go hunting, instead of facing the enemy in battle. They would not doubt his courage, but they would be puzzled by his eccentricities.

What would his sons think? He didn't care too much what his men thought; Manu-baal and the others would do as he said. They would give a good account of themselves in a battle.

But he cared what his sons thought. Eliphaz knew him best, and perhaps Eliphaz alone of all this company understood his need for solitude. He was the only one who had heard Mahalath tell him to go to the ford of the Jabbok River before he took action against Jacob. Would Eliphaz understand his need to go there tomorrow? Or why he had to go hunting today?

He looked again at his men. They were waiting for him to say something. "The day after tomorrow," he said, not sure just what he wanted to say to them, "we may or may not fight. What happens is in God's hands."

The men sat silent, staring at him. That should give them something to think about. Mahalath's reputation as a seer had spread throughout Moab, and these superstitious worshipers of Qaus were sure some momentous events were destined to take place soon.

Perhaps they were right. Esau himself was looking forward to the next two days. He had a feeling of awe, that these events were foreordained, in God's hands, the outcome not determined by plans and actions of mere mortals.

As he looked at his men, their faces stony and unreadable, he became aware of Reuel staring at him with a frown. His oldest son would be mystified by these events. Would he think his father afraid of the battle? Or would he merely be disappointed that his vengeance was postponed for another day?

Esau shrugged as he turned away to find a place to sleep. The boy would be dealt with later. There were more important things at hand now.

30

The sun was filtering through the branches of the balsam trees when Esau awoke. Today was the day. He would learn the meaning of Mahalath's strange message. *Go to the ford of the Jabbok.* His indecision, his ambivalence, his unwanted delays would be over.

He picked up his bow and slung his quiver on his back. He glanced around the clearing. Most of his men still slept. Some stirred up the fires to prepare for a long day of waiting.

As he crossed the clearing toward the trail which led to the ford of the Jabbok, he paused. Someone was running up the trail toward him. It was Manu-baal.

"Esau!"

Manu-baal's deep voice sounded loud in the still morning air. There was an excited ring to it. What was happening?

"What is it, man?"

"They're coming, my lord. From Jacob's camp!"

Esau hand tightened on his bow, his senses

suddenly alert. "How many men?"

Manu-baal shook his head. "Only about five, sir. They're unarmed. But . . . they've got a herd of goats!"

"*Goats!*"

"Yes, Esau. Goats. I don't now what they're up to, but we'd better be ready."

Jacob's devious mind was plotting a diversion. His army might even now be sneaking around for a flank attack.

"Call the men, Manu-baal. Send out scouting parties, and keep an extra watch on Jacob's camp. We don't want to be taken by surprise."

Manu-baal nodded, turned, and went toward the camp. He shouted orders as he went, kicking the men out of their blankets. He dispatched the men quickly and efficiently. The clearing was suddenly bare; the warriors were either scouting or hidden in the forest, ready to surprise their attackers. They were all accomplished bowmen; no enemy with hand-held weapons would stand up to them, no matter what the odds.

And here came the enemy. A herd of goats. Esau heard them first; their plaintive *baas* echoed in the silence of the morning. Then he saw them coming up the trail from the west: gray and speckled creatures, their horns and beards tossing as they were herded and pushed by only four men.

No — five men. The tall one, who seemed to be their leader, was just a little past middle age, his bushy black beard cropped short. He wore a burnoose, but the cowl was lying on his back, leaving his straight black hair visible.

Esau stood alone in the clearing as they approached. The bareheaded man came directly toward him.

At twenty feet, the man prostrated himself on the ground, his arms extended in front. "My lord Esau. May you live forever! May your sons rise up and call you blessed! If your humble servant has found favor in your sight, please accept this small gift as a token of love and affection."

"Stand up, man!" The authority in Esau's voice brought the groveling servant instantly to his feet. "What does all this mean? Who are you and who does this herd belong to?"

The man bowed his head. "My lord Esau, I am Omri, servant of your brother Jacob. These goats belong to you, a gift from your brother, your humble servant."

Esau watched in astonishment as the goats spread out in the clearing. The herdsmen no longer driving them, they began to crop the grass. There must be over two hundred. Esau remembered his father's herd of goats; it was about the same size. What did Jacob expect to accomplish by this? Esau still suspected a trick; he glanced around furtively to make sure his men remained concealed and alert.

His glance included the trail from the west. There was more coming! Another herd. Sheep, from the sound of them. Here they came — a huge flock, probably as many sheep as goats. Strange. They were speckled or black, not the pure white he was familiar with.

"My lord Esau," said Omri, "your brother sends you these sheep as an offering of love and affection. Let there be peace between you."

Still another herd came out of the forest, this time cows. About fifty of them. They added their *moos* to the noise.

"May you live forever, my lord," said Omri. "These are all gifts from your brother, who seeks your good will."

The clearing was now filled with livestock, milling around and cropping the grass. Their cries filled the air — moos, baas, snorts. What had been a peaceful clearing minutes before was now a crowded pasture!

But more were coming. A herd of about thirty asses plodded up the trail and pushed their way into the clearing. Their brays added to the cacophony of the meadow.

Omri raised his voice to be heard above the din. "This completes your brother's humble gift to you. Two hundred she-goats and twenty he-goats; two hundred ewes and rams; forty cows and ten bulls; twenty she-asses and ten he-asses. May they bring you happiness and prosperity, for with them comes the good will of your servant Jacob."

If this were true, then Esau was suddenly a wealthy man. Jacob must have turned over to him half of his livestock herd. But why? What cunning plot was this by his grasping brother?

Esau turned to Omri. "Where's my brother now?" he thundered.

Omri stepped back, his eyes widening in fear. "He — he's at his camp, my lord. In Mahanaim."

"And his warriors? Where are they?"

Omri looked puzzled. "He has no warriors, my lord. All his servants are simple herdsmen. Jacob is a man of peace, sir, and he is helpless, at your mercy. My lord, I beg you, do not harm him. Give him the hand of peace, for he loves you and seeks only your good will."

Esau snorted. "So that's why he sent me these gifts! To buy me off!"

"My lord!" Omri bowed his black head. "If these gifts have found favor in your sight, spare your brother Jacob. Even now, he waits with his family at Mahanaim for your answer. Be merciful to him, I beg of you."

If this were true, that Jacob's men were

shepherds and not warriors, then his brother was truly defenseless. But Esau did not believe this. He knew his brother too well. Jacob was "The Grasper," who even now was plotting and scheming his way out of a delicate predicament.

"My lord!" Omri's wrinkled brow reflected his discomfort. An honest servant carrying a message, he was obviously not enjoying facing a dangerous enemy. "If it pleases you, your brother would like to see you. He begs forgiveness from you for past wrongs. He wants nothing more than to hear from your own lips your forgiveness and desire to live in peace."

Esau shook his head. He didn't want to talk to Jacob. He only wanted to face him in battle, to kill him, to erase forever from the earth that despicable creature. If the brothers came face-to-face for a talk, Jacob would surely find the smooth words or schemes to outwit his older brother. Esau's strong memories of treachery and deceit made him unwilling to face Jacob except in battle.

Esau gritted his teeth. He couldn't help admiring Jacob's devious but shrewd mind. He was helpless before Esau's strength, yet he devised a scheme to buy his brother's forgiveness and plead for mercy. Jacob would be confident his brother would accept his generosity in exchange for peace.

Esau chewed on his mustache as he confronted another dilemma. Should he accept this gift from his brother, then kill him? Well, why not? Esau could return home a wealthy man. This was a more equitable payment for his birthright than a pot of red stew. He could provide well for his family now and continue to hunt the wilderness of Edom. He could teach his sons to hunt, including Reuel, finding some way to overcome his oldest son's hatred of him —

His thoughts were interrupted by the sight of Markesh making his way toward Esau through a flock of sheep. He pushed a she-ass away and waved his hands at goats in his path.

Then Markesh stood before Esau. "My lord Esau!" he said.

"What is it, Markesh?" Esau noted the worried frown on the servant's forehead. "Are my sons all right?"

"My lord, Eliphaz is fine. He is ready with his bow, and even now stands at the edge of the clearing ready to fight if need be. But Reuel —"

"Where's Reuel?"

"I don't know, my lord. He's gone. I don't know where."

No wonder Markesh frowned; he had been charged with Reuel's safekeeping. Esau smiled grimly. He knew where Reuel had gone. He would be expecting a fight, and he wanted to be sure he was on the right side.

Esau frowned, suddenly angry. Reuel was his son, his firstborn, his heir. It didn't matter what he thought of his father; he belonged by Esau's side. If he fought with Jacob, it would be difficult for him to survive the battle unhurt. He could caution his men to be careful not to injure his son when they fired their arrows. Even so —

But how could he return to Edom with a son who hated him? If Reuel survived the battle and were led home a captive, would his resentment build even more? His son — his heir — would have to live in Esau's house, but would he ever accept Esau as his father?

Suddenly Esau was disgusted with the way things were working out. He had wanted to come here to fight, to kill Jacob, to fulfill his old vow of vengeance. Nothing more. No complicated plots, responsibilities, burdens. He was face-to-face with a herd of livestock to take back to Punon, a son who had deserted him for Jacob's camp, and a brother who was scheming and plotting for peace.

Esau was breathing hard. He turned on Omri, scowling. "Go back to that pig brother of mine," he roared, watching with satisfaction as Omri quailed before him. "Tell him I'll come to him tomorrow morning! But I won't be talking! I want my son back, do you hear? And I want Jacob *dead!*"

When Omri and his herdsmen had gone, Esau's warriors came out of the forest, gaping at the crowded pasture. Manubaal pushed his way through the animals and stood before Esau.

"What shall we do with them?" he shouted above the din.

Esau took a deep breath. He was still trembling from his anger and disgust with Jacob. He focused his mind to deal with the problem before him. "We're going to be herdsmen for a while, my friend."

Manu-baal's eyes widened in dismay. Then he shook his head vigorously. "Esau, we're warriors, not herdsmen. We have had no experience as drovers."

"I think you'll learn quickly enough. It's a long way back to Edom."

"To Edom! Do you mean we're going to nursemaid these brutes all the way home?"

Esau nodded. Manu-baal struck a large bull on its flank with his bow. The beast swung around and lowered his head. Manubaal backed up, reaching for an arrow, confusion on his face.

Suddenly Esau's anger evaporated. The sight of Manu-baal, a bowman, confronting a bull armed only with horns brought a smile to his face. "No, no, my friend. Be gentle. First you will need a staff. We'll carry our bows on our backs for the trip home."

Manu-baal muttered, still eying the bull. "We'll never make it, Esau. None of us knows what to do."

"Markesh does," said Esau. "He'll show you."

By this time several of the men had pushed their way through the herd. They, like Manu-baal, were aghast at the prospect of exchanging their bows for staffs and fighting a menagerie of unfamiliar beasts all the way to Edom.

Several of the more enterprising cattle had pushed into the forest around the clearing. Esau gave orders. The men, muttering and shaking their heads, went after them to drive them back. Keeping them together for a trip taking several weeks would be a problem — with inexperienced herdsmen, and with the *yoreh* and its rains not far away.

Manu-baal called in his scouts, who confirmed Omri's insistence that Jacob's men were herdsmen, not warriors. They had seen no weapon among them, just shepherds' staffs. No need for guards, then. The men could be assigned new duties, take turns keeping track of the livestock, watching them at night —

He caught his breath; he had almost forgotten. Tomorrow they would fight a battle! The men needed rest, not work. He looked around. The men were yelling, waving their arms, trying to keep the animals in the clearing. Somehow he must organize them, train them to be herdsmen, and still allow them some rest.

"Markesh!" he shouted. The servant was at the edge of the clearing, remonstrating a warrior for shouting at the skittish sheep. *"Markesh!"* The man heard his second call and turned to come immediately. Esau waved toward the herd.

"What shall we do, Markesh? We face a battle tomorrow. The men need rest. How can we manage until after the fight?"

Markesh wrinkled his brow. "It won't be easy, sir. We can divide the men into four shifts to take turns watching the livestock. But getting them back to Edom may be a problem."

"Let's worry about that later. Right now, we have to get through tonight."

Markesh nodded. "We can assign ten men to a shift. I'll have to tell the men not to yell at the animals. It scares them."

"Manu-baal!" shouted Esau, scaring a pair of sheep grazing nearby.

Markesh frowned at him. His shout was the very thing Markesh was talking about.

"Manu-baal, we must organize the men to guard the livestock. And they need to rest tonight for the battle tomorrow."

"Yes, Esau. It shall be done."

Several hours later, Esau looked up into the sky. The sun was almost gone. The entire day had been spent talking with Omri and organizing the men. His stomach growled; he hadn't eaten anything since last night. And he had not gone to the ford of the Jabbok yet. Well, there was an easy answer to that. He would go tonight. Now. Then he would see why Mahalath had sent him.

He sighed and started down the path. At last, he'd be doing something. Finally his confrontation with his destiny had arrived!

31

Although the afternoon light was fading, Esau had no trouble following the broad trail leading to the ford of the Jabbok River. He could hear the muted sound of water flowing in a swift stream on his left; just ahead he heard the splash of a small waterfall. He recalled the place: the small clearing, the hyssop growing by the rocks, the overhanging ledge where he and Mahalath had spent three days and nights.

He stepped out of the forest at the edge of the stream. The ledge was dimly visible in the twilight, and he made his way cautiously up to the rock. No need to go inside; he squatted on a stone still warm from the afternoon sun. Soon the chill of the night would be felt, but he shrugged; he had spent cold nights in the wilderness before. Solitude and the discomforts of nature were no strangers to him.

As he chewed a twist of venison, he listened to the night, trying to attune himself to the small clearing where the trail crossed the stream. He blocked out the flow and splash of water, straining for anything which would disturb the peace of the night. There was nothing. The dry season was far advanced, and soon the *yoreh* would come, the first rain which was always a welcome relief to the parched land. He felt so much a part of the land that his skin prickled in anticipation of that first deluge.

He finished eating and drank water from the stream. Then, as he had done so often when hunting, he controlled his body, tuning it to a state of alertness which would respond to any stimulus in the natural world around him. His breathing was shallow and slow, his bow ready in his hand. His eyes pierced the deepening night. He was ready.

Ready for what? If he were hunting, he would watch for a gazelle or an ibex, or even a wildcat or bear. They would be coming to drink soon, and he could easily make his kill and go home. But that wasn't why he was here.

He didn't know why he was here. Mahalath had told him to be here, and he trusted Mahalath's gift.

He recalled the night Mahalath had told him about her gift. It happened right here, in the cave to his right, the light of the fire flickering on her face. He had not believed her then; in fact, he had scoffed at her. He knew better now. He believed in Mahalath's gift.

In spite of his iron discipline, he couldn't stop thinking of another scene which took place inside that low cave. He saw Mahalath, her slim body bared somewhat because of the strip she had torn from her dress to bind his wounds. He had wanted her then. She was willing, although he hadn't known at the time she was a virgin. Had she been older, experienced, and not as innocent, he would have taken her that night. But he couldn't. And his wanting her had seared itself into him deeply, unexplainably. Maybe that was when he started to love her.

He had never loved a woman before as he loved Mahalath. He recalled Basemath and Judith, his concubines at Beersheba. He had enjoyed them greatly as sexual companions, but they were playthings. Not Mahalath. Mahalath was more than just an outlet for his lust. She was someone to share every phase of his life with. That's why he could not take her that night.

And Adah. How strange was his love for the Hittite girl he had found in the wilderness! His first sight of her was when she lay naked, raped and mauled by the Horites. A skinny child, with welts on her body where they had beaten her. And shivering. Yet when he bent down to cut her loose, she had spit in his face.

His fondness for Adah had grown as she matured, her body filling out to a young woman's. It was she who gave him his son. She and Mahalath were his only loves.

Of course, there was Oholibamah. But the Horite girl who gave him so many sons was no more to him than Basemath and Judith. She was voluptuous and insatiable, but he had never quite developed a love for her as he had for Mahalath and Adah.

He blinked his eyes, wondering at the unaccustomed wetness in them. Thinking of home could easily dull his awareness of the night around him.

The hours passed swiftly as he waited in the night. The moon had come out, a half moon which offered considerably more light than the stars alone. Its silver splattered the Jabbok River, splashed across the rocks, and put filigree fingers on the pine and balsam trees. This was a peaceful place with fond memories; no wonder he loved it so much.

Just a few miles away was his brother.

His eyes narrowed and his forehead creased in a frown. Jacob. The old hatred rose in him. He gripped his bow more tightly. Tomorrow he would end the long and bitter rivalry between them. Tomorrow he would kill.

It might even be the last thing he would do.

He recalled all the warnings against his fulfilling his vow of vengeance. First, Isaac. His father's blessing — or was it a curse? — had placed him inferior to his younger brother, in a position of eternal servitude. His mother's curse had promised him suffering if he fulfilled his vow. And Mahalath's gift had warned him repeatedly that the way of revenge was the way of disaster.

Nevertheless, he could not lay aside the compulsion for vengeance. He had made a vow. Never, in the long years since he had left Beersheba, had he wavered in his need to fulfill the oath to take his brother's life. It was his mission in life; he had no other purpose. And the events of this day only strengthened his resolve.

He was casting aside everything: his family, loves, hunting, new wealth — even his life itself. Sacrificed on the altar of vengeance. Hate was stronger than love.

He smiled grimly as he recalled his wives' strategy to overwhelm him with love to make him forget his hate. They had done well; he had for a while succumbed to the easy life of love in his family. It was pleasant, fulfilling — but not his mission in life, which must not be denied. Nothing, not even his family's love, could prevent his revenge.

He didn't know yet how he would do it. He

would confront Jacob, refuse to listen to his pleas for forgiveness and peace, and then somehow kill him — regardless of the consequences. He himself might even be killed. He hoped his sons would not. But that didn't matter. The only thing that mattered was that his vow of vengeance be fulfilled.

This might well be the last night of his life. He shrugged. So be it. Whatever would be would be. He had had a good life, and now he had arrived at its climax. And this climax would happen tomorrow . . . possibly even tonight.

In spite of his thoughts, his mind and senses were alert. A movement in the shadows on his right, across the river to the north, caught his eye. Something or someone stood in the shadows of the pine trees at the foot of the hill. Esau focused his attention there.

Whatever it was moved to the edge of the darkened forest. Then it stepped out into the moonlight.

It was a man.

32

The man stood on the north bank of the stream. He had come up the trail from the south. Now he prepared to cross the shallow ford. Yet he hesitated, looking around, uncertain.

The hood of his long burnoose covered his head. Only the tip of his beard showed; it was short and curly. He was of medium height, and as far as Esau could tell, middle-aged.

He stepped into the stream and splashed across. He hadn't seen Esau yet. Esau was in shadows and hadn't moved. The man, if he continued coming, would pass right by him.

No, he wouldn't. Esau wouldn't let him. Mahalath had sent him here, for a reason. He didn't know the reason — but this stranger might be it.

The man was across the stream now. Water dripping from his sandals and the hem of his burnoose sparkled in the moonlight. He stepped onto the rock just a few feet from where Esau crouched in the shadow.

With a lithe motion, Esau stepped in front of the man.

The stranger gasped, then flung himself, head down, into Esau's stomach. The force of his charge sent them both flying off the rock onto the soft ground at the edge of the clearing.

When they struck the ground, they separated. Esau leaped to his feet, crouching, hands forward. He had dropped his bow. The man rolled over, staggered to his feet, and charged again. This time Esau was ready. He sidestepped to the left, grasping the stranger's right wrist. Then he pulled, and the man twisted around to come into Esau's arms. The big muscular arms circled his back, and they struggled face-to-face.

Esau could hear the man gasping. He tightened the force of his bear hug, and heard a choking sound. Then Esau flung him to the ground. There was a crunch, as though a bone were breaking, and the stranger's sharp cry of pain.

The battle was over now. Esau had won. He stepped over to where the man lay writhing on the ground, moaning.

"Who are you?" asked Esau.

The cowl of the burnoose still hid the man's face. Esau reached to pull it back, but the stranger's hands shot out and grasped Esau's wrist, jerking him over on top of him. Esau fell on the man, who grunted as the air went out of his lungs.

The man writhed beneath him, gasping for breath. He was badly hurt, reminding Esau of a wounded animal. No one, man or beast, should suffer pain.

Esau felt a moment of sympathy for his fallen adversary. "Who are you?" he said again.

The man writhing beneath him finally regained his breath. But pain and fear muted his voice.

"Jacob *ben* Isaac," he whispered between clenched teeth.

Esau gasped. Jacob! His brother, his enemy, lay beneath him, badly hurt — within his power!

Esau straddled his brother's body on his knees and reached for the throat. So easy. He could choke out his brother's life right now. Then his vow, his mission in life, would be complete.

Now the cowl fell back, and Jacob's features became distinguishable in the moonlight. He had aged some since Esau last saw him, but he was still the same Jacob. The narrow eyes, high cheekbones, sharp nose, curly hair and beard — how he hated that face! His grip tightened on Jacob's throat.

"Who are you?" Jacob gasped.

Esau's grip slackened. It hadn't occurred to him that Jacob would not know him. But he didn't. The moon was behind Esau; what Jacob saw was a face blackened by shadow. To his brother, Esau was just a man who leaped out of the shadows and confronted him. A robber. A murderer. A madman.

Jacob's eyes were wide, reflecting the moonlight. They also reflected the man's inner being — fear, treachery, selfishness. Same old Jacob. "The Grasper." The baby who grasped his brother's heel at birth, still reaching for what didn't belong to him. Only now what the Grasper was reaching for was his life!

Fear of death was reflected in those eyes. Terror. Jacob's breath came in short gasps. Esau should do it quickly. Kill. Swiftly. Mercifully. That was what he would do for a wounded beast.

Then why couldn't he do it? For years he had killed, quickly and easily. He would never allow a beast to suffer. Always before, there was that brief moment of sympathy, of respect, of kinship for a forest brother — then the swift killing blow.

Now! Kill! Fulfill that vow! Bring your life to its fruition — now!

Jacob reached up and feebly grasped Esau's tunic. "Who are you?" he asked again.

Esau stared at the hands clutching his brother's throat. Why couldn't he do it? Jacob's hand tightened on Esau's tunic.

"Let me go," Esau muttered. "It's almost daylight."

"No." The voice was as feeble as the hands. "I won't let you go. Give me your blessing."

"What!"

"Bless me! Now!"

Esau stared into the face of his brother. The wide eyes, pupils dilated, showed fear and resignation. He expected to die. And he would, just as soon as Esau could force his hands to squeeze the soft throat. But to ask for a blessing? Who did he think Esau was?

The moonlight faded and clouded Jacob's face. With a grunt, Esau knew the answer to his own question. Jacob thought he was . . . *God!*

But to ask for a blessing! He already had the birthright! The voice of Isaac came into Esau's mind, a voice blessing the son and heir: *Be lord over your brother; may your mother's son bow to you!*

How absurd. Here he was, bending over Jacob, the man's life literally in his hands, his brother thinking he was God, begging for a blessing! Who was bowing down to whom?

Then Isaac's voice came to him once more out of the past: *Cursed be every one who curses you, and blessed be every one who blesses you!*

He snorted. "Jacob," he muttered. "You aren't Jacob any more." He looked down at the pitiful face before him, still twisted with pain and fear. "Not Jacob, the Grasper. You should have a new name before you die."

The night was almost gone. He could clearly see Jacob's features. Yet his brother still did not recognize him. Jacob's mind seemed clouded with fear and pain. He was transfixed with the notion that his mysterious assailant was God himself.

Esau grunted. In a way, perhaps he was. It must have been God, through Mahalath's gift, who had brought him here, against his understanding, to this ford of the River Jabbok. It must have been God who had allowed him to wrestle with his brother. It must have been God who had also stayed his hands when he tried to use them to bring his brother's death.

And so it must be God's hand reaching down, touching Jacob's life in this moment through the hairy red hand on Jacob's throat. Yes, he might well be God's messenger for this occasion.

Cursed be every one who curses you, and blessed be every one who blesses you. Isaac's words seared through Esau's mind. Jacob, not Esau, was God's chosen one. Jacob, not Esau, had God's blessing. Jacob, not Esau, was the heir of the Promise. Esau bowed his head in mute acceptance.

"You are no longer Jacob," he said softly, "but Israel. *One who struggles with God.* For you have fought with God — *and won!*"

Esau's shoulders slumped. He released Jacob's throat and let his breath rush out. Something left him with that exhalation. Something which tore out of his windpipe, scraped his throat, and set his teeth tingling. He heard it then — the sound of his own voice, a screech, a roar, a scream! He felt empty inside, drained of energy, purged of emotion, inexpressibly weary.

Esau stood. Below him, his brother gasped and slipped into unconsciousness. He looked so frail, so fragile, like the morning mist fading into the dawn. Yet in all his weakness, Jacob was the one who would be strong. He had the Promise.

And Esau accepted it. The hate which had burned in him for years was gone, torn from him in his mighty shout as he bent over Jacob. He was purged, clean and free. Esau took a deep breath. His mission in life was accomplished. He could go home.

He turned and trudged through the hyssop into the dawn.

33

"And did you see Jacob at Mahanaim?" asked Mahalath.

Esau and Mahalath had walked onto the plain below Punon to inspect his herds. He moved his bow from his left hand to his right. He still would not carry a staff, even when surrounded by his own sheep.

"Yes," he replied. "But briefly. I only asked for my son to return."

He gazed across the flock grazing on the flat grassy plain of the Arabah. To the north was the Salt Sea. To the east rose the red hills of Edom, at the foot of which nestled Punon and his home. His eyes returned to the flock.

Several shepherds stood with the sheep. Esau noted with satisfaction that Markesh's father, Jubal, was there, with the other herdsmen from Beersheba. They had come to Edom to be with Esau, rather than wait to be absorbed into Jacob's vast herds and household.

He smiled as he recognized one of the shepherds. The young man turned his head, saw Esau and Mahalath, and waved. Mahalath waved back. It was Esau's oldest son, Reuel.

"Did Reuel come willingly?" asked Mahalath.

Esau nodded. "Not only that, but he felt differently about me. He doesn't hate me any more."

"How do you explain that?"

Esau shrugged and said nothing. He didn't know the answer. Reuel had spent three days in Jacob's camp at Mahanaim before Esau appeared before them to demand his son's return. During those three days, the boy had chosen Esau over Jacob, and all the way home — the journey took three months because of the herds — he was respectful and obedient to his father.

"I wonder. . . ." Mahalath turned toward her husband, a frown on her face. "He was in both your camp and Jacob's, and he had an opportunity to get to know you both. He saw Jacob for what he was — and you, too."

Again Esau shrugged. "Maybe someone told him the truth about Jacob — and how he got the birthright. I don't know."

"Why don't you ask him?"

Again there was silence between them. The bleating of the sheep seemed unnaturally loud in the hot basin.

Finally Esau spoke. "He'll tell me if he wants to."

Mahalath's voice had a petulant edge. "Esau, my husband!" She stood directly in front of him, looking up into his face. "You are exasperating sometimes!"

Esau smiled. "Would you like me to talk and talk and talk, like your father used to?"

Esau's comment was rewarded by a smile from Mahalath. The dimples showed on her face at last.

"No." Suddenly her tinkling laugh blended with the bleating of the sheep. "No, never! You are who you are, and you always will be. Thank God for that!"

Esau's smile faded. "And who am I?"

Mahalath's face became suddenly solemn. "You are a man without a birthright," she said.

Esau nodded. "Is that so bad?"

"No. In fact, I wonder if Jacob will find the burden of the birthright heavy. His descendants, too."

"Possibly."

Mahalath looked up at her husband and spoke softly. "Mediocrity may be a much more comfortable burden to bear." She smiled again, but her eyes were serious. "Tell me, my husband, who do *you* say you are?"

His reply was instantaneous. "I am the

Hunter of Edom!" He held up his bow. "*This is my birthright!*"

"And nothing more?"

"Nothing more."

"For the rest of your life?"

"And for the life of our descendants."

She moved closer to him, then reached out and gently touched the hand which held the bow. When she spoke, her voice was soft and loving. "God has blessed you richly, indeed!"

She looked at him. Esau was aware of the depth of her eyes, as she probed his soul. Sunlight glistened on them, and he wondered if it was reflecting a tear.

"You're right, Mahalath. I have been richly blessed."

Suddenly the dimples returned to Mahalath's face, and her tinkling laugh again mingled with the bleats of the sheep.

Esau breathed deeply. Tomorrow he would go hunting, leaving the sheep in the capable hands of Jubal and his men. He would take Reuel and Eliphaz with him. They would go into the *mishor,* where the almond trees would be in blossom, and follow the hidden trail into the grove of oaks, then to the clearing at the stream where the herd of gazelles came to drink.

He lifted his eyes to the red hills of Edom behind Punon. Sunlight reflected on his house, its white walls gleaming boldly on the crest of a hill. His wife Adah was there, and Oholibamah, and his sons and daughters. And Basemath too; she had come to Edom with Jubal and the others.

Esau smiled. Did Jacob have any more than he?

The employees of Thorndike Press hope you have enjoyed this Large Print book. All our Large Print titles are designed for easy reading, and all our books are made to last. Other Thorndike Press Large Print books are available at your library, through selected bookstores, or directly from the publishers.

For more information about titles, please call:

(800) 223-1244
(800) 223-6121

To share your comments, please write:

Publisher
Thorndike Press
295 Kennedy Memorial Drive
Waterville, ME 04901